Praise for

'A twisty and pacey thriller 1
stakes and jeopardy that bu

'*Her New Best Friend* is a slow burn with a hot finish ... An intriguing read' *Jane Lythell*

'Riveting, twisty and tense, *Her New Best Friend* will keep you guessing until the last sentence! A page-turning psychological thriller' *E.C. Scullion*

'A twisty look at obsession and motherhood. You're in for a treat!' *Louise Mumford*

'A twisty and engrossing story of motherhood, friendship and betrayal. A great read for lovers of domestic thrillers' *A.J. Campbell*

'This is the perfect blend of beautifully written, taut psychological drama. Suspicion and anxiety build until you find yourself turning the light off at dawn. Fabulous!' *Victoria Dowd*

'A fast-paced thriller looking at obsession, whether you can trust your own instincts, and how the past can come back to haunt you when you least expect it. Compelling' *Catherine Cooper*

Praise for *My Perfect Sister*

'Claustrophobic and thrilling – a true page-turner in which no one can be trusted' *Catherine Cooper*

'Pacey and entertaining and I whizzed through it. Great for anyone (like me) who loves to be hooked into a psychological thriller' *Philippa East*

Reader reviews

'This is a brilliant first novel. A fascinating story of family dynamics and secrets'

'A wonderful twisty thriller. A truly fantastic debut novel'

'This is a fabulous book! An incredibly gripping story with a host of intriguing and sensitively drawn characters'

'A truly engaging read from start to finish. A triumph of a first book from a really promising new author'

'I really enjoyed *My Perfect Sister*; from the outset it sweeps you along and keeps you guessing, and there's a smart twist too!'

'This is a great read for anyone who likes a bit of a mystery, I read it over a weekend and couldn't wait to find out if my hunch on what happened was right – it wasn't!'

'Really captivating story. An excellent debut novel and an ending with lots of twists and turns'

'A great lockdown read … had me gripped and guessing right until the end'

'A good story with a twist at the end. A page-turner and refreshing to see a disabled character as one of the main characters'

'A fantastic thriller, with plenty of twists and turns. A real page-turner. Now I need more books from this author'

'I loved reading this book! It is well written with believable characters and plot. It has lots of twist and turns right up to the end. Kept me guessing! An excellent book'

her

new

best

friend

PENNY BATCHELOR

Red Door

Published by RedDoor
www.reddoorpress.co.uk

ISBN 978-1-913062-71-2

A CIP catalogue record for this book is available from the British Library

Cover design: Emily Courdelle

Typesetting: Jen Parker, Fuzzy Flamingo
www.fuzzyflamingo.co.uk

Printed and bound in Denmark by Nørhaven

For Chris, who shielded by my side whilst I wrote this novel

Part One

Audrey

~ 1 ~

I didn't turn my back on the pram for much longer than a snatched handful of seconds, a few heartbeats, but that was all the time it took for my five-year-old daughter, Antonia, to turn on her heel and dash after the fluttering wings of a yellow-breasted great tit in the local park.

Seconds. Ordinary passages of time which, on a regular day, we don't think twice about the passing of or maybe even long to pass by more quickly. A few of them, however, as every mother knows and fears, is all it takes.

'Antonia!' I anxiously call out. 'Don't run off!' I let go of the pram's handles and try to walk as fast as I can to reach my daughter who is heading in the direction of the trees, following her quarry. 'Come back!'

It has felt like such a long day, as if twenty-four hours have passed before 3.30 p.m. My voice cracks slightly when I try to prevent my usual singsong mummy tone from turning into barbed impatience. Having short legs seems to make it more difficult today for me to catch up with my child on whom my husband James and I always impress the importance of staying close by when venturing outside the home. Easy to say isn't it, but not so simple for easily distracted children to do when something has caught their eye.

3

Antonia turns when she hears her name and I see the expression on her little flushed face betray her internal debate on whether to continue her wild bird chase or come back to me. I win. Antonia starts to do as she's told and run back to me when we both hear a shout coming from near the pond at the centre of the municipal park.

Instinctively I turn back to the pram.

It's not there.

My heart beats ferociously and I sense the acrid taste of adrenaline in my mouth. For a split second I'm frozen. I stare down towards the bottom of the path the three of us walk on nearly every day. A soggy, small blonde figure is pulling a pram out of the shallow area of the pond. My pram.

Time freezes into an icy shock until I scream 'Wilfred!' in fear. I reach for Antonia's gloved hand and pull her as quickly as I can towards the pond. Most of the water is surrounded by a low concrete wall adorned with the usual detritus of crisp packets and drinks cans visitors couldn't be bothered to put in the nearby litter bin, but this small area, where ducks paddle and wait to be fed, isn't; instead there is a little sorry patch of grass between the end of the paved, sloping path and the brown sludge that the pond's waters gently lap against.

'It's OK, I've got the baby!' shouts the soggy figure, a woman wearing a now-wet, hooded, long black puffa jacket and bright peach lipstick that makes her resemble a portly penguin. 'The baby's alright!'

A high-pitched wail punctuates the end of the sentence: Wilfred expressing his displeasure, a noise I've sighed at so many times in the middle of the night but now couldn't be happier to hear.

At last I reach the pram, dragging my daughter with one hand and stretching out for my son with another. Wilfred is still tucked in under the knitted patchwork blanket my mother-in-law knitted for him. He's safe. Thank God he's alive and evidently still has good use of his lungs. What have I done? How can I have put him in danger, this little boy who means the world to us all?

An older man walking his dog comes over after hearing the commotion. 'Is everything alright? Do you need any help?' he asks. His black Labrador, despite being on a lead, sniffs too close to Wilfred's wrinkled up, sobbing face for my liking, and I lean further into the pram to create a protective barrier between them.

'Everything's fine,' the penguin replies, yielding the pram to me.

The man, sporting a green wax jacket and a white moustache that needs a good trim, beckons his dog towards him. There's a deep crease between his eyebrows.

'Well then, no harm done. Accidents happen. It's not easy with two children is it,' he says, moving to leave and then adding, 'Perhaps next time you're out with both you could bring someone else with you?' With that he clears his throat and goes on his way in the direction of the bandstand.

Never have I felt so small.

'Patronising git. Ignore him, the old duffer,' the penguin woman says, rolling her eyes. Immediately I feel a kindred spirit. That's the sort of thing I think but my Catholic upbringing would ever let pass my lips. If you haven't anything nice to say then don't say anything at all. I force a weak smile in thanks.

Guilt and shame seep through my pores. I turn to the woman who now, up close, I can see is quite a bit younger than me, without the worry lines and dark eye circles of a mother of two in her mid- to late-thirties who hasn't got the time, inclination or head space to apply make-up before she leaves the house.

'Can you hold onto my daughter for a minute? Thanks,' I say. As soon as the kindly stranger holds Antonia's hand I lean into the pram and scoop up an unharmed Wilfred in his mercifully dry coat and snuggle him close to me, rocking him gently. 'I'm so sorry. Mummy's so sorry. I'll never let it happen again my darling poppet.' I force myself not to cry as many tears as he is. What would James say?

Wilfred has calmed down now, even if I haven't. I gently place him back in his pram. The wheels are covered in green gunge, a mixture of duck excrement and goodness knows what is at the bottom of the pond. The water hadn't reached the seat, therefore the pram hadn't gone very far into the water. But how could it have rolled away from me in the first place? I'm sure I put on the brake. At least I think I'm sure; it's the sort of automatic, unthinking task I always do, like locking the front door when I leave the house or double-checking the hob rings are turned off after cooking.

I didn't get much sleep last night. Wilfred was up half the night and although James offered to help I said no and let him rest, soothing Wilfred myself through the monotony of the breaking dawn and the Shipping Forecast on BBC Radio 4. The names even sunk into my consciousness, speaking 'Rockall, Malin, Hebrides, Bailey,' soothingly to Wilf as if they were a nursery rhyme. The birth of a new

6

day may be magical on a wildlife programme in Tanzania but when looking out of the window of a suburban bungalow at a chipped climbing frame and a garden that screams 'weed me', the rising sun doesn't hold the same attraction.

It was my decision to do the night shift. Thankfully Antonia now usually sleeps right through until 7 a.m. unless she is feeling poorly or has had such a busy day that we forgo her usual bedtime routine of bath, milk, story, bed. James has been particularly busy at work recently trying to prove he is worthy of his promotion last month to a level above the one we were both on in the government department I worked for too until I resigned after maternity leave with Wilfred. Now we are a one-income household we rely on James's salary and there isn't much wiggle room when all the bills are paid, unlike the more profligate past when it was just the two of us, both on decent salaries, choosing to eat out on Friday nights and have romantic weekends away in boutique hotels.

Is my memory failing me? Have I made a terrible error of judgement? In my haste to watch over Antonia did I clean forget to put the pram's brake on? Surely I'm not the sort of mother who would put my much longed-for children in danger? I know I'm my own worst critic. The voice in my head never fails to point out when I haven't lived up to my own standards. Maybe I set them too high but those standards can mean the difference between life and death.

I cling to my son penitently. Underneath the hat the downy hair on the top of his head still smells of the comforting aroma of baby shampoo that I washed it with yesterday evening, mingled with his own unique scent that I would know anywhere.

'Mummy, why did Wilfred's pram roll into the pond?' asks Antonia who has now forgotten about the bird and reverted into big sister mode, pulling silly faces at her brother and sticking her tongue out at him to make him smile. Thank goodness she hasn't realised the danger that Wilfred had been in. My eldest is rather down-to-earth in character and not, unlike a couple of her school friends who try my patience, a child who relishes histrionics and drama.

'I don't know darling. I don't know,' I reply, shaking my head. Antonia lets go of the lady's hand to hug me. I pull her close and give silent thanks that both my children are safe.

The penguin woman tells me what happened. 'I was walking round the corner and I saw the buggy roll down to the pond, that's when I ran to pull it out. It didn't go very far into the water, it can't have been moving very quickly.'

'Thank you. Thank you. I'd never do anything to harm him. Thank you so much. I'm so grateful. I thought I put the brake on, I could have sworn I had,' I gabble.

The woman smiles reassuringly. 'I'm sure you did. The council should have built the wall all the way around the pond. Health and safety. Their responsibility. Perhaps the buggy's brake is faulty? It might be a good idea to get it checked.'

A chill wind blows across my cheeks. 'Yes, great idea. I don't know how to thank you.'

'I'm Claire by the way,' the woman says, offering a pink-mittened hand for me to shake. 'You don't have to thank me, I'm glad I was around. It's getting quite cold though and you've had a shock. How about we go to the café and warm up?' Her eyes move from me to Antonia and twinkle. 'I bet you're a hot chocolate fan.'

My daughter's face lights up. 'With extra marshmallows?'

It *had* been a shock and it *is* cold. I can't face going back to the empty house with my thoughts just yet. My heart is still pounding with consternation and remorse. Some company would do me good. Also I haven't been to a café with an adult for a long time, nor had a conversation with anyone over five who isn't James. I decide to break my daily routine and go. A snack at the café will keep Antonia and Wilfred happy until a slightly later tea-time.

'Another great idea Claire, but I insist that the cake and hot chocolate are on me. I'm Audrey by the way and this is Antonia and Wilfred.'

'Hello!' says Antonia, who wants to prove she is grown-up by shaking hands too. She does so with gusto and I notice that Claire tries not to smile at her pink knitted mitten being pumped up and down by Antonia's much smaller stripy gloves.

We began to walk towards the park's exit with me gripping onto the pram's handles whilst making polite conversation about which café to go to. Is Claire judging me? No, she doesn't appear to be, she hasn't blamed me for taking my eye off Wilfred. I think she wants to help and not criticise. Not that I deserve it. Did I really put the brake on? What if the pram had rolled further in to the pond? What if Claire hadn't been around to pull the pram out before I got there? Could Wilfred, my miracle baby, have drowned? It's a thought too horrific for me even to contemplate.

I make sure Antonia holds on to the side of the pram in our

usual fashion as we walk out of the park gates and along the high street to a well-known coffee shop chain. The blown-up photos of seductive sugary treats and drinks topped with frothy dairy-free milk in the window steer the eye away from the smeared glass. By now the after primary school crowd has headed home and the tables are mainly taken by silver-haired shoppers interspersed with a smattering of lanky teenagers in school uniform. We find a table in a corner that has four seats and enough room to park the pram without it getting in the way of the other customers.

'What would everyone like? I'll go up and order.' I cringe when I realise I'm still using my mummy tone of voice even though an adult, Claire, is included in the conversation. I make a mental note to speak in the way that used to be normal but now is a welcome change.

'Latte please,' Claire replies.

'Cake as well? Go on, we can't have Antonia being the only one eating cake.'

Antonia has taken off her coat and it's in danger of falling from the back of her chair onto the floor. I quickly rescue it. My daughter crosses her arms and looks at me seriously. 'Mummy you have to have cake too because when you don't order cake you always eat some of mine.'

Too true. 'You've got me there darling. I'll order my own. Red velvet for me I think. Which cake would you like Antonia? Chocolate, carrot or Victoria sponge?'

'Chocolate, of course.' In a heartbeat Antonia's face changes from dour to a grin that shows off her wobbly front tooth.

'Well in that case I'll have what she's having. Want any help carrying the tray Audrey?' says Claire.

'I'm fine thanks, I'll ask them to bring it over.'

The couple at the front of the queue take ages deciding what to order. I chastise myself for my impatience when the server offers them a loyalty card, which takes the pair another few minutes to sign up for along with a lengthy explanation on how it works. Just don't tell them about the app I pray, or we'll be here 'til kingdom come.

Suddenly conscious that my children are sitting with a stranger, albeit a friendly one, I look back to check on them. Antonia is chatting away to Claire who smiles with interest whilst rocking Wilfred in his pram at the same time. Usually I don't like non-family or close friends to hold my son; you never can be too careful about colds and viruses that can be so easily passed on, or trust that an acquaintance actually knows how to handle a baby properly. This time, however, I deliberately squash my agitation. I should relax. Claire has earned a free pass and the children look happy enough.

Eventually the loyalty card couple carry their tray to a table. After one other customer it's my turn to order. Wilfred has a bottle of emergency formula in the pram and I buy him a small organic cookie to suck on. He usually has a low-sugar diet but a treat won't hurt him. Poor little lad deserves one after what I put him through today.

I head back to the table a few minutes before the server arrives with our food and drink. 'What have I missed?' I ask brightly, taking Wilfred out of his pram and sitting him on my knee. Thankfully today he doesn't try to wriggle off, he is gurglingly happy to escape the confines of the pram, and tries to grab my specs.

'Claire writes lots of letters every day in an office,' says

Antonia hurriedly, rushing her words with the pleasure of being the first to know this information about our new friend.

'Oh yes? Are you a secretary?' As soon as I say it I wonder if it is still the correct term or if I sound terribly out of date. In the civil service secretaries are called something like administrative officers and what they call a secretary is actually the person in charge of the whole department.

'Office assistant. Filing, typing, making the tea… that sort of thing. Whatever I'm asked to do. A general dogsbody really.'

'What's a dogsbody? Do you have to dress up as a puppy?' Antonia has a very curious mind and never lets adult talk go over her head.

Claire smiles. 'No, no dressing up involved. A dogsbody is someone who has to do all the jobs at work that other people don't want to do.'

'I like dressing up. I was a pumpkin at Halloween.'

'I wish I had someone at home to do all the jobs I don't want to do!' I say, tapping on my phone to show Claire the picture of Antonia wearing an orange costume. Other parents spent hours making bespoke outfits whilst I, not being the creative type, bought Antonia's from a supermarket and kept quiet about its provenance, thankfully remembering to rip the price tag off at the last minute. 'Have you worked there for long?'

'No, a few months. I moved to this area for the job. It's my first permanent contract and even though the job is shi—' she stops herself mid-word, 'I mean not great, it's so much better than being on a zero-hours contract and never knowing when I'll be working or if I'll earn enough in the week to pay my rent.'

I'm relieved I'm just out of the millennial bracket and

was able to buy a home with James before prices went really stupidly sky-high. If we were starting out now there would be no way we could afford our three-bedroom bungalow, never mind have enough put by to enable me to be a full-time mother. The thought makes me feel slightly protective of Claire. No doubt she lives in a crummy flat-share with a bath the others don't clean and her food goes missing from a mouldy fridge. I endured six months of that before James and I moved in together. A friend joked at the time that it was worth getting a partner just to be able to share the rent to afford your own place.

There's a lull in conversation, which I break by asking Claire, 'Do you like it round here? It's great for young families but perhaps a bit quiet for younger people who have to travel to the city for nightlife that's not the local pub.' James and I bought in this area in anticipation of parenthood. Parks, close to the countryside, a primary school with an outstanding Ofsted report.

'I like it quiet. City life is not for me.'

'Where did you live before?'

Claire hesitates slightly. 'Er, Bristol.'

'I wouldn't be able to tell by your voice. You've not got a Bristolian accent.' Claire's voice isn't posh but it doesn't have any burrs, elongated vowels or dropped consonants that would place her from a specific region.

'I never had much of an accent and when I went to uni I lost it.'

'What did you study? Sorry, I'm interrogating you, aren't I? It's just nice to have a conversation with another grown-up!' I inwardly cringe that didn't use the word 'adult' instead.

Antonia jumps into the conversation. 'I'm nearly grown up. I'll be six next birthday,' before stuffing the last of the chocolate cake into her mouth. I shoot her a look to remind her not to speak with her mouth full.

Claire waits until I start eating and, like me, uses a cake fork. 'Business. I thought it would be the best course to get me a job. Like I said, I'm grateful for the permanent contract but I don't know many people around here yet. I'm the youngest one in the office and the others don't go to the pub after work. They've all got families to go home to.'

'It's tricky when you move to a new town for a job. I did that after university too but I was fortunate because at work there was a group of us who all started at the same time. Do you get chance to go home at the weekends?'

'I don't, no.' There's something in the slightly pained expression that crosses Claire's face that tells me not to ask any more questions. Not everyone considers where they grew up to still be home. Perhaps it was a place she was glad to leave.

The conversation turns to the old stalwart of the weather and the week of rain that weather forecasters have predicted to hit our region.

Wilfred, who has been happily babbling away, starts to grizzle. 'OK little man, I get the message. Time to take you home now for a nappy change and bath. Do you need a wee-wee before we go Antonia?' My daughter shakes her head fervently.

'OK, coat on please. Sorry to rush off, Claire. Thanks again for everything. I'm in your debt.'

'Audrey, you're starting to bore me with your thanks. I told you, I don't need them.'

🍂

I'm slightly taken aback at these words until I register her teasing laughter. Claire really is a no-nonsense breath of fresh air. 'Right, no more thanks. But let me give you my phone number. If you're at a loose end sometime and want the company of two children and me then give me a call.'

It's one of those things that people say to be polite, not thinking that the person they're talking to will take them up on it. I'm good at politeness. It's people who aren't that draw attention to themselves.

Claire takes her mobile out of her coat pocket and types in my number then sends a text to me so I have hers too.

We leave her behind in the coffee shop to finish off her cake. On the way home I remember that I'd asked all the questions. Was that rude of me? Claire hadn't asked me anything back. I soon forget this thought when I unlock the front door of our bungalow and my mind turns to plans for the evening ahead and then back to the park incident. In the hallway, just before I lift Wilfred out, I try the brake on the pram again. It works perfectly. To double and triple check I click it off again and again, yet every time all works fine. When I try to push the pram with the brake on the wheels don't budge.

It *must* have been my fault. A bit of bile rises to my throat. I don't have the certainty of it to swear on the Bible in a court of law but there is no other explanation. A prosecution barrister would tear me to shreds. Yet I can't help feeling that failing to do such a simple thing just isn't like me. It is completely out of character, however tired I am. The safety of my children is paramount. If anything I'm probably a bit too overprotective rather than lax. Do I not know myself any more? Is it true what the man in the park implied? Am I not coping well enough? Surely all mums made the odd mistake? Or can I not trust myself?

A sixth sense tells me something isn't quite right.

It also tells me that James needn't know about the pond incident.

~ 2 ~

Antonia is at the end of the lounge that we call the playroom. There are two washable beanbags there; clear plastic boxes full of toys made of wood or fabric wherever possible; crayons and colouring paper; and the baby mat with gym (why do they call it that? There are no exercise bikes, weights or running machines) that Wilfred used to love but now is growing slightly too old for. He's at the stage where he's trying to crawl and flops on his stomach a lot, wriggling like a fish missing the limbs it never had.

I've put on an audiobook for her to listen to and, as I pop my head round the door, see that she's unusually quiet, curled up in the foetal position on the beanbag with the yellow lion's head on that she's claimed as hers. Antonia hardly ever admits that she's tired because she hates to miss out on anything. Her latest mission is to find out what Daddy and I get up to when she's gone to bed. Two nights last week she got up saying she needed a glass of water and asked us if she could join in what we were doing. When she realised, however, that Daddy had brought work home from the office and I was sorting the laundry it didn't take much to persuade her to return to bed. Daddy doing paid work whilst Mummy finishes the housework are definitely not the gender role models we want to set for her though. James and I spent ten minutes laughing and working out what to do the next time Antonia is nosy. We decided on him demonstrating the fluffy duster and me dashing to fix the leaky tap in the kitchen. All pretend of course, I don't know one end of a spanner from the other. We must get round to calling a plumber.

Nevertheless I've noticed that the excitement and stimulation of school does take it out of Antonia sometimes and I'm pleased to see her resting instead of winding herself up into a state of over-tiredness. She looks so sweet lying there, her eyelashes fluttering during a dream and a soft snore sighing between her lips. Our darling daughter. My heart swells with love for her.

Dinner is nearly ready. Wilfred is playing with a cuddly toy in his bouncy chair that I've positioned in the kitchen as far away as I can from cupboards and simmering pans placed on the back hobs. I'm desperate for a quick loo trip so I turn the heat down on the hob and drag the bouncy chair with me into the bathroom. We don't have a lock – James took it off when we were child-proofing the house for Antonia. Privacy in the bath is an historical concept in this house.

As soon as I've pulled my leggings down Wilf throws his toy out of reach, his little face starts to redden and then the bawling begins. I stand up, leggings around my ankles and my greying knickers below my knees, and waddle over to pick up the bear cuddly toy and give it back to him. The crying doesn't stop. I wiggle bear's left hand in a wave to make Wilf smile but unusually this trick doesn't work. It's late in his day. What Wilf no doubt wants is a cuddle then food. It's not long since I weaned him and I still occasionally get tell-tale leaks from my nipples.

Just for once I long for a blasted wee in peace. 'Give me a minute Wilfred darling, Mummy won't be long.' I waddle back and am in mid-flow on the loo when the door creaks open and Antonia, now evidently not listening to her audiobook, barges in.

'Why's Wilfred crying, Mummy?'

'I'm on the loo sweetheart, I'll see to him in a tic. Remember that we knock before we go into the bathroom.' My daughter looks at me with impatience for her brother and then lifts him out of the bouncy chair to hug him. 'There there, Wilfred, Antonia's here.' I turn my head away so she doesn't see me smirk at her grown-up mothering attempt. She really is five going on fifteen, particularly when she copies both her paternal grandma's tuts at my supposed lapse in motherhood duties and my technique for rocking a baby.

I pull up my knickers and leggings, flush the loo then make a show of explaining to Antonia the importance of washing my hands afterwards. 'Yes I know, Mummy,' she says rolling her eyes. 'You and Daddy have told me lots of times before. Then you've got to dry your hands on the towel until they're not wet any more.'

'That's right, well remembered.' I give her a kiss in acknowledgement then take Wilfred from her arms and carry him through to the highchair in the kitchen, tying his bib behind his neck. Antonia sits on her chair around the table. Like mine, her seat has a padded cushion on top. Hers is blue with yellow stars on whilst mine is a cheap, slightly stained white one from IKEA.

I serve up dinner, mine in a pasta dish, Antonia's in a smaller bowl and Wilfred's pureed version in his plastic tray. He likes having his own spoon and trying to feed himself, although his hand co-ordination isn't quite up to it yet. We have a good three minutes of eating time before the pasta sauce I spent over half an hour simmering, which oozes with organic tomatoes, fresh basil, garlic, ground pepper and carrots cut up so infinitesimally small they won't be noticed by little eyes or taste buds, slides down the once-sparkling kitchen cupboard door globule by red globule, slithering snake-like down towards the slate floor.

I can't jump up to grab some kitchen roll and stop it in its tracks because the thrower of the dinner, Wilfred, who evidently has decided once again that lobbing his food is much more fun than eating it, turns bright red with anger and threatens to hyperventilate. I calm him down just in time to stop him throwing his plastic spoon in the same direction and whisk the bowl, emptied now of its expertly cooked nutritious contents, out of his reach, all the while saying in a sing-song voice, 'That's not what we do Wilfred is it? Food is for our tummies, not the walls!'

If it's possible to get to the end of your tether I'm very nearly there, clinging on to the edge with my fingernails ripping off millimetre by millimetre. Chairing an important meeting at work was ten times easier than this.

Antonia looks on with the indignation of a superior five-year-old who of course doesn't remember how she behaved as a baby. 'Wilfred is very naughty, isn't he Mummy?' she says. She is devouring her own portion and it won't be long before she finishes. I know she'll be bored if she has to sit and wait for her yoghurt pudding until Wilfred has settled and I've finally fed him with some of the leftovers in the pan that I was saving for James when he gets in. Still, I know that although right now she is enjoying watching her brother being mischievous, later Antonia will want to snap back into big sister mode and want to help bathe her brother and read him a bedtime picture book. I adore how much she obviously loves Wilfred and it's a joy to see his happy, chubby face as he holds out his arms to be picked up when she plays with him.

I love my children, I really do with all my soul. It took so many years of heartache for James and I to start and then complete our family, years when I felt so low and desperate every time my period came right on time, more punctual than a credit card statement dropping onto the doormat. I'd wanted to howl and scream out my pain and I begrudged every pregnant woman I saw in the street even though I knew logically that them having a baby didn't make it any less likely that I would. I never told anyone other than James.

I feel so guilty about thinking, albeit only in the dark corner of my mind, that however much I adore my children and wouldn't want to be without them, if I'd known before about how all-encompassing motherhood really is then perhaps, just perhaps, I'd have thought twice.

My joints are hurting. I avoid taking Wilf out of his highchair just yet because the mood he's in he'll arch his body to make it much harder for me to carry him. I suppress my urge to clean up the pile of tomato sauce now sludging on the floor. I virulently hate mess but instead reach for my smartphone to play nursery rhyme songs through the kitchen speaker via Bluetooth.

Time to reach for the only parenting strategy my exhausted brain can think of at the moment. 'Let's see if Wilf remembers all the animal sounds we taught him!' I say to Antonia using my overly enthusiastic mummy tone. 'Can you show your brother how to sing "Old Macdonald"?' Antonia, having a theatrical bent and always keen to show willing, launches straight in with gusto. In cahoots we make Wilfred giggle with our animal impressions and I kiss his forehead when he joins in with 'E-i-e-i-o!'

Surreptitiously whilst we're singing I slip Wilfred a piece of breadstick to suck on and put the rest, broken into pieces, with a few raisins on his tray. I've had second thoughts about risking a re-run of the Spanish Tomatina Festival in the kitchen. Wilfred is much more amenable to feeding himself with his tiny fingers than being spoon-fed by his mother. When the carbohydrate and fruit combo has disappeared I switch the music off, declaring that Antonia and Wilf sang so well that they can pick their own flavour of yoghurt for dessert. Antonia asks for strawberry and I feed a banana and mango puree to Wilfred who, this time, is happy enough to play trains and open his mouth for me to get some fruit into him. Instead of a yoghurt I focus on the one chilled glass of Sauvignon Blanc I'll be having at wine o'clock when the children are in bed and James is home.

When I've settled Wilfred down in his cot I usually spend time reading a story to Antonia and then tuck her up in bed. Tonight Wilfred is fractious and is wriggling in his sleep sack when I've closed the picture book, drawn the blackout blinds in the nursery and switched his night light and baby monitor on. On a good day James is home from work in time to help out but recently he's been missing quite a few bedtimes because his boss wants him to stay late at the office. His new manager is a woman but doesn't fly the feminist flag. She's not a mother herself and despite the existence of the department's official parental policies, doesn't cut James any slack as a father. I joked that she fancied him and was making excuses to keep him in the office but apparently she's married to a woman, so no worries there then – not that I would ever think James is the kind to cheat.

I know he's having a hard time at work but at times I envy him for not being permanently on childcare-call. I miss meetings, going for lunch with colleagues and using my brain. But I have no right to complain. We made the decision together that I would give up work and look after the children. I wanted to stay at home.

When I worked part-time after Antonia joined us I felt that I was failing at both being a mother and an employee, not having enough time to dedicate properly to both. No doubt though that if the boot was on the other foot and James was the stay-at-home parent I'd dreadfully miss having one-on-one time with the children and resent him for being able to do so. He often says he wishes he could take an equal parenting role but we both know the finances don't stack up for that to happen.

Finally, after I've sung to him for ten minutes, crouching in the dark by his cot, Wilfred drops off to sleep and I creep back into the kitchen, not wanting to turn the television on in the lounge yet in case the noise wakes the children up. My mobile rings and it's James apologising for his no-show and saying that he'll be home in about half an hour. I tell him we've all missed him and he replies he loves us. In my chest my heart flutters a little – even after more than ten years of marriage he still has that effect on me.

I press the on button on the digital radio and put Radio 4 on at low volume. It's a documentary about regional inequality in health care provision and I quickly retune to an easy-listening music station, deciding that it's all my brain can take at the moment, whilst I'm cleaning up and loading the dishwasher. Andy Williams, the Lighthouse Family and the Bee Gees keep me company.

I'm drying my hands on a now-dirty tea-towel when the phone rings again. James probably, saying he's stuck in a traffic jam and will be even later home. But it's not him. The caller has a woman's voice.

'Hello. Is that Audrey?'

'Speaking.' I can't place the voice and slip into 'work answering the telephone' mode. Chipper, professional and emotionless. I hope it's not someone selling something. Despite me placing my number on a register to not receive cold callers occasionally one gets through. Then I check if there's a number on the screen – I'd answered without looking – and there are three words appearing: 'Claire from park'.

I switch the radio off in the background hoping she hadn't heard Barry Manilow singing out. It takes a second for my brain to place 'Claire from park' and when I do the guilt at not putting the pram brake on roars again with a biting nausea. The baby monitor is quiet when I turn to double check and see if there are any lights on, not fully trusting my ears.

'It's Claire here, I met you today in the park.'

There's a silence before I reply. 'Yes, hello?'

'I just wanted to thank you for the drink and cake. It was nice to meet you all.'

'No problem. Thanks for helping us out. I really appreciate it.' I don't say what for.

'I'm not interrupting anything, am I?'

'Only loading the dishwasher!'

There's a brief laugh on the other end of the line. 'I don't have to do any dishes tonight because I bought a takeaway burger. The house I live in doesn't have a dishwasher anyway. I'm calling because I found a little blue giraffe toy when you left the coffee shop. I wonder if it might be Wilfred's? It was on the floor under our table.'

George the Giraffe is one of the few toys I usually tuck in Wilfred's pram. My son is used to being without George for a few hours when I fling him in the washing machine (the toy, not my son I hasten to add) to remove the dribble – Wilfred is going through a stage of wanting to put everything in his mouth at the moment – but no doubt he'll want him soon. He must have thrown George out of the pram when I wasn't looking.

Another time today when I wasn't looking.

'Oh thanks! I didn't realise George was missing.' What must Claire think of me? I fail to put the pram's brake on and manage to lose a soft toy all in one day. A flashback comes into my head and I quickly dismiss it. I won't go there, I *can't* go there again. Deep breaths. Control your thoughts Audrey.

'George?'

'The giraffe! Don't worry, George isn't a child. He's a

giraffe. Well a toy one anyway.' What am I saying? Why am I nervous? I realise it's because I don't want her to think I'm a terrible failure of a mother.

'I had a teddy when I was a child that I wouldn't be without, but I wasn't very imaginative. I called it Teddy.'

I smiled. 'Fitting name!'

I heard Claire laugh down the phone. There's a lull in conversation before she says: 'Shall I drop George round or do you want to meet up sometime? If you've not been "out out" for a while do you fancy a quick drink after the kids' bedtime?'

Of course I didn't drink when I was pregnant with Wilfred but since then I've enjoyed my one glass of wine in the evening when the children are in bed. I suppose it wouldn't do any harm to have it in a pub rather than at home. I have rather got into a routine and it might be nice to go out when the children are in bed. Not for long though, in case they won't settle and I'm needed at home. They're not used to being without me for very long. I'll ask James, see what he thinks.

But then again why should I? I cover for him when he works late. It's not babysitting when it's your own children, is it? Yes, going to the pub will be something different, a chance to put some make-up on and see if I still fit into my pre-maternity going out clothes.

I'm mentally flicking through the contents of my wardrobe when another thought surfaces. Claire is quite a bit younger than me. Will she think I'm middle-aged, boring and frumpy? I've been living in old tunics and leggings with stretched elastic. And will we have anything in common?

Nowadays I have little to talk about other than the children. Or facts I've heard on TV.

Nevertheless I decide to be brave. 'Yes, a quick drink would be great. I'll have to check with James about which evening he knows he'll be able to come home from work on time so I can go out. Is it alright if I text you with a few dates?'

'Sure, I don't have much going on at the moment, I'm free most evenings. I always try to leave work on time, I'm paid so little for what I do that I'm not giving them free labour! I could do tomorrow or the day after. Which area do you live in?'

I tell her and we agree that I'll text her to confirm a night. The click of the front door opening – James's arrival – prompts me to say goodbye and end the call.

It's about ten minutes later, when James is dishing up the sorry-looking reheated pasta, that I realise that Claire asked me where I live but never said where she does.

~ 3 ~

There are two secrets I hold inside my head, locked in with a heavy-duty padlock in an indestructible box. One is that I envy my husband's ability to come and go when he pleases with the excuse of being the sole breadwinner, his promotion, and having to work late to impress the management. The other I keep to myself because I don't know if I'm imagining it.

Back to my first secret. When I took into account the trauma of all the negative pregnancy tests and the arrival of my period that bled over all our hopes, it was inconceivable to me to miss out on Wilfred's early childhood. When Antonia had arrived and I worked part-time after a year, I'd hated having to rush and drop her off at nursery when she was crying and also when the nursery staff told me she'd said a new word or achieved something that I wasn't there to witness. Even though I was part-time I felt I had to do extra to prove myself as the one in the office who had to leave on the dot to pick up Antonia, although, to be fair James did share pick-up duties. Yet even when I came home from work and James was there bouncing Antonia on his knee, the achievement I'd felt at clearing my desk for the day was kicked into touch by the aching longing to have more time to spend with her, slightly begrudging the extra time James had with his daughter. Stupid and immature I know, that's why it's a secret I keep to myself.

James hates having to work late but he does so because austerity and redundancies have hit the public sector hard. Nobody's job is guaranteed. I wasn't replaced after I resigned. Fewer people in the department doesn't mean there's less work to do, but in an occasional fit of pique I do wonder occasionally whether sometimes him staying late at the office is down to personal choice rather than necessity; a break from the mealtime struggle to feed Wilfred, Antonia's tired tantrums and free time to go to the loo in peace. I bet he even takes the newspaper in there.

It's years now since I had the luxury of presenteeism. I used to be keen to arrive at the office early and stay late to finish as much of my to-do list as I could, keen to use my brain and make my mark in the happy knowledge that I had James, a takeaway and our warm bed to go home to.

Once I passed my mid-twenties and the thrill of adulthood had ebbed away, I began to wonder exactly what the point was to all this. Did what I do for a living define me as a person? Was this it until retirement? Shouldn't life be more spiritually fulfilling? It was about the same time that my biological clock began to tick with a loud beat.

We always knew we wanted to start a family at some point but that point always hovered a few years into the future. I know I'm incredibly fortunate to have two children when James and I thought, following those excruciating years, that we wouldn't be able to have any. I'd shared my trials with one of my best friends who also couldn't conceive. When

I found out I was pregnant, coinciding with Sophie's IVF failing for a fourth time, she sent me an email saying she was sorry but she couldn't be around me any more because it was too upsetting. She ignored my emails and phone calls back. I felt her pain at my joy, but the hole she left in my life has never quite healed. Would I have been noble enough to keep our friendship if it had been the other way around?

James finishes his pasta and then pops into a slumbering Antonia's room to check on her. Looking in from the doorway I see our daughter wake up to hug her daddy and tell him what she's done that day. I hold my breath as I wonder if she's going to tell him about the pram incident. She doesn't, however; her excited chatter focuses on our coffee shop trip, a rare treat, and a description of how many marshmallows were on top of her hot chocolate. Guess Daddy, guess!

'Glad you treated yourselves, you should do it more often. Antonia seems to have enjoyed it!' says James as we creep along the corridor to the lounge and shut the door quietly behind us. It's time to put the TV on low and find a drama to watch on Netflix. We sit next to each other on the sofa that I'd earlier removed toys from.

I know I should tell him what happened.

'We met a nice woman in the park, Claire, and she suggested we all go to the coffee shop. After she'd suggested it I couldn't disappoint Antonia and not go.'

'How did you start talking with Claire? Not like you to chat with strangers.'

'I, I…'

I chicken out. The sixth sense wins. I don't want him to think I'm incapable of keeping our two children safe.

'Passing the time of day, the weather, that sort of thing.' I scratch my nose and look away.

It's true I'm quite shy and like to keep myself to myself. I don't make new friends easily. I'm the sort of person who would much rather have dinner with one or two friends than go to a party. At least motherhood is a perfect excuse to get me out of the rare invitations we are offered.

I decide to tell a half-truth. 'Actually, Wilfred dropped George and she found him after we'd left the coffee shop. Claire has suggested that we meet up for a drink in the evening to give him back to me.'

James picks up the remote control, turns on our huge TV (his choice) that hangs on the wall, immediately mutes the sound and beings to flick through the dramas available.

'So you have to go out for a drink to get George back?' He looks bemused.

'We got on. She suggested a drink. She's new around here and younger than me. I think she's a bit lonely. I remember what it was like when I moved here after uni and didn't know anyone. You didn't go through that of course.' I laugh. His university girlfriend moved here with him until she dumped James for her new boss.

He smiles at our running joke about the girlfriend from hell. 'When are you going out? I'll mind the children. Do you want the sci-fi one or the American drug cartel series?'

'Is tomorrow alright? Will you be able to come home from work on time? If we all eat together then I'll get ready and nip out afterwards. I won't be long. Sci-fi please.'

'OK to both!'

We snuggle up together with James's arm around me to

watch the drama set in a futuristic world where Earth has colonised Mars but there's a rival company trying to destroy the shanty town built there. Daft but enjoyable. I savour this adult time, being with each other but not feeling the need to talk or having to make decisions, just the two of us as one. I cocoon my head under his shoulder, leaning in and inhaling the familiar musky scent of his aftershave, a smell that always makes me feel like I'm home and safe. A five o'clock dark brown shadow has appeared on his chin and under his top lip and he's wearing the hoodie he reserves for wearing around the house after work. Family time. This is the side of him only I get to see: relaxed, natural, slightly dishevelled, a far cry from his workday suits or weekend uniform of jeans and a T-shirt or jumper.

I'm so comfortable I could easily nod off but the programme ends with a shocking cliffhanger – has the Earth Commander died in the HQ blast started by the rebels? – and it grabs my attention. Addictive plotting designed for people who can binge-watch TV all night. We reluctantly agree to watch the next episode another time and I have to pull myself away from James's warm body to get ready for bed.

There's a loud crack when James stands up and we both wince in case it was loud enough to wake the children up. He's stood on and broken a painted wooden child figurine of Antonia's that escaped me during my clean-up. It has split through the torso and a few jagged splinters are sticking out at will. The face on the figurine now appears to have more of a grimace than a smile. How easy it is to make a mistake, to forget something, only for it be irreparable. Some things superglue can't fix.

James says to throw the figurine away and Antonia probably won't notice it's missing. I'll know it is though. The blue dot eyes glaring out from the cracked figure seem to taunt me for my oversight. Another one. I put it in kitchen bin and hide its face under some other plastic packaging but still get the feeling that it's watching me. It *knows*.

I creep into my children's rooms to check they're safely sleeping. They are, like little cherubs, so innocent and so vulnerable. A single thought plays on an infinite loop in my head: What if it wasn't a figurine I let break, but my child?

In bed it feels very ironic that Wilfred and Antonia are fast asleep and yet I'm wide awake, staring at the shadows on the ceiling, my thoughts in an interminable loop, knotting and tying themselves together until I'm stuck rigid to the bed in blind panic.

James is lightly snoring in an almost endearing, rhythmic manner. I turn over to check the digital number on the alarm clock. It's only five minutes later than when I looked before. I try and use a mindfulness technique I read about in a magazine: take slow breaths, in and out, and think of a time I treasure for being one of the happiest.

Behind my eyelids I see Antonia wearing her new pirate outfit, a party hat on her head, clapping excitedly as she blows out the three candles on her birthday cake. All the people I love are there; James, his parents, my mum before she died last year, Sophie and her husband Gary, Rob – my best friend from university and Antonia's godfather – and Alex and Emma, James's sisters, who live far away but are proud godmothers. I can almost taste the Victoria sponge sugared icing on James's lips when we kiss and he holds me close, exultant to finally have the happy family we'd striven for. We all sing happy birthday to Antonia… but then the memory stops and another pushes it violently aside and takes its place.

And my second secret? I think someone may be stalking me.

~ 4 ~

It's the sort of chilly morning that can turn sunny or rainy at the drop of a hat. The wind blows itself out then quietens down to take a breather before swaying branches in a silent dance again with its second puff. There's a nip in the air, the smell of the melting frost on the soil, but if the sun does peek outside from behind the clouds it will feel much warmer than the thermometer says. I've wrapped up the children in their winter coats. Antonia has pulled the zip down on hers and is not playing the zip game as per usual to see if she can do it in one long sweep because she says she's too hot. My daughter definitely knows her own mind and I love her for it. At five she has a fearlessness and confidence I sometimes struggle to have at more than thirty years older.

Like every other school day Wilfred and I walk Antonia to the school gates about a quarter of a mile away from our home, and again like every other school day I've factored in an extra quarter of an hour in timings for the last-minute delays that often happen: Antonia needing another wee, Wilfred being sick or, as happened a fortnight ago, the toaster spontaneously combusting. I want Antonia to arrive at the school gates calm, collected and in good time, and for me to not be one of those mothers who drags her child along with seconds to spare.

There's a new tarpaulin hanging from the playground railings announcing the school's recent outstanding Ofsted rating. Before I moved here I didn't realise that the school's great rating was partly due to the lack of social housing and families on low incomes in the area. I'm embarrassed that it's people like James and me who could afford the rising house prices which ended up forcing young locals out to cheaper areas. That doesn't mean I'll move though. That's another thing to feel guilty about, not putting my money where my principles are.

Wilfred is a little grouchy today. I think he's teething and I can't imagine how that must feel to a baby who can't understand what's going on. I rock the pram gently whilst Antonia spots her friend Ophelia in the playground and runs off to play with her.

I nod at a few other women at the gates I've met before. The school gates are very tribal and I am not aligned with any of the groups. I never was a clique person. At school I had two or three close friends but never a gang.

There are the glam mums who always have full make-up on, even if it's the look that's supposed to appear au naturel (so why bother?), and I can tell they're the sort who have thought about their outfit the night before rather than pulling on any old thing that the baby hasn't been sick on. They waft past in a haze of expensive perfume and laugh loudly with each other wanting to show everyone else what a great time they're having together.

A few women at the gates are nannies or au pairs. They stick together and, if they don't have another child with them, huddle outside the gates to share a cigarette like rebellious teenagers.

There is a smattering of dads – the glam mums align themselves with the handsome one but leave the less-salubrious men alone to hang out with the few grandparents roped in to do the school drop-off and pick-ups. I recognise three women who are usually late and run up the path trailing their child behind them, sprinting towards the gate before it is shut and locked. I'm always setting off back home with Wilfred then. There's one mum who looks a lot younger than the rest of us that I say hi to because, like me, she's usually standing on her own. Antonia has had a few playdates with daughters of the glam mums but, however polite they are outside school, the parents don't include me in their playground circle.

I'm lost in my own thoughts when I nearly push Wilfred's pram into a woman on the way out of the school yard. I really should be more careful. I apologise but she doesn't acknowledge me, then walks away in the opposite direction. How rude. Am I that invisible? At least it wasn't one of the glam mums, then I'd probably be the talk of the playground gossip all day. Mum in out-of-control of her pram shocker!

My daily routine carries on like clockwork as per usual. As Wilfred won't settle there's little time for fun play with him. Finally he goes down for his afternoon nap and I look through my wardrobe to decide what to wear tonight. The decision does not take long at all thanks to me having very few clothes that aren't for work or hanging around with the children. I settle on a blue flowery wrap dress I can wear with boots. Thankfully when I try it on, with one ear out listening if Wilfred is waking up, it fits – that's the beauty of the wrap style, you can let it out a bit around your body's padded parts.

Today's big job is batch cooking some vegetarian mince Bolognese. Most is headed for the freezer but I reserve some to top with mash potato for tonight's fake shepherd's pie dinner, baked in a Pyrex dish I inherited from my mum after she died. The white dish with an orange and brown flower on the outside instantly reminds me of home. We often had shepherd's pie for dinner. Mum always made it with beef mince and it was only years later, when watching a cookery show on the television, that I learnt its proper name is cottage pie. Shepherd's pie is made with lamb mince. When I think of a shepherd I think of a sheepdog and I certainly don't want to imagine eating dog mince, so today it's veggie mince all round. Mum laughed when I told her about the meal's proper name. It doesn't matter what it's called as long as it tastes good, she said. I can almost hear her say it now in her high voice, which sounded frailer near the end. Thinking of Mum brings up a pang of grief that I don't have time to acknowledge. It's nearly school pick-up time and Mum would tell me off if I was late meeting Antonia at the gates.

I finish making little potato tufts with a fork on top of the mash, cover it with a clean tea-towel (I've banned clingfilm from the kitchen) and carefully slide it onto the lower shelf in the fridge. By the time I've coaxed Wilfred into his pram and we're heading off down the road, avoiding the lumpy tree roots protruding from the cracked pavement stones and the cars blocking the dropped kerbs, we still have a few minutes to spare. 'Mummy's going out tonight for a drink,' I tell my wide-eyed son as I walk along. 'I haven't done that since before you came along, my poppet.' He responds by dribbling, which I quickly wipe away with a muslin cloth I keep handy.

I'm tucking the cloth away when a fleeting shadow renders me rigid mid-movement. I see it out of the corner of my eye darting behind some trees on the other side of the road. I did see it, didn't I? A few times now near the school I've seen a shadow slip away or felt eyes watching me, causing the hairs on the back of my neck to bristle. But what if I'm imagining it?

Now once again, mother's instinct puts my body on alert. I jerk my head around. There's no one there. 'Hello?' I call. 'Can I help you?' I walk up to densely packed conifers planted to shield the house behind them from the road. I'm not very brave. I don't really want to investigate but I need to know what I saw. If anything. I think I hear a rustle but I can't be sure because a car drives past and dominates the soundscape. I clutch the handles of the pram with sweaty palms. Wilfred, thank goodness, is happy dribbling away, oblivious. The soft soles of my trainers make no noise on the entrance to the driveway but the muscles of my heart pumping blood are as loud in my ears as a pneumatic drill. How can anyone else not hear it? I take a few tentative steps more. My head is level to the conifers now – all I need to do is peek behind. I take a deep breath, trying to be as silent as possible. Wilfred for once is as quiet as a mouse. My heart's decibels crank up. I begin to move my head…

'What are you doing? Are you alright?' a woman's voice with a slightly muted tone says behind me, making me jump a few steps back before turning around to face the road, fingers still gripped to the pram's handles.

I instantly recognise the woman who is looking at me quizzically, no doubt thinking I'm some sort of intruder or weirdo pram lady. It's the woman from school I nearly hit with the pram this morning. She's about thirty, wearing jeans and a blue sweatshirt with a sunshine happy face printed on it, and a leather jacket. Around her neck is a chunky, multicoloured knitted cowl. She's average height for an adult woman, although everyone looks tall to me, and she's carrying a battered brown leather handbag with a not-quite-shut zip that's struggling to keep all the contents inside. Her stunning curly black hair is tied up in a ponytail and now I realise why she didn't acknowledge me this morning. In each ear she's wearing a hearing aid, the visible sort with a brown plastic case tucked behind the helix. She's deaf and won't have heard me this morning because she wasn't looking at me. I instantly feel relieved that she hadn't been ignoring me until the embarrassment at being found snooping in a stranger's garden returns with a bang.

'Hello, I thought I saw someone dash behind the trees. It scared me. I'm not burgling the joint, honestly,' I jest, trying to make light of the situation.

'Do you want me to have a look with you?'

'Well, if you don't mind. I'm probably just being silly though.'

The woman walks up to me and together we look behind the conifers. There's no one there, not even a dog or cat I might have mistaken for something else. What a fool I must look to her.

'Thank you. You've got a child at the Church of England primary school haven't you? I'm on my way there to pick up my daughter.'

'No problem. You can't be too careful these days,

40

especially near a school. I suppose you could have seen someone and they went down the side path to the back garden.' The driveway is at the right-hand side of the house as we're facing it. I see now what she's referring to, a path beginning at the left-hand side of the house. A gate there is half open. Could she be right? Did I see someone and they ran through there? I can hardly trespass into a stranger's back garden to check. Maybe it was the owner I saw returning to their house, or perhaps I didn't see anything at all. What with all this pram brake business I'm doubting my own senses.

'I don't know. It may have been a trick of the light.'

'I'm Tina by the way and yes, my son recently started at the school.' Tina offers her hand confidently for me to shake. I notice short, bitten nails and the lack of glossy manicure. My kind of mother, unlike the glam mums at school who think it's a crime to turn up at the gates in leggings sans glossy manicure. I shake her hand. 'Audrey. My daughter Antonia is in Miss Abidi's class.'

She smiles, a real one from her eyes and not just a polite, toothy gesture. 'So is my son! We've moved here recently to be near my partner's parents. More help with childcare and the like. It's a bit daunting actually at the school gates. All the mums seem to know each other already.'

'It is a bit cliquey,' I reply. 'I know some parents to say hello to but that's about it.'

'Well let's stick together then. Your daughter is called Antonia did you say? My son is Jordan. I work freelance at home and I'm usually the one who does the school runs although of course the one time Daddy does it is always Jordan's favourite!'

I feel at ease around Tina. We start walking towards the

school, leaving behind the conifers and whatever I may or may not have seen.

'Same here. Antonia loves it when my husband has a day off and takes her to school. It's because it's a novelty though. That's what I tell myself anyway!'

'And who is this?' I can tell she's being polite because she doesn't know whether my baby is a boy or a girl. He's wearing a green coat today, visible under the crochet primary colour baby blanket handcrafted by James's mum. Thankfully she made it before Wilfred was born and she didn't know which sex he would be. I avoid dressing him in blue most of the time even though most of the clothes that were given to us as new baby gifts fitted the boy stereotype.

'My son, Wilfred. Antonia's little brother. Do you have any more?'

'No, we've been trying but it hasn't happened yet.'

'I know what that's like,' I empathise, and don't press her further.

'What do you think of the school? We were lucky they had a place for Jordan, the Ofsted reports are good.'

'So far Antonia's very happy there.'

We continue chatting amiably about the school, Miss Abidi, and other children in the class until we reach the gates a minute before the children start to stream out. The glam mums are huddled together laughing again with such extravagance it could be part of a pre-scheduled performance designed to make other parents feel inadequate that they don't know the joke. A couple of the grandparents say hello and comment on the weather. One toddler is having a red-faced, heartfelt tantrum.

The doors open and some children start to run out into the playground with scuffed trouser knees, undone shoelaces and big smiles on their faces. I look out for Antonia. She emerges a minute or so later linking arms with Megan, her current best friend, although that title is proffered to a different child seemingly every week. Megan skips off to a woman I presume is her grandma and Antonia waves at me, looking very cute carrying her oversized school bag. No doubt by the time she reaches Year 6 it'll be far too small.

'Mummy, guess what I did today? I saw a frog!' Antonia is buzzing with excitement, unable to contain all she wants to tell me. She starts to tell me about the nature walk her class had been on when a young boy runs up, narrowly avoiding charging directly into his mum, Tina. Jordan has darker skin than her lighter black complexion and instantly wants to add his story of the frog. He and Antonia both battle to get a word in edgeways.

'Do you play much with Antonia in class?' Tina asks her son to change the topic.

Antonia butts in, 'Jordan is new. He doesn't play with many people.'

'Would you like to play with him?' I say, then regret it in case she says no.

Antonia looks at Jordan who is jumping from foot to foot.

'Do you like football and stories?' she asks him. Jordan nods.

'Then I'd like to play with you. We can take it in turns to be the goalkeeper.'

'Why don't I arrange with your mum for you to come over for dinner after school one night? We've got a garden

43

to run around in and it doesn't matter where you hit the ball because we haven't had time to plant anything yet!' Tina says.

'Yes please,' Antonia replies politely. I'm proud of her and sense that Megan may soon be demoted. She and Jordan chat away whilst Tina and I swap numbers and look at our calendars on our mobile phones, settling on Thursday next week.

A familiar scent hits me and I sniff Wilfred in his pram. 'Time to go home Antonia, Wilfred needs a nappy change.' Jordan screws up his nose and wafts his hand in front of his face until Tina tells him to stop it.

'Mummy, have you got your nappy on today?' my dearest daughter blurts out insouciantly. 'Mummy's nappy is smaller than Wilfred's. It's from a different packet in the loo.'

Tina tries not to laugh and shoots me a sympathetic look. 'Mummies don't wear nappies, silly. Babies do,' Jordan says.

'My mummy does.'

'Doesn't.'

'Does!'

'I've explained to you haven't I Antonia that it's not a nappy, it's a special pad, something that grown-up ladies have to wear now and again.'

'Why?' asks Jordan.

'Chips and sausages for dinner?' Tina interjects hurriedly and Jordan cheers, the subject of menstruation soon forgotten. I smile at her in thanks.

'Mummy, can we have chips?' At my house frozen chips and Quorn nuggets are an emergency meal for if there's nothing else in the house, but that rarely happens.

'I've made a shepherd's pie.'

'Awww…'

'You love shepherd's pie. I'll stir up lots of gravy.'

'I love gravy!'

'I know you do. That's why I'm making it.'

We say goodbye to Tina and Jordan and I walk us home a different route from the way we came, even though it takes longer. I skip the park. Today I want to get my children home, safely behind a locked door, and batten down the hatches. In the road next to ours I see a dog run out from behind a front-garden hedge. It's obvious to me, by the size and shape of its shadow, that it's a dog. I know in my heart that I saw someone, a person, earlier on.

But if I'm right, who on earth could it have been?

~ 5 ~

As promised James arrives home at six o'clock having worked through his lunch break. The children have had a snack but not enough to put them off their dinner. I've pureed a big ladleful of the shepherd's pie for Wilfred, and I dish out portions for the rest of us from the Pyrex dish.

James being home makes me feel safe and, when I quickly tell him when the children are out of earshot what I thought I saw this afternoon, he reassures me by saying it was probably nothing but if it happens again I should call the police if I'm worried. He looks up the telephone number of the local police and saves it on my phone. All I want to do after dinner and putting the children to bed is stay in, watch a bit of television with James and get an early night. Then I remember my drink with Claire. It'd be bad manners to cancel now without a decent excuse, wouldn't it? Then again it's not like I know her.

'Just go for one,' says James. 'You never know, you might enjoy yourself and want to stay out later.' We're in the bedroom and the blue wrap dress is lying on top of the duvet, where I left it earlier on, ready for me to change into. It seems as if it's detritus from another life, when I was another person, not a stay-at-home mum of two.

I start to take off my clothes. 'It feels like I'm going on a first date or something. Sophie used to tell me tales from when she went internet dating before she got together with Gary. She once met up with a man who was so boring that she said she was going to the loo and left the restaurant.'

'Really?' James laughs. 'Poor bloke. He probably didn't think he was boring.'

'She said she couldn't bear another minute listening to him talk about house price changes in the area. He was an estate agent.'

'Maybe he was nervous? I can imagine Sophie didn't take long to make up her mind.' Typical James supporting the underdog. He's right though, Sophie always was quite opinionated and headstrong. It was one of the things I liked about her, something that made her so different from me. Something I miss.

'What if I'm the boring one? She doesn't want to hear me talk about the children all night. I haven't got anything else to say.'

'Of course you have.' James comes up behind me and massages my shoulders the way he knows I like. 'Current affairs. That's always a winner. Or ask her about herself. People always like talking about themselves.'

'I don't.'

He kisses my neck in the special spot he knows I adore and I close my eyes, savouring the moment. Perhaps I could not turn up and James and I could make the most of Antonia and Wilf being asleep before one of them wakes up and needs attention. I press myself against his lips but he stops suddenly and passes the blue dress with one hand.

'That's because you're modest. You deserve a change. How about we have a code? If you're having an awful time send me a text saying "Wilf" and I'll call you and ask you to come home, make up some story about him being sick or something.'

'You want to get rid of me?' I smile.

'Of course not. I want you to enjoy yourself and then come back home happy and in the mood.'

'Ah, that's your ulterior motive.'

'Of course.' He helps me tie the bow at the back of the dress. 'You look beautiful.' This time he kisses me on top of the head, knowing it's safe to do so because I haven't brushed my hair yet.

'OK, I'll go and I'll text you if I want to come home. I won't be late anyway. No chance of lying in tomorrow with our two for an alarm clock.'

Beside the wardrobe is a freestanding long mirror. I pick up the hairbrush from a basket on top of the chest of drawers and then look at myself, brushing my shoulder-length brown hair until it falls straight and starts to shine. Next I swap the brush for a little make-up bag containing products that are all at least three years old except the SPF primer I usually put on over my moisturiser to stave off skin cancer. I open a half-used compact of rosy-peach powder blusher and pat some on my cheeks with a finger. Then it's black mascara, a nude-coloured lipstick and I'm actually pleased with the way I look.

The taxi I order to take me to the pub so I can have a drink turns up on time. The Crooked Crown is one of those local pubs that has recently had a renovation to attract more diners. Outside of the dining area are some little booths and larger tables with cushion-covered benches. There are plants and flexible wooden tall screens dotted about to make the area feel more socially distanced yet intimate than it actually is.

I have no qualms about arriving alone at a work meeting with people I don't know. If there's somewhere I have to take the children, such as to a health visitor or new GP, I'm fine with it yet walking into a pub on my own is far out of my comfort zone. Think well outside the Kármán line at the edge of space. I pull my shoulders back to try to feel confident and concentrate on looking for Claire rather than wondering if the pubgoers are staring at me.

The bar is relatively empty. She's not standing by it – all I can see there are the backs of balding men sitting on stools. On the right-hand side is a group of three young women with two bottles of wine and three glasses in front of them. One is gesticulating dramatically with her hands, perilously close to her half-full wine glass, as she talks.

Claire is not sitting near the door as I would to be easily spotted. Perhaps she's not here yet? I'm about to put my head around one of the screens when I hear the door close behind me and the word 'Audrey!'

Claire is flush-cheeked, she has rushed to the pub she says after having to stay late at work. She tells me about the internet going down and the panic it caused her boss whilst we head for the nearest booth. It consists of two fake leather brown armchairs facing each other with fat patchwork cushions resting against the backs, and a small table, enough to hold a few drinks and a packet of crisps, in between. Claire takes off her coat and throws it over the back of her chosen armchair whilst I carefully place my padded jacket over mine.

'So I finally finished photocopying the reports my boss managed to download from head office for tomorrow's meeting once the internet was back up and he let me go home.'

'Good' I say, not knowing what else to add. I wonder what James is doing.

'Drink?' she asks. I reach for my going out handbag – the small one because there's nothing to do with children in it – and take out my purse that's on top of the EpiPen I always carry around with me, my keys, phone and lipstick. How much do drinks cost these days? I pull out a new twenty-pound note from the wallet section. 'Let me pay for them,' I say. 'I'll have a glass of dry white please.'

'Thanks, that's kind of you.' Claire takes the note from me and scrumples it up in her hand. 'I'll go up to the bar. Won't be long – I don't think it will take long to get served!' We both turn to look at the barman who is idly flicking through a newspaper.

Whilst she is up at the bar I send James a quick text to let him know I'm at the pub. I laugh when I remember Sophie's internet dating tales. She has left such a hole in my life. It has been a long time now since she said she couldn't bear to see me again. Can female friendships break your heart? If so that's close to what she did. I've always been more of a loner and not one for gangs or groups. At university of course I had a few friends who faded away with the years after we graduated. I spent most of my time though with my best friend Rob. We're still as close as ever; whenever we chat or meet up, straight away we slip back into our comfortable friendship and it is as if we are both eighteen again, chatting in the communal university halls kitchen over a large cup of tea.

Sophie was the first time in my adult life I ever had a best female friend. When we met at a work colleague's party we immediately got on well, she the ying to my yang, me the water to her fire. She's forthright and energetic, loud and can be moody. I noticed people were either drawn towards her or found her too much to handle. I was surprised I was the former despite often feeling insignificant and energy-drained next to people who enjoy being the centre of attention. Yet Sophie, when she liked you, could instantly make you feel special. I spent most of that party laughing with her, seeing the world differently through her eyes. It wasn't long before she told me all about her life and I felt as if I'd known her for a long time. We fitted. I miss that. I miss unspoken jokes and a woman to talk to who instinctively knows what I'm thinking.

Claire interrupts my daydreaming with a bang on the table. 'It was buy two glasses and get the rest of the bottle free so I went for that.' It's an open bottle of chilled house dry white with a few drops of water from the chiller trickling down the outside. From the other hand she sets down two huge wine glasses on the table and pours them about four-fifths full.

'Right, let's start as we mean to go on. Cheers!' Claire lifts her glass with a big grin and I copy her, masking my alarm that she's obviously forgotten the concept of a school night. I'll just have to sip slowly. The glass is warm, probably straight out of a dishwasher, but the alcohol is cool on my lips.

'Nearly forgot.' She stands up, reaches into her jeans pocket and produces some coins. 'Here's your change.'

'Thanks.' I have another small mouthful of the wine before picking up the coins and putting them in my purse. The wine's actually rather nice.

What can we talk about? I can't ask Claire about her day because she's already told me. Instead, thinking of James's advice, I plump for current affairs.

'Shocking that stabbing in the news today, isn't it?'

'Has there been a stabbing? I don't follow the news. Too depressing.'

Not a good start there then. I take another sip and wonder whether Wilfred has stayed settled and how long is an acceptable time to wait before I text James to ask him to give me a call.

'Look at that group over there,' she says, inclining her head towards the three young women. They're probably about her age. 'The dark-haired one is a local celebrity, did you know?'

'Really? I don't recognise her.'

'Yes, she's the girlfriend of the Premier League footballer Lee Stormer. I've heard lots of things about her. Crystalle, I think she calls herself. She dated another footballer before him but ditched him to climb up the ladder to be a Premier League WAG.'

'Antonia likes playing football but I don't follow it. Crystalle doesn't look famous, she's not dressed up to the nines.'

'Probably trying to go incognito, although she always makes sure she gets papped for the gossip websites when she's near anyone who calls themselves a celebrity. Did you hear what she and the other WAGs got up to at a London nightclub last month?'

I lean in, interested. Usually I have no time for celebrity gossip but with the woman concerned sitting about ten metres away from me, too far to hear what we're saying, I'm intrigued and there's a frisson of naughtiness about it. A glass smashes on the floor, it's Crystalle's gesticulating friend, the one I saw when I first arrived. Claire and I turn to look at them out of our booth and then sit back and laugh. Claire pretends to swipe her glass off the table and I mime doing a karate chop on the wine bottle. I take another drink and start to feel my muscles relax and my shoulders drop. Maybe tonight might turn out to be fun after all.

By the time Claire has finished telling me all there is to know about the debauched lives of those with more fame than sense, and we've discussed which TV presenters we love and hate (I haven't heard of half the ones she mentions), the wine bottle is empty. My watch says that one and a half hours have passed by. I haven't laughed so much in ages but I ought to be thinking about getting home. Thankfully I'm still sober enough to be aware that I'm certainly merry with the warm and fuzzy feeling of the alcohol I've drunk – more than I usually would at home with James on a weekend.

'Just nipping to the toilet,' Claire says and I check my phone to see if there are any messages. There's only one, a text from James saying that the children are fine and he hopes I'm enjoying myself. I put the phone back into my handbag and quickly add another coat of lipstick. When Claire gets back I'll make my excuses. The three women are quite rowdy now, laughing loudly at something one of them has said. I wonder how many bottles down they are, then count the hours that are left before Wilfred is likely to wake up for good in the morning.

'I'm back!' Claire says, bringing two large glasses of wine with her and the rest of the bottle tucked under her arm. We carry on chatting about our favourite films and the TV programmes we watched as children for about quarter of an hour. The wine sips down nicely, cooling my throat in the stuffy room.

When she finishes reminiscing about the Teletubbies, Claire disappears again then returns back a few minutes later and thumps another bottle of wine down on our table. She is obviously wanting to carry on drinking. I glance at my watch. Before I set out this evening I thought I'd be home kicking off my shoes and getting ready for bed by now.

'It's not technically my round but I'm having so much fun I bought another bottle,' Claire says, beginning to pour some more wine into my nearly empty glass. I've never really thought before how nice the glug sound is.

I put my hand over my glass to stop her. 'Sorry, I ought to be getting off. Antonia and Wilfred get up early. It's school tomorrow.'

She looks at me mimicking a puppy's sad eyes. 'How about just the one? I've bought the bottle now and I can't drink it all on my own. Well I could, but it wouldn't be any fun.'

I'm wavering. It would be rude to leave when she has bought the bottle and I *am* having a good time. James is right,

I deserve a night out. I rarely get to do anything that doesn't involve the children. I pull my hand back. Just the one. Claire fills up my glass and then her own. 'So tell me about Antonia and Wilfred. They're adorable children.'

I don't need asking twice. My children are a subject that I can talk about for ever. I tell her all about their little habits and some funny stories about Antonia, including today's sanitary pad incident. Claire roars with laughter and presses me for more. I go on to say about how Antonia has been trying to find out what Daddy and I get up to after she's gone to bed, Wilfred's funny expressions when he's dreaming and the very loud burp he did the first time he met James's parents. Time passes quickly. Claire fills my glass up again and we continue laughing and putting the world to rights.

A bell rings loudly, cutting through the ambient background chatter. 'Time to drink up!' the barman says loudly. I look at my watch. My eyes take a few seconds to focus on the hands and I wonder if I need to have an eye test at the opticians before I realise that, although Claire has drunk slightly more than me, I must still have had more than a bottle and haven't drunk any water in between the wine refills. I work out where the clock hands are. The barman is right, it's closing time already.

'Oh bugger,' I exclaim.

'What's wrong?'

'I told James I would be home ages ago.' I reach for my handbag and delve around in it for my phone. There's a missed call from James and one text from him that says:

You still at the pub? All OK? ☺ x

55

'Text him to tell him you're on your way.'

'I need to book a cab.'

'I'll sort an Uber out for you.'

I've never had an Uber before. Gosh I'm getting down with the kids. I rarely take taxis. I don't go anywhere to need to. Claire taps away on her mobile and says the car will be here in five minutes.

It's my turn to go to the loo and I'm conscious that I'm not walking in a straight line. I try and drink some water from my scooped palms under the bathroom sink. Most of the water slips through my fingers and I chuckle at my attempts. I go to leave the bathroom and then turn back, spinning on one leg, when I remember I haven't dried my hands.

When I get back to our booth Claire has her coat on and passes me mine. It seems extremely difficult to work out which arm goes in which hole.

'Audrey, you've put it on inside out.'

We both burst into laughter, which impedes Claire's attempts to help me shrug the coat off and put it on the right way round. Her phone beeps. It's my Uber. 'Are you coming too?' I ask. 'How are you getting home?'

'I'll walk, it's not far.'

I've enough sense left in me to realise that her walking home alone isn't a safe idea.

'Where do you live? You could stay in the taxi after it drops me off?'

'I'm not that far away. Some fresh air will do me good. Sober me up.'

'I've had a fabulous evening. I'm so glad I met you,' I hear myself saying, or rather slurring.

She hugs me tightly. 'You too. And I'm so glad you're up for meeting up this weekend with the kids. Let's not leave it long before we have another girls' night.'

'Meeting up with the kids?'

'Yes, on Saturday at the city farm. Remember?'

It sounds a bit familiar but I don't remember. I thought I knew all that had happened this evening but it's actually a bit blurry. I haven't been this drunk since getting my finals results at university. At our wedding I stuck to one glass of champagne only.

'City farm will be great. Text me where and what time.' I make a mental note to write it in my diary.

'Don't forget George!'

Claire ushers me outside to the waiting car and passes me the cuddly toy she's clinging on to. I start to tell the driver my address but Claire says the driver knows it already because she gave it with the booking. I open my handbag, pull out my purse and give Claire a twenty pound note to pay for the cab booking and to go towards the second bottle of wine. She takes it gratefully and we say slurred goodbyes before the car sets off.

'Good night I see, eh?' the female driver remarks. She can't be that much younger than my mum was when she died and the thought sends prickles of tears into my eyes.

'Very good, yes.' I press the button to put the window down and take some gulps of fresh air. I need to sober up. I mustn't wake the children. What's James going to say when I walk in sweating out Chardonnay? That mental image turns my tears to giggles.

The car parks on my street and I clumsily climb out.

Over the road there's a dark figure, probably a man, walking a dog. The taxi starts its engine and sets off. I wait until the man passes out of view and then walk the few metres up my drive. All the lights are off, James evidently hasn't stayed up. I slowly put my key in the lock but it won't turn. I try again with no luck. I hesitate because I don't want to ring the doorbell and wake Antonia and Wilf up. I'm just about to knock on the door quietly when I notice it's green.

Our front door is blue. I'm at next door's bungalow. No wonder James's car isn't parked in the drive!

Stifling my chuckle I retrace my steps to the main pavement. A bark makes me jump and I turn straight round to see the man with the large dog walking slowly back towards me along the street, pulling on the lead. I dart into my own drive. The lights are on in the front kitchen. I squint when our porch light on a sensor beams on, illuminating the darkness. Before I can get my key out of my handbag again the door opens. It's James, pressing his forefinger against his frowning lips to silence me.

'Sorry,' I slur, holding on to him with my hand precariously close to his groin.

'I think you need to sleep.'

'Noo, not sleep…'

He leads me to the bedroom, takes off my shoes, leaves and then reappears with a pint glass of water.

'Drink that.'

The water is cool and refreshing. 'It's much better drinking out of a glass than my palms,' I say.

'Lie down now Audrey. I'll get up in the night for Wilfred. I don't think you'll be in a state to. I'm off to the bathroom,

I won't be long.' He turns on the bedside lamp and switches the overhead bulb off.

Before I pass out into the blackness of dreamless sleep two thoughts cross my mind: the first that it's strange that the dogwalker retraced his steps to walk back down the street again, did he do it deliberately to watch me? The second is that I didn't remember giving Claire my home address to book the Uber.

~6~

The next morning I recall why I rarely drink much. I wake with a raging thirst, the headache from hell, a revolting taste of stale wine in my mouth and an urgent need to evacuate my bowels. When I stagger back from the bathroom, still wearing last night's blue, now very crumpled dress, James pushes his side of the duvet back and turns to look at me. I imagine he's seeing the swamp creature before him. Is he very cross?

'Morning alkie.'

Oh the shame.

'How are you feeling?'

'I think that's rather obvious.' My voice sounds in my head like I'm speaking through a megaphone.

'Come on, let's get this off.' I sit on the bed and he undoes the knot on my wrap dress then pulls it up over my head as I lift my arms up like Antonia does when I help her undress. He reaches under my pillow and passes me the neatly folded, oversized T-shirt with a black and white picture of Audrey Hepburn on the front that he gave me couple of Christmases ago and that I love to wear in bed. I pull it on quickly.

James can't sleep in total darkness therefore we always leave the curtains open a few centimetres so he knows when morning has arrived. The colour of the sky peeking through is an ombre dark grey and orange. Not time yet for Antonia to get up.

'Wilfred! How is he? Should I go and see to him?'

'Not with breath like yours,' jests James. 'You'll gas him. He's fine, he woke up a couple of times in the night but settled straight away when I went in there.'

'I'm so sorry James. I didn't mean to stay out that late.'

He hugs me from behind, trying to be funny by taking a deep breath and avoiding smelling the air around me. 'Never mind. It's not as though you stay out late and get drunk every day, is it? I'm glad you enjoyed yourself. Just don't do it every night.'

'No, Dad. My head hurts.'

'I'm not surprised. How much did you drink? You were gabbling away when you got in then collapsed on the bed and started snoring. I'll be back in a minute.'

I turn the pillow over so I can gingerly rest my head on the cool side. I hope Claire doesn't think I'm a drunken idiot. I don't usually let myself go like that. It is as if I am a snake that has shed its deceptively scaly skin and now has to mould my flesh back into it and sew it on as quick as I can to avoid attack from predators.

James comes back in again. He's brought a glass of water from the kitchen and a strip of paracetamol from the locked medicine box we hide behind unused tubes of toothpaste in the bathroom cabinet.

I smile gratefully, take the two paracetamol tablets he has popped out of the blister pack for me, and gulp them down with three-quarters of the water. Right now a glass of cool water tastes so much better than the house white from last night that I can still taste on the fur covering my teeth.

'I *am* glad you had a good time but seriously though, I was worried when you didn't call or text. I didn't want you stranded somewhere with problems getting a taxi. Or walking home. You said yesterday you thought someone was following you on the way to school.'

Waves of contriteness break over the nausea. 'I know. I'm sorry. We got chatting and time passed quickly, I didn't think to check my phone.'

'So you got on well then?' He slithers under the duvet next to me, where I'm lying prostrate, and reaches for my hand to squeeze.

'We did. She's fun. Totally different from me and outspoken you know? In the end I didn't have to think of things to talk about. I don't know whether *she* thinks I'm fun though or a cliché of a mum who doesn't get out much and drinks to make up for it.' I remember it was Claire who bought the third bottle. She didn't force me to drink it though.

'Get some sleep. There's an hour and a half left before the alarm goes off. I'll get up if Wilfred cries.'

Antonia is like me, she wakes up at the same time each morning whether it's a weekday or the weekend.

'Thank you. I love you.'

'Love you more. Well, when you've brushed your teeth anyway,' he laughs, the exhalation of breath tickling my exposed neck. I squeeze his hand back.

'Auds, do you think you'll be up to taking the Antonia to school today and looking after Wilfred? I can always ring work and say there's an emergency and I need to stay at home this morning.'

My stomach churns at his words. One night out doesn't make me an emergency. What if his colleagues found out he was taking the morning off work because his wife got herself intoxicated the night before? I know he's being caring but him thinking that I can't look after my own children gets my goat.

'I'll be fine. Another hour and a half's sleep and I'll be raring to go.'

'Really? I don't mind.'

'I am capable of looking after my own children.'

'Of course you are, you're a brilliant mum. But if you're feeling ill you might want some help.'

'But I'm not feeling ill.'

'You just said your head hurts.'

'The paracetamol is doing its job.'

'Alright, it was just a suggestion.' I can tell he's on the defence. I squeeze his hand again as a peace offering.

'Thanks. Let's get some sleep.'

With that I slip back into the other side of consciousness, walking the children down to the school gates totally naked, oblivious as to why the glam mums' jaws drop wide open when they spot me.

A minute after the alarm goes off James comes in and brings me toast. I look at the clock, he's reset the alarm for twenty minutes later than usual. He must have got the children up himself.

'Are you in tonight or you are going clubbing?' he laughs. The joke is starting to wear a little thin.

'I'm joining a convent,' I reply.

It's only when he's gone that the image comes into my head of the man walking his dog last night. I'm sure he was walking down the street away from me when I got out of the taxi. I'd waited until he'd passed because I was embarrassed about being seen swaying in my inebriated state. When I finally made it to my own front door (thank goodness I didn't wake the next-door neighbours up) I could swear I saw him walking back this way. The orange glow from the nearest lamp post barely reached him and all I could see was a dark grey silhouette. With that description he could have been anyone but I'm sure it was the same man from a few minutes before, coming back retracing his steps, because of the dog. I don't know that much about dogs, not having had one myself, but it was a large one, about the shape and size of a Labrador. Once the taxi had left, the dog's bark was the only sound breaking the stillness of the gloomy suburban night.

Do people usually walk their dogs when it's nearly midnight? When I'm up at that time it's because I'm soothing Wilfred and I'm sheltered inside our bungalow, oblivious as to what's going on in the street outside. I suppose people who find it hard to sleep may do, men at least for I doubt few women would walk the streets on their own at that time even if they do have a big dog to protect them. Perhaps the dog hadn't had any exercise that day and needed to go outside to perform its ablutions.

But why would the man walk to the end of our street and then back again so quickly? Was he watching me, checking if I was OK, or could it have been something more sinister? Could he be the man I think has followed me before? I think hard back to the figure I think I saw dart behind the trees near Antonia's school. That person definitely didn't have a dog but try as I might, last night's memory is too hazy, too wine-fuelled to work out whether it might have been the same person. Or maybe I'm dramatising things; all I saw the other day was a trick of the light and the dogwalker had turned back because he'd only gone on a short walk.

Nevertheless the incident adds to my hungover unease. My eyes search the shadows on the walk to school, the adrenaline pumping through my body setting my nerves on edge, waiting for something to happen. The day passes painfully slowly, each second ticking by taking longer than it does for a child to wait for Christmas Eve to pass. When I've dropped Antonia off at school, Wilfred seems to need more attention than usual and I over-compensate for my thankfully receding hangover by ignoring the household chores and giving him my full attention instead, which he loves so much that he doesn't want to go to sleep for his afternoon nap and therefore I don't get a chance to doze.

When he eventually does I receive a text from Claire thanking me for a great night and giving me the details for the city farm trip on Saturday. I'd vaguely heard of it before but have never been and I think Antonia will love showing her brother the animals that make the sounds they've been singing. I don't have anything planned for that afternoon anyway. James has a bike ride with the local cycling group on Saturday. He previously said he wouldn't go if we wanted a family day instead but after my performance last night I think he deserves some time out on his own too.

Claire's text reminds me that I haven't thought to find

out whether she got home safely; my concerns regarding her were around whether she thought I made a fool of myself last night. I chastise myself for not checking up on her but am pleased that she evidently enjoyed herself. I tell Antonia on the way home from school that we're going to the city farm and she is very excited, jumping up and down on both feet to see how high she can go. 'Will there be cows Mummy, and horses? And chickens? And pigs? And lambs?' I check the website on my phone and say yes. The news that they have an alpaca, an animal she hasn't heard of, sends her further into a frenzy.

'Can Jordan come too?' Evidently the pair had played football together in the lunch break and she scored more goals than him.

I think that it would be impolite to invite Tina and Jordan along too when Claire had invited only us.

'Not this time Antonia, Claire invited us, the nice lady from the park.'

'The dogsbody lady that likes cake?'

'That's the one.'

'I liked her. She pulled Wilfred out of the water.'

I nod but secretly wish that was a part that she had forgotten.

Not long after dinner Rob rings me on my mobile. James takes over bath time knowing that since he and I had children me and Rob don't often get the chance to catch up. He's ringing to organise a weekend to visit us. When I tell him I got drunk last night he bursts out laughing.

'You, the convent schoolgirl? What would Mother Superior have to say?'

'She'd probably have expelled me.' I curl up on the sofa with the phone wedged between my left ear and shoulder.

'I wish I'd seen it. I've only ever seen you really wasted once. When we got our finals results. And even then you went to bed early. I had to carry you back to your room when you fell asleep at the table after we all got back from the bar to carry on drinking in the kitchen. Do you remember?'

'No, as you just said, I was asleep!'

'Ha ha, those were the good old days. How're things with you?'

I hesitate then decide not to tell him about the pram or the figure following me.

'Fine, same old. The children are lovely. Your god-daughter misses you. You? How's Kieran?'

There's a silence.

'Oh dear, have I said the wrong thing?'

'We split up last week. He said he's not very good at commitment.'

'I'm sorry, his loss. You'd been with him a while hadn't you?'

'Six months. I saw it coming.'

Rob tends to move from relationship to relationship but with none of them lasting much longer than a year.

'You OK?' There's an itch on my foot and I insert two fingers under my sock to scratch it. Rob seems tough to the outside world but, knowing him as well as I do, emotions hit him harder than he makes out.

'Yeah fine. He came half an hour ago to pick up the things he'd left in my flat.'

'Had he moved in?

'No, but he spent a lot of time here because he's in a shared house.'

I'd forgotten Kieran is nearly ten years younger than Rob. I only met him once when they both visited for an hour. Wilfred had colic and I was a very poor hostess.

'So I thought I'd give my best friend a call. It has been a while; would you like me to visit soon? To be honest I could do with the company.'

'Of course. Antonia will be in seventh heaven. You know you're always welcome here. We'll have a great catch-up when the children are in bed.'

We settle on a date for him to arrive on a Friday night and leave on the Sunday. Rob is about the only visitor I can be myself with when he's staying. I love James's parents but feel I have to be looking after them all the time they're here for the weekend. They say they want to help me out in the house but to be honest them trying to cook dinner or do the dusting ends up being more of a hindrance than a help. By the time I've explained where everything is and how things work I could have done it myself.

'Audrey, are you sure everything's fine?' he adds when we're about to say our goodbyes and hang up.

'Yes, why do you ask?' My stomach starts to churn.

'You don't sound quite yourself. Not the getting drunk – I mean, it's about time you let your hair down – but your voice. As if you're holding something back. Like the time when you had that health scare and you didn't tell me.'

I'd been recalled after a smear test and didn't want to talk about it. Doing so would open the pressure cooker of my catastrophising thoughts. Rob had known something was wrong though. Luckily the second test was all clear.

'It's nothing, I'm just tired. I thought I saw someone watching me, following me a couple of times, but I was probably imagining it. I'm so tired all the time Rob, it's hard to trust my own senses. And there was something else…'

'What? You know you can tell me.'

'I haven't told James yet. I don't want to worry him. I thought I'd put the brake on the pram and it rolled away a bit. Everything was OK, Wilfred was unhurt, but I could have sworn I'd put the brake on. I've checked and triple-checked it many times since and it works perfectly.'

'Perhaps you'd thought you'd put it on but it hadn't clicked fully? You know like when you put a plug in a socket but it's not firmly in far enough to work properly?'

I perk up. The itch stops. 'I hadn't thought of that. You could be right. I'll try the brake tomorrow and see if it does that.'

'Audrey, you are the most diligent and sane person I know. You're the one everyone goes to to organise things. Nothing gets past you. Don't doubt yourself. Let's talk about it when I visit.'

James comes into the room and asks to say a few words to Rob. When I first met James he was wary of my friendship with Rob, despite knowing he was gay. They circled each other like tigers wanting to be the dominant one in the pack. Now they rub along well together. I say bye and pass the phone over to James then walk outside to our porch where the pram is.

It's dark already, the shadowy gloom enveloping suburbia with its creeping tendrils. I take the pram outside to the drive and experiment with the brake. There's a nip in the air and I shiver without a coat on, feeling goosebumps pop up on the lower parts of my arms uncovered by my three-quarter sleeve woolly jumper. Nine times out of ten when I press the brake it clicks on fully. The tenth time I deliberately don't push as hard and the brake is in limbo – it looks as if it is on but when I push the pram it clearly isn't and it clicks back to the off position. I try again, now seemingly knowing the trick and two times out of three the same thing happens. A design fault? I heave a sigh of relief. That must have been what happened, I put the brake on but not fully. One of those freakish things to happen. I'm not going mad. I *am* a good mother.

Smiling I turn the pram around to wheel it back to the porch where it will stay overnight. I'm about to lift it over the door frame when I hear a noise. A bark. *The* bark.

Turning my head to see where the noise comes from I see the Labrador-sized dog, the one from last night, and a man staring at me. When he sees me look his way he starts to walk quickly along the street.

'James!' I shout. 'James, come now!'

Barely ten seconds have gone by when he arrives, shaken-faced, my mobile phone still in his hand.

'What's wrong?'

'It's the man' I point in the direction of the street. 'The one I think is following me.'

'Where?'

We both rush to the end of our driveway, James taking my hand in his.

'He was over there, with a dog, when I called you.'

'Audrey, I can't see anyone. There's no one there.'

'But there must be, he can't have disappeared. He'd have to have run pretty fast to get to the end of the street in that time.'

James, however, is right. My eyes skirt along the road, searching, but there's no one and nothing at the end of the street bar a lone wheelie bin someone has forgotten to wheel back into their drive and the wind whistling past it.

~7~

The next few days I try to carry on as per some kind of normal, going through my usual routine, struggling not to pass my anxiety on to the children who have the gift of remaining oblivious to everything that's outside of their own little bubble. James says he believes me that I saw the man with a dog again that night but I'm not sure if he means it or if he really suspects my sighting was the product of an overly imaginative hangover. He and I are usually so close but his unspoken doubt makes me glad I never mentioned the pram incident. That was explained away by Rob anyway. I don't want James to use it as a reason to doubt what I say I saw. I *know* what I saw. But why would anyone be following me now? I wish my heart would believe what my brain tells it to, that I'm not paying the price now, being hunted down for my sins.

'Are you sure you don't mind me going cycling?' says James on Saturday morning. I can tell by the way he's fidgeting with his fingers that he's itching to put on his Lycra gear. 'You've not been yourself this week, I can always come along with you to the city farm instead.'

I bristle at the term 'not been yourself'. When others have questioned my ability in the past James has always been chief champion. Does he now think that because of my man with dog sightings I need chaperoning? Besides, it would be awkward going with both Claire and James. She'd probably feel like a spare part on a family outing.

We're in the bedroom sitting on the bed taking a brief respite as Wilfred is in his bouncer and Antonia is playing with her toy cars nearby. James takes a furtive look at the wardrobe. I can read him like a book.

'You go cycling, I'll be fine. Honestly.' I peck him on the cheek and he moves in for a longer kiss. He probably didn't doubt me at all, I'm just being over-sensitive. He's a good dad and husband. The best.

Whilst Wilfred sleeps through much of the city farm visit, Antonia is in her element. She is in her blue wellies, I'm wearing walking boots because I guessed it might be muddy, and Claire's off-white trainers turn brown by the end of our visit. We see the pigs, chickens and sheep, and Antonia is beyond excited when the kindly assistant shows her how to hold hay in her hand for the old carthorse to eat.

I was concerned it might be a bit boring for Claire being stuck with two children all afternoon but she takes it in her stride and goes hand in hand with Antonia to see the cows when I have to head to the facilities to change Wilfred when he wakes up and starts crying.

We arranged to rendezvous in the café and, with a few minutes to spare, I take Wilfred to pat a docile sheep.

'Mummy!' I hear behind me and two wellied feet run towards me, deliberately splashing in the few muddy puddles around. I turn to see Antonia with Claire a couple of metres behind.

'The café is shut! We can't have a hot chocolate and cake again!' She sticks out her bottom lip in mock misery, then does the thumbs down sign with her right hand. I think that's something she picked up at school this week.

'It's true, they've closed early. A sign on the door says it's due to a leak.'

Antonia will be getting hungry now and all I have in my bag is a packet of raisins, which she turns her nose up at. 'That's Wilfred's food, not mine.'

'Right madam, how about we go home then and I can make some hot chocolate and a sandwich there. Claire, would you like to join us?'

Her face lights up. We haven't had chance for any personal talk but I once again get the sense that she's lonely and keen to get out of her room in the shared house.

'Yes, if it's not putting you out…'

'No trouble at all. You can come back in the car with us. Is it far from where you live?'

'Not that far. I can walk home.'

It crosses my mind that she hasn't been to my house before and so won't know where it is, but then remember she knew my address when she booked the Uber the night we went to the pub. I must have told her it and forgotten.

I strap the children into the child seats in the back of the car and Claire hops in the front with me. It beings to rain profusely and that, along with bad traffic, means it's three-quarters of an hour before we get back home. Both the children are grouchy so I set to feeding them in the kitchen and make mugs of steaming hot chocolate for Claire, Antonia and me.

'I love your kitchen, it's really homely,' says Claire.

'Thanks, we had a new one put in not long after we moved in. The old one was on its last legs. The elderly gentleman who lived here before us apparently didn't spend any money on the house for thirty years. Only one hob on the cooker worked and you had to light the oven and the hob with a match!'

'You're very lucky having such a lovely home and family.'

'Thanks, I know.' I hold back because I don't want to sound smug. 'Hard work though! Hardly any time to myself.' I feel I should say something about missing my freedom years but the truth is I don't. As much as I miss work I wouldn't swap my children and James for Claire's life for a million pounds.

'Mummy, can I watch television please?' Antonia asks. We usually let her watch an hour of television at the weekends, normally something like *Bagpuss* that we've downloaded from YouTube. We know our era programmes are suitable for her to watch. Now she's at school she says she's too old for CBeebies.

'Of course, let's go into the playroom and I'll set it up for you.' Claire sits with Wilfred whilst I find the programme on the television and then I suggest that she and I go and sit in the lounge, taking Wilfred's playmat and toys with us.

The lounge is in a far better state that the playroom. We don't receive many guests but I like to keep it in a state that's fit for adults. Wilfred is happy lying on a blanket on the carpet playing with his squeaky cuddly toy. Claire waits for me to sit down on the sofa and I move a couple of cushions out of the way so there's room for her to sit down at the other end without having to hunch up next to me.

'I really enjoyed today. Do you want to go out for a meal next week? A woman at work recommended an all you can eat Chinese buffet. I'd like to try it.'

I haven't been out for a meal since before Wilfred was born and then it was with James for our last date night before the baby came. It seems unfair and rather profligate of me to spend money on going out without James now I'm not earning a salary.

'It's very cheap,' she adds, as if sensing my money concerns. 'Only if you want to of course. It'd make a change for me from my manky bedroom.'

I take this to mean she doesn't have anyone else to go with. Claire has been really kind to me and the children and she could do with a friend. Why should I not go out for a meal? I should be able to spare a couple of hours.

'Yes, sounds good. I won't be drinking this time though. Did I tell you I went up to the wrong house when the taxi dropped me off?'

'Really?!' Claire laughs and her shoulders drop down. I sense she's relieved that I said yes to her invitation. It can't be easy trying to make new friends in a strange city.

'It's strange but I saw a man walking his dog up and down the road twice. I thought he was watching me. And the other day on the way to school in the afternoon I felt like I was being followed.'

'Hmm…' Claire looks pensive then she takes a deep breath before going on. 'I have heard at work that a few women have reported being followed. The MD's PA said a car followed her back home last week until she drove into a police station's car park. You can't be too careful, not these days.'

I knew it. I *knew* I wasn't making things up.

'Did she report it to the police?'

'I don't know, I didn't ask.'

There's a conversation lull and we both watch Wilfred trying to chew the carriage of his wooden train. I take it from his mouth and go to the kitchen to bring him a sterilised dummy.

When I get back Claire is standing by the mantelpiece that surrounds our electric fire, looking at the line of photos and knick-knacks we have on top.

'Is that your wedding photo? Mind if I have a look?' Claire points at the picture in a wedding gift silver frame on the left-hand side of the others. I've seen it so many times it has become part of the furniture next to the expensive scented candle I burn occasionally as a special treat. On the other side of the mantelpiece is a card Antonia drew for me for Mother's Day, which I put in a clip frame. The blobs, holding spindly hands, are supposed to be James and me. My blob has a big pink grin and Daddy's blob has eyes on top of his forehead, like an alien cartoon character. For good measure there's a pencil-swish's worth of brown hair on top. Wilfred is a small, hairless blob lying on the floor.

I pop the dummy in Wilfred's mouth and lift him up, sitting him on my knee on the sofa, moving my knees up and down to make him chuckle.

Claire picks up the frame then sits down next to me to examine the photo. The colours have slightly faded from the print behind the glass but the moment the photographer captured is still magical. I remember it so clearly: the late June sunshine twinkling off the crystal champagne glasses at the outside drinks reception at the hotel we went to for the wedding breakfast following a church ceremony; the feel of the long, handmade, beaded long silk dress that I've never worn since brushing against my skin; James insisting he needed a few practice goes when the photographer asked us to kiss for the camera; the sweet scent of the lilies in my bouquet that I kept a hold of until I threw it behind my head to the single women (thanks to my wonky aim nobody caught it but there was a scrum to pick it up from the floor); and the rings of laughter as our two families gathered together on the lawn to record this moment for posterity.

It's special to me but maybe through someone else's eyes this snap, over a decade old, just looks dated and is a testament to how James and I have aged. A little less hair for James, a little more weight for both of us and tired bags around the eyes for me.

'Your dress is lovely,' says Claire, her jabbing finger leaving a smear on the glass. I think it'd be rude to wipe it in front of her but my fingers itch to do so. I keep my hands busy playing with Wilfred.

'Where was it from?'

'A local dressmaker my mum discovered designed and made it for me. Obviously the ones in bridal boutiques wouldn't fit and I didn't want all that fuss of trying on anyway. I told her what sort of styles I liked, brought in a few examples I'd torn out of magazines, she sourced some cream silk and voila! Bob's your wedding dress.'

'And James?'

'John Lewis. He went with his dad and his best man and they bought matching suits. It has made an appearance at every wedding and christening we've been invited to since.'

Claire is peering at the picture now, bringing it closer to her eyes as if she were short-sighted.

'Who is the kid standing next to you?'

Her question sends me back in time before I answer her. The photographer had told James and me to stand in the centre of the shot with his family and friends to the left and mine to the right. A barrage of conflicting outfit colours mingle together along with smiling and somewhat tipsy faces, overpowering fascinators rising up from some women's hairstyles, and a young boy dressed in smart trousers and a white shirt he's yet to spill anything down stands on my right. He was nearly eight and the same height as me.

I was born with restricted growth. When my peers shot up I didn't make it past four feet four. It's a genetic condition of which there's no history in the family. I'm used to it of course, being the same size as my cousin's son who on my wedding day loved telling everyone that day that he'd soon be taller than the bride. His jaw dropped wide with admiration when he asked me why I was born short and I told him it was a result of a spontaneous genetic mutation. He then kept asking if I was able to fly like Superman and offered to lend me his Batman costume. Mutations, to a seven-year-old, are cool. Sadly, they're not to some other people. A partner of one of James's friends who'd never met me thought at first I was the flower girl and one elderly relative after imbibing multiple glasses of free champagne clasped my hands warmly in hers and declared that it was so wonderful I was married, she always hoped someone would see how special I was, and what a kind and caring man James must be. I blanked out her words, ignoring the subtext that she thought Saint James was doing me a favour, rather than the other way around, and moved politely on to talk to another guest.

I've been there before with the carer inferences, the surprised looks, the assumptions that I'd be single and if I did happen to meet anyone it would be a man of my 'own kind'. I wasn't going to let anything spoil my day, nothing was going to pierce the cocoon of happiness gently wrapped around James and I. I wouldn't let it, and it didn't. So why do I feel a little embarrassed that Claire has pointed out the height situation? It's not as if she didn't already know. All my life anyone who looks at me knows immediately of my disability. It's not as if I can pretend to be a five-foot-eight marathon runner. I've had to develop a thick skin to ignore the stares, gawps and the idiotic assumptions about my abilities and my intelligence. My height isn't the only thing that defines me. At school and university I worked hard to prove naysayers wrong. With my first-class degree I knew that employers would want to hire me because of my intelligence and not despite my disability. Yet I still had to put up with the patronising comments from a small number of others, that my tutors only gave me good marks because they felt sorry for me (hello, have they not heard of blind marking?) and the Civil Service employed me so they could tick an HR minorities box. At the other end of the scale were those who said it was so inspiring that 'someone like you' could get a job. Mother Mary give me strength.

James doesn't care about my height. Neither does Rob, and Sophie used to say she kept forgetting to look down when chatting to me walking side by side. Claire didn't seem bothered when we met. I can't help feeling tense though, that she's going to ask me lots of personal questions she's saved up in her head. What's it like being that small? How do you and James have sex? It has all happened before and I brace myself for the inevitable barrage. I don't want her to be one of those people and for me to have to cut this friendship short.

I answer Claire's question. 'That's my cousin's son Jake. He's in his first year at university now over in America,' I reply gingerly.

'That's a long way to go to study. Did he want to make sure he can't come home to his family for the holidays then?' she laughs.

'He got an athletics scholarship.'

'Ooh! Very posh. Fat chance of me having got one of those. I told the games teacher I had my period every week at school to try and get out of PE lessons.'

She stands up and puts the frame back in its spot on the mantelpiece, slightly skew-whiff but I'll fix that when she's gone.

To my relief that's the topic over with. Antonia comes through with her cuddly Bagpuss toy keen to tell us the latest story she's watched and act it out for Wilfred. As the director she gives Claire and I parts to play as well. Basically that involves her telling us what we have to say. She even sings the theme tune at breakneck speed before we begin and at the end, then takes a bow.

'I'd better start the night-time routine now if you don't mind Claire.'

'No problem, I was going to head off anyway.'

'Are you sure you're OK to walk home? I'd ask James to give you a lift but he won't be back from his cycle trip for a while yet. His group usually goes to the pub afterwards to socialise and it's the only time he really goes out.'

'Less free time now he's a dad?'

'No, he was like that before the children came. He's a homebird, never liked being the life and soul of the party. Like me, I guess that's why we get on so well. We can both stay in together.'

Wilfred, Antonia and I say goodbye and I realise I'm looking forward to seeing Claire again at the restaurant. She's really easy company and James was right, despite preferring to be at home it has done me good to go out a few times. I'm not just a mum, I'm Audrey too.

'How was your afternoon?' asks James when he gets home in his sweaty black Lycra. There's no scent of alcohol on him because he stuck to cola, not wanting his cycling to be impaired on the road home. When Antonia arrived we both took out life insurance, realising that becoming parents came with a huge financial responsibility for a long time to come.

'I really enjoyed it, thanks. Wilfred's asleep and Antonia's just gone back to bed after getting up a couple of times. She wanted to see if you were home yet. If you go and see her now she'll probably be awake and will tell you all about the animals we saw.'

He fills up a pint glass from the sink and glugs down

82

the water rapidly. 'And Claire? How was your new best friend?'

'Good. We had fun and she's great with the children. We're going to go out for a cheap Chinese soon if you don't mind. Don't worry, I'll stay on the soft drinks and will probably drive.'

'OK.' He bends down to kiss me and I wrinkle my nose smelling the odour emanating from his sweaty armpits.

'Better have a shower when you've seen Antonia, I think, if you want to get close to me tonight.' I smile.

He lifts his arm to smell his armpit in mock horror. 'Deal.' We both laugh, the distance between us that was there this morning melting away into the ether.

James walks to the kitchen door to go to Antonia's bedroom then turns round unexpectedly.

'Auds, it's great to see you happy. I mean it, there's not been a lot of that recently.'

'I'm good.' I put my secrets out of my mind. 'We're good.'

He heads off and my mobile rings. It's 'Claire from park'.

'Hi, you home alright?' I ask.

'Yes, safe and sound,' she replies, in a more serious tone than earlier.

'Everything OK?'

'Well, yes and no. I don't want to worry you but when I was leaving I saw a man loitering outside your house. He was wearing a black coat and beanie. I didn't get much of a look at him because when I walked towards him he went off in the other direction. Could be nothing but after what you told me today…'

My heart sinks. 'Did he follow you?'

83

'No. I checked on the way home and stuck to busy streets. No one followed me.'

'Thank goodness for that. Are you sure he was loitering outside my house?'

'Yes, he didn't see me for about thirty seconds. He was standing opposite, staring at the house. Not having a fag or anything like that. There didn't seem any reason for him to be there.'

I don't know what to say. The hairs on the back of my neck prickle. My stomach churns. What do I do? I go to the front door and look outside. Nobody's there.

'I'm looking outside now and I can't see anyone.'

'He hasn't come back then. Good. Keep an eye out, I believe you when you said you thought you were being followed. If I were you I'd call the police if you spot him again.'

We say the obligatory farewells and I put the phone down. James is still in Antonia's room. I rush to check on Wilfred and he is sound asleep exactly where I left him. I close the curtains in all the rooms and double check the lock on the front door. We need to get an extra bolt added I think as I stand in the hallway, for the first time not feeling safe in my own home.

Is this man following me or lots of women? Does he think I'm a target because of my height and lack of ability to fight back? Vomit rises in my throat and I run to the bathroom to purge myself of it.

~ 8 ~

On Monday evening a week later I meet Claire again at her
chosen Chinese restaurant at the studenty side of town.
She's right, it is cheap and cheerful, offering a ten-pound all
you can eat buffet deal. In fact it's so cheap that it makes me
wonder what's in it and bet the meat isn't free range. I keep
those middle-aged thoughts to myself.

The savings that the owners have made from not
changing the décor since around 1970 explain how they can
afford to offer the Monday-night only deal. Claire is already
waiting, sitting on a faded red-quilted chair near the window,
near the flashing orange pagoda lamp. It's quite busy here
and full of what my mum would have called 'young people'.
By the amount of food on their plates they've come to eat
enough food to last them until next Monday when they can
repeat the cycle.

I managed to park only a few doors away and was on my
guard as I walked the few strides to the restaurant. I haven't
seen anyone follow me since last week but as the saying goes,
just because you are paranoid doesn't mean they aren't after
you. I did wonder about cancelling, concerned about being
out alone after dark, but then thought twice. I can't let fear
rule my life. Plus James bought me a piercing alarm to go in

my handbag. If I'm worried all I have to do is pull the cord.

I breathe in the delicious scent of spicy fried food and hear the sizzle of the wok. All the dishes to choose from are on a conveyor belt that the chef switches on when they're running out. Then the belt moves and more huge bowls of stir fries, noodles, fried rice and curries miraculously appear alongside a temple-sized pile of prawn crackers. Later I skip those because I see others reach into the pile with their hands and touch some of the crackers they're not going to eat. Who knows what germs they might have deposited on them?

'Hi!' says Claire, standing up to hug me when I arrive. We sit down to chat about our week and it's not long before the waiter comes over to take our order. As well as the buffet I order a sparkling water and Claire plumps for a bottle of Chinese lager.

We take it in turns to go up and get our food because I don't want to leave our coats and my handbag unattended. Claire's phone and small purse are tucked in her jeans' pockets. I forgot to swap handbags and am carrying around my huge mummy survival bag.

She returns to our sticky table, which rocks when you put a plate down on it, with a massive heap of different dishes all merged together. When I get back I have a more modest portion of egg fried rice and stir fry chicken and mushroom. Having placed it on the table I'm in the process of sitting down when I hear a loud braying voice, an unmistakeable one, behind me. It's *her*, a fact I confirm with a sneak peek, then sit hurriedly sit down trying to hide behind the coat I've hung on the back of my chair.

'What are you doing? That woman who's speaking too loudly, do you know her?'

I nod.

'Who is she? Do you know the woman she's with too?'

I quickly turn my head then shake it. She is sitting down three tables away with a grey-haired woman I don't recognise.

'Looks like it could be her mum. Come on then Audrey, what's the gossip?'

I wish I was at home, back with James and the children, watching some rubbish television. Anywhere rather than near that woman.

A sigh escapes my lips. I'm going to have to tell the tale now.

'She's Mary Adair. James and I met her at our adoption meetings.'

'Adoption?' Claire furrows her forehead.

'Yes, we adopted Antonia not long before her first birthday.'

Claire puts down her fork. No chopsticks for her. 'Really? I didn't know that.'

'It's not a secret, Antonia knows she had a mummy and daddy who couldn't look after her and James and I wanted her so much that we became her mummy and daddy.'

Although my appetite has receded I use my chopsticks to eat a mouthful of rice. It's actually delicious.

'Do you know much about her real parents?'

'Birth parents,' I correct her. 'They were young, there were issues and social services decided it was an unsafe environment for Antonia.' I don't mention their drug use in case Claire ever inadvertently lets it slip in front of Antonia. It's something we're waiting until she's much older to tell her.

Claire picks up her fork and begins to eat again, looking down at her plate. I copy her. When she stops to swill it down with some lager she asks me what Mary did at the adoption sessions.

'She and her partner were looking to adopt as well,' I answer. They were a few years older than James and me. They'd used up all their rounds of IVF on the NHS and decided to adopt instead.

'Is Wilfred adopted as well?'

'No. He's our genetic child. I'd tried for a long time to get pregnant before we looked into adoption. Wilfred was a wonderful, natural surprise when I came off the pill after Antonia had been with us for less than three years.'

Over the general hubbub I hear Mary's voice screeching about how her neighbour is annoying her. Good for him I think, then inwardly chastise myself for my uncharitable thoughts.

Claire points her fork in Mary's direction. 'She's getting on my nerves already and she's only been here a few minutes. Why are you hiding from her?'

I've curled inwards without even realising. That sort of person makes me shrink instead of standing proud and tall. Words may not physically harm you but they stay in your psyche like tiny barbed spikes.

'As I said, she was in our adoption group. After the introductory meetings, when we decided to go ahead, as well as being assessed by a social worker we went to group sessions where we were all taught parenting skills and such. We discussed what we'd do in different scenarios. Some of it was a bit like group therapy, the point was being able to understand the lives of people very different from us. Most of the children who are up for adoption have had a traumatic start to life, far different from our own upbringings.'

I take sip of water. The bubbles pop in my mouth and wash away the taste of oyster sauce.

'She and her partner seemed nice enough. That was until she found out in a session that we were open to adopting a non-disabled child. James mentioned it in the meeting. Afterwards she accosted me in the car park, said it was political correctness gone mad that I should be given a normal baby when so many women like her, without a disability, want to adopt. She crouched down and asked me how I'd know how to bring up a child without a disability when I'd never had that experience myself. I was astonished. I couldn't get a word in edgeways.'

Claire's jaw drops open. 'What a bitch! I can't believe she did that! What happened next?'

'James came out of the building. I'd gone ahead to the car whilst he had a quick chat with one of the other men. When he saw my face he came running over and asked what was going on. She stormed off without a word and I got into the car and burst into tears. It was that sort of situation where later on I thought of lots of great retorts but at the time I was too stunned, too upset to say anything.'

'That must have been awful for you.'

'She said every bigoted thing I'd worried people might think.'

'I hope you said something. She shouldn't be allowed to care for a child with an attitude like that.'

'I didn't. James wanted to but I said no. I didn't want

to play tit for tat. Didn't want to make a fuss. It turned out though that another social worker in the car park witnessed the lot. Mary and her partner weren't at the next session, which, ironically, was all about respecting difference in religion, culture, sexuality, race and ability.'

A grain of rice escapes her mouth as Claire snorts with laughter.

'She got what was coming to her then. Did she adopt in the end?'

'Haven't a clue. I never saw again thankfully. Until now.'

'Just ignore her. Silly cow. The adoption people obviously thought you were wonderful seeing as they allowed you to adopt Antonia. I'll give her the dead eye. Maybe with any luck she'll choke on her chow mein.'

I can't help but laugh. I begin to relax again, though cross my legs to avoid having to walk past Mary to go to the loo. The evening carries on. Claire tells me about a woeful book she's reading written by a man who keeps describing a woman's pert breasts and peachy bottom. 'What's wrong with saggy tits and a lardy arse? Hasn't he met any real women?' she jokes, now on lager number three. I've moved on to tap water.

'Then it goes on to describe his throbbing member. A member of what? Parliament? Just call a dick a dick.' By now I can't stop laughing, but blushing too at her candour, and Mary Adair has been pushed to the edge of my conscious.

I'd promised James I'd be back by 10 p.m. and at 9.30 I ask the waiter for the bill. Claire again refuses the offer of a lift, saying she wants to stop off at the convenience store on the walk home to pick up a few bits and bobs. I pay on my credit card and tell her it's my treat. On the way out it's unavoidable to walk past the table where Mary Adair is sitting. I'd resolved to keep my eyes focused in front on the door but as I walk past she looks at me, her gaze burning my cheek; recognition registers on her face and she holds my gaze a few seconds too long.

Claire deliberately walks right up to the table and swiftly whirls her right elbow round. The glass of red wine in front of Mary spills its half-finished contents all over the tablecloth, swooshing right into Mary's lap.

'Oops, sorry! My bad,' smiles Claire and walks out brazenly with me following behind, trying to curb my astonishment until I'm outside. I go quickly hoping that Mary isn't going to come running after us, then, out of sight of the restaurant, double over with laughter.

'I can't believe you just did that!'

'She deserved far worse. No one messes with my friends. Did you see her face though? Priceless!'

'No, I was too busy trying to get out of the door.'

'She didn't know what had hit her! Probably will have a huge dry-cleaning bill as well.' Claire hugs me goodbye.

'Thanks for tonight, in more ways than one. I'd never have done that in a million years but, well, you doing it is a different matter…'

'Anytime. I'll call you tomorrow.'

'I look forward to it.'

As I pull out of the space in my car, cocooned in the safety of the locked doors and lulled by Marvin Gaye on the radio, I forget all about the shadows, the dog walker and the man watching our house. Tonight I was free to be me.

I'm still smiling when I quietly let myself into the house and walk into the kitchen where James is sitting drinking a cup of tea. One look at his expression obliterates the smile from my face. There are worry lines around his eyes and he looks at me with concern.

'What's wrong?' I ask hurriedly. 'Has something happened to the children?'

'No,' he says. 'They're fine. Both asleep and haven't woken up since you left. Will you sit down please?'

'Why? What's happened?'

'I'm so glad you're home. I've been looking out for you.'

I take a seat, glad to do so as my knees reactively start to wobble. It's not my usual seat and the chair is hard underneath without my cushion on it.

'I took the bin outside tonight and I saw him. The dog walker, going slowly up and down our street. He was as you described. He walked to one end of the street and then came back again, stopping outside our house to stare. I would have confronted him but didn't want to leave the front door unlocked with the children inside. So instead I shouted, "Can I help you?" in his direction. He hurried away.'

'You saw him? What does he want? Why us?'

'I believe you Audrey, I really do. I'm sorry for being a bit flippant before. I'm going to call the police tomorrow. There's no point now, he's probably long gone. I probably should have called them earlier but I didn't want to disturb the children if they came to the house.'

James holds his hand out to hold mine, his fingers coiling themselves around my smaller ones. 'Maybe he's a burglar. Maybe he gets his kicks out of scaring people. I don't want

92

you going out on your own after dark Audrey. I don't want to be all heavy-handed but I don't think it's safe, not until this gets sorted. Promise me.'

'I promise.'

In bed the minutes collectively click past as I try to rest. Sleep eludes me until I eventually pass out with exhaustion. My body might be dozing but my mind is still on high alert. My old headmistress appears at the front door, ringing and knocking until I let her in. Her black dress is uncreased, not a wisp of hair falls from under her wimple. 'We all reap what we sow Audrey and now it's your turn. Punishment time.' With that she disappears to be replaced by the dark figure of the man, his dog jumping up at me, biting me in his struggle to get past me to reach the children.

I wake up in a sweat. It's not yet dawn but I've never been so glad to be awake in all my life.

~9~

James calls the police from work. He rings to tell me that they have recorded what he and I both saw, along with the times and dates, and are going to send a patrol car regularly around the area for the next few evenings. It's little help but I can't think what more they could do. Nervousness purrs along in the background of my day like a car engine that won't switch off. I jump at the slightest noise. Is it just me the man is targeting or, as Claire said, is he getting his kicks out of trying to scare lots of women?

Of course we say nothing to Antonia. James fixes a new bolt to the front and back doors. I spend the next few weeks on edge, looking out of the window, making sure that the car and front doors are locked and only going out with the children in daylight hours. I meet Claire for lunch at a café quite regularly or take soup in a flask to the park where she eats the remnants of last night's takeaway. A few times the children and I meet up with her in the park. When I'm outside in her company and not on my own with the children I feel the tension ease and the worries about the safety of Antonia and Wilfred lessen. I even pluck up the courage to go out for a cheap pizza with her, getting a taxi door to door, all the time staring out of the windows in case the menacing dog walker is there. He isn't. James and I hope that he's moved on to someone else or, even better, stopped altogether.

The day for Antonia's playdate with Jordan, postponed due to him being off school with some sort of bug, finally comes around. Although it's on the calendar in the kitchen and in the computer diary James and I share, I nearly forget on the day. Tina wasn't at the gates this morning, her partner's mother had brought Jordan in. I think Tina had said something about having an early Zoom meeting with a client. In the morning an ex-colleague of mine calls to ask if I'd be available to do some paid freelance accounts work for his sister's beauty salon business. A spark of joy ignites inside me when I think about working with numbers again and earning my own money. If I can find a nursery space for Wilfred for one day a week then I reckon I'm ready to do it. Perhaps eventually I could start my own little part-time business. When Wilfred is old enough for a free childcare place I'll have time to work but still be around for the school run and at home for Antonia and Wilfred after school. The beep alert on my phone, reminding me of Antonia's playdate today, which Wilfred and I are joining in with, interrupts my thoughts, but for once there's a smile on my face as Wilfred and I set off in the afternoon to the school gates.

Instead of taking the car to pick Antonia up I decide to walk. We wouldn't fit all five of us in my car and anyway I don't have a spare car seat for Jordan. We'll walk to Tina's house with them and then perhaps take a taxi home that provides child car seats if it's too early to call James to come and pick us up. I text him and he says he'll try and get back home from work a bit earlier than usual. He still doesn't want me walking home in the dark.

Jordan and Antonia chatter away as we amble along with Tina and Wilfred to their newbuild house in a small development about a mile away. It's pristine, still with that 'out of the box' smell of paint and new carpet. Jordan and Antonia don't even bother taking their coats off; they go straight into the back garden to play on the swing and with bats and soft balls. Tina and I take it in turns to keep Wilfred amused whilst we chat.

'I'm thinking of joining a book club,' Tina says, 'but I'm not going on my own, I need an ally. Want to come too? It's advertised in that free magazine that comes through the door every month.' She looks at me imploringly.

'I want to meet some more people round here and if you come too it will be fun. We can be the naughty ones at the back who looked up the story on Wikipedia ten minutes before the meeting.'

'When is it?'

'First Tuesday of every month in a private room in the pub. Don't worry, it's not one of those where you have to invite everyone to your house or anything.'

It's ages since I've read a novel for the sheer pleasure of it. The only books I've read in the last year are childcare manuals and baby food recipes. Why not? I nod my agreement before I think twice about it and chicken out. I'm starting to become quite the social animal.

'Great! I'll email the co-ordinator and find out what the latest book is. I'm glad we met, Audrey. It's great having a mum friend. There's no way I'd want to hang around with the group of school-gate mums whose highlight of the day is getting a manicure.'

I look down to my unvarnished fingernails, clipped short for practicality, and laugh. 'Who says I don't?'

The early evening passes quickly with us talking about the school, the funny things that the children say and looking out of the window to keep an eye on the whooping twosome.

'Do you mind if I ask you a question?' I ask Tina when there's a lull in conversation. It's something I've been wondering about for a while.

'Fire away!'

'You usually wear your hair up. Is that because you prefer the style or because you want people to see your hearing aids?'

Tina smiles. Today she has plastic rainbows clipped on to the brown part of her hearing aids that contain, I think, the computer chip or whatever and the battery.

'A bit of both. It's easier and quicker to tie my hair back. I rarely have time to make an effort what with work and running after Jordan. I also got sick of explaining to people that I'm deaf and need them to speak clearly and not cover their mouths. If they can see the hearing aids then they usually figure that one out for themselves. Or I can make them feel guilty if I do still have to explain and can point to the hearing aids for evidence. What do you think of the rainbows?'

'I love them! Antonia said that she wants a hearing aid because she loves your rainbows so much.'

'They're great aren't they! Do you mind if I ask you a

question too? Was there a possibility that your children would inherit your disability? It wasn't with us because we had genetic testing before we started trying for a family and my husband Kofi hasn't got the recessive gene.'

Strangely enough I don't mind Tina asking me this because she's in the same boat as me. 'Antonia is adopted. There was a chance that Wilfred could have but James and I decided we'd have what nature gave us. If Wilfred had been born with restricted growth it wouldn't matter to us.'

'I agree. Same with Kofi and I but we did the testing to know if it might be a possibility. I've noticed, if you don't mind me saying, a few people staring at you. They do at me as well sometimes with the hearing aids.'

'I tend to ignore them. I've trained myself to. If I let it get to me I wouldn't go out of the house. They're the ignorant ones, not me. I did once buy a pair of three-inch heels though because I wanted to see what it was like to be taller. I found a website that sold adult shoes in smaller sizes – I'm a size two. I wore them once. I could barely walk in them, they hurt my feet and three inches hardly made any difference! Since then I've stuck with flats or courts.'

'I know what you mean about stilettos. I mangled my feet when I was eighteen and nineteen wearing them to go out clubbing. Loads of corns and plasters! Then one night I slipped on a spilt drink whilst wearing them and badly sprained my ankle. The shoes went to the charity shop!'

We both laugh and share more fashion failure tales. The hands on my watch seem to move quickly. Tina is in the middle of telling me how she and Kofi met when the ring of my mobile phone – just the standard one it came with, I never got around to changing it – interrupts our conversation. I delve in my handbag and pull it out. It's Claire. I don't answer, thinking it rude to whilst I'm with Tina and that Claire will leave a message. A minute later it rings again and then, a minute after that as well.

'It might be urgent,' says Tina, folding her legs underneath her on the battered leather easy chair she's sitting on. There are lines of felt tip on the side and I smile in recognition that there's no point buying fancy new furniture when you've got young children. In a funny way the colours add to the homely feel of the room, you can sense that it's lived in and loved in.

Tina's got a point. I worry that I should have answered the call first time. To call three times on the trot, rather than sending a text or messaging me, is odd. Perhaps it's important. My phone beeps again to tell me I've got a message.

'I'm sorry, I'd better listen to this.' Tina nods and starts to play incy wincy spider with Wilfred who claps his hands delightedly.

'Audrey, can you call me back please when you pick this up? Bye,' is the message. Claire assumes I know it's her. Her tone is difficult to read, neither friendly nor concerned.

'I don't know what she wants. I'll call her back. Sorry, I won't be long.' I walk out of the room, accompanied by Wilfred's excited giggles, into the white hallway, a blank canvas waiting to be decorated. In the other room I can hear Antonia and Jordan chattering away.

Claire picks up after two rings.

'Hi Audrey.'

'Hi, how are you? Is something wrong?'

I hear her taking a sip from a drink at the other end and wince at the slurping sound.

'No, nothing's wrong, I said I'd call you today, remember?'

'Yes, you did, sorry I forgot. It has been manic here. I haven't got much time to chat now I'm afraid. Can I call you later, when the children have gone to bed?'

'Sure. Where are you? I wondered if you fancied meeting up for a drink tonight or tomorrow?'

I cast my mind back to the number of times I've seen Claire over the past month. More than I've seen my few long-term friends in two years.

'I'm at the house of a friend of Antonia's. I'm sorry, I can't do this week. I've been going out a lot recently, don't get me wrong I've really enjoyed it, but I need to try and spend some time with James. I'll call you though. How's work?'

'Same old shite.' She sounds low. I know she's said her job is lots of work for very little money.

'Sorry to hear that,' I commiserate, looking at the time on my watch. Tina has cooked dinner for the children, including Wilfred, and if I don't take him home within the hour he'll be wanting to sleep in his pram. The nights are getting darker and the grey is closing in already. If it's alright with Tina I'll definitely stay here until James gets home from work and can come and pick us up in the car. At the back of my mind is the memory of the shadow behind the trees and the man walking his dog, along with James's warnings to be careful. As I thought earlier, tonight's not a night I want to walk home with the children in the twilight, even though it's still a very respectable time of the evening.

'But you've got the time to go to somebody else's house. Who's Antonia's friend?' Claire's voice is sharp with an edge I haven't heard before. I hope I haven't offended her.

'It's Jordan's mum, Tina. Do you remember he and Antonia are best friends now? I'm sorry you're having a hard time. I'll call you tonight.'

'Oh don't worry, I didn't mean to be off. It's one of those days. I'm hormonal. I'll see you soon then? Hope we can meet up again soon. Give me a call when you have some spare time.'

'Will do. Bye then.'

'Bye.' She hangs up. My shoulders hunch when I walk back into the living room and a knot of guilt winds around my stomach. Wilfred is on Tina's knee, chuckling as Tina pulls silly faces at him, wobbling her bottom lip with her finger. I can't help but smile and the knot loosens a little.

'Everything OK?' she asks.

'Fine, it's a friend. She wanted to know if I was free to meet up with her.'

'Free? A mum with two young children?!' she laughs, eyes rolling.

I sit down on the sofa next to her and pull a rabbit face for Wilfred. He's loving the attention.

'I feel a bit bad, I told her I don't have any time this week. Or next week really. I've spent quite a lot of time with her recently and think I've rather neglected James. She sounded put out.'

'Well he is your husband, it's not a surprise you want to prioritise him! How long have you known this friend?'

'Claire? Just over a month. I've seen her lots, on my own

and with the children. We've had fun. She's younger than me, new here and doesn't know many people yet. I think she's a bit lonely.'

'How did you meet her?'

I cross my fingers under my knee and give a vague answer. 'In the park, we got chatting and went to a coffee shop.'

'Don't feel bad. Family comes first doesn't it, especially if you've only known her a month.'

'Hmm.' My set mode is to worry about things. I hate letting people down but Claire's words come back to me: 'But you've got the time to go to somebody else's house.' What an odd thing to say. It's not really her business who else I socialise with, is it?

Tina offers me some food when she gives dinner – vegetarian lasagne, salad and garlic bread – to the children but I decline, wanting to eat later with James instead when the children are in bed. I do, however, accept the offer of a slice of toast to keep me going seeing as it's not the done thing at someone else's house to finish up Antonia's leftovers, not that there was any with her being so ravenous after wearing herself out playing with Jordan.

Antonia has just finished her dessert of fruit and ice cream when the doorbell rings.

'That must be Daddy,' I say to her, causing a huge grin to light up her face. Jordan sticks out his bottom lip. 'I don't want you to go, I want to carry on playing.'

'You'll see Antonia again tomorrow at school,' says Tina as she gets up to go and answer the front door.

'How about you come to play at our house next?'

The bottom lip goes in.

I hear James's deep voice with its hint of Devon accent coming from the hallway.

'Right darling, time to say your goodbyes and get your coat.' Antonia jumps off her chair and follows me through to the hall with Jordan trailing behind.

'James this is Tina, Tina this James,' I say feeling like I ought to give them a formal introduction although it's obvious who they both are.

'Hello Tina, good to meet you.' James shakes Tina's hand rather formally whilst she is far more laid back. He doesn't find meeting new people particularly easy and I'm quite protective of him in case other people interpret his social reticence to be standoffish.

'Great to meet you too.'

'Er, busy weekend coming up?' he asks quietly whilst gently rocking the pushchair Wilfred is sleeping in. There are a couple of dark circles under his eyes. I can tell he'd rather get home as soon as possible. I start to help Antonia put her coat on but she remonstrates with me saying she can do it herself. With a shudder I try to block from my thoughts that James had to come and pick us up because I don't feel safe walking home with the children after dark. What if the man with the dog follows me or God knows what else?

Tina's voice snaps me back into following the conversation. 'We've got my partner's sister coming to visit. She hasn't been to our new house before.' Jordan jumps up and down with excitement, waving his arms about. 'Aunty Amma! Yay!'

Tina puts her hand on her son's shoulder to calm him down and looks at us conspiratorially. 'He loves his Aunty Amma. Probably something to do with the fact that she spoils him and never arrives empty handed.'

'My sisters are like that too but we don't get to see them that often. They usually make up for it with presents though.'

'Presents!' shouts Antonia.

'Settle down sweetie, we'll be home soon then it's bath and bedtime.'

Tina turns to me. 'What about you Audrey? Have you got any brothers or sisters?'

I feel a vice tighten around my chest, compressing my lungs and squeezing the oxygen out of my body like a reverse ventilator.

'No.'

I try to take a deep breath but the room begins to spin and however much I gulp the air isn't entering into my lungs. Breathe normally Audrey I tell myself as my heart races in panic. I swallow down the small bit of vomit that comes up into my throat, thrusting my hand into my handbag for my eco water bottle. With a shaky hand I screw off the top and take a mouthful.

James places a firm hand on my shoulder and strokes me gently. I manage to bring my breathing back to some form of normality – with his hand holding me I know I won't fall. Tina looks at me with concern. 'Are you alright? Do you want to sit down?'

'I'm fine, just tired. It has been a long day. Wilfred was up super early this morning. We'd better get back, thanks so much for having us. Why don't you two come to our house after school next week?'

'Love to. We can sort out a day at the school gates tomorrow. Are you sure you're OK?'

I lie and nod.

With that the children say goodbye, Antonia thanks Tina for having her as I've taught her to, and we head off to the car, Jordan waving and Tina watching at the door until James has strapped Wilfred into the car seat and dismantled the pram to go into the boot.

As we drive the short distance home through dimly lit streets, Antonia chats away to James about what she's been doing and he chats back, squeezing my hand between gear changes. When we stop at a red light, the windscreen wipers shooing away the bleak drizzle, he looks over to me and mouths 'tell me later'.

Our road seems extra busy today with cars parked on the street. I wonder if someone is having a party, and I'm thankful that we have our own drive and don't have to park a way away and walk to our house in the drizzle. James unstraps Wilfred and wraps our still-sleeping son tightly in his arms and dashes for the front door with Antonia, as instructed, holding on to the end of his coat. I use the car key fob to open the boot, lift the pram out, press the fob again to automatically close the boot and pull the folded pram up to the front door so it's ready for tomorrow's walk to school. Probably because I'm rushing to get out of the wet the pram's wheels don't play ball and by the time I get to our porch the others are inside, having left the front door open for me.

There's a loud bark. Instantly I jump out of my skin. I look over to the road. A man with a large dog is standing opposite watching me. Staring. I'm not imagining it – his eyes are boring into me.

It's *him* again.

There's a crash as the pram tips over onto the floor. In my shock I've let go.

'James! James!' I bend over to try and grab the metal pole of the pram but my shaky hand can't grasp it.

'What is it?' He comes to the door and bends down to lift the pram inside.

'There's the man over there. With a dog. Watching me. The one I've seen before.'

We both turn to the street. The rain is thicker now, I can hear the pouncing sound as it hits the windowpanes and car roof, staccato notes mirroring the ferocity of my heartbeats.

I jerk my head left and then right. A shadow disappears into the darkness at the end of the road.

~ 10 ~

The days pass by swathed in a curtain of unease. I fall into a routine of meeting Tina at the school gates and I'm thankful for the reassuring presence of my new friend who makes me feel less alone in the gaggle of noisy mums. Looking behind me and keeping my eyes open for anything suspicious has become second nature. I meet Claire with the children a couple of times after school but my heart isn't in it, what I really want to do is get home, back to my sanctuary, where I know that I, and the children, are safe behind the bolted doors.

James and I pull together. In front of the children we try to act normally. Any mention of our fears is banned. It's extra difficult though after another parent reports a suspicious-looking male watching the school gates. The school gives an assembly on stranger danger and is extra vigilant about the list of people permitted by parents to pick up their children. The police check the school's CCTV but find nothing. Either the parent is mistaken or the man has done his homework and knows exactly where to stand to not be caught on camera. The community liaison officer tries to up her patrols of the area but with other issues going on for her to deal with, her visits are infrequent.

To keep up the appearance of normality for the children we decide to celebrate James's birthday with a family lunch at a pizza restaurant. We each have the choice of the food we want to eat on our birthdays – a tradition James and I have long held and one that we introduced Antonia to on her fifth birthday (fish and chips followed by chocolate cake was her choice).

'Why don't you pick pizza Daddy, I love pizza! Pizza will make you grow even bigger and stronger!' Antonia had said to James daily every day for the last week as part of her one-child pizza propaganda campaign. There's a family-friendly chain with crayons and colouring-in table mats in an out-of-town retail park about fifteen minutes' drive away that she went to for a children's party a month ago which gave her the Italian bug. At least there we won't feel like we're disturbing other diners with our baby because at that time of the day they will all be families with children, too.

Wilfred eats a stew I've brought from home whilst the rest of us enjoy our favourite pizza toppings. My shoulders drop as I start to feel tension release in my body. Antonia is entertaining us with her favourite jokes and James tries to up the ante by teaching her some 'knock knock' ones he remembers.

'Knock knock.'

'Who's there?' Antonia asks excitedly.

'Annie.'

'Annie who?'

'Annie joke you can tell I can tell better,' laughs James. Antonia's squeals of delight set Wilfred in his high-chair and me off laughing too. To be out spending normal family time together is wonderful and I start to think that maybe I can put the strain of the past few weeks behind me. I smile with genuine happiness, the muscles in my face almost having forgotten how. I've made some new friends, have an ally at school and last night had a discussion with James when he said he thought it was a great idea my taking on the freelance accountancy work that's on offer. Maybe now I can look forward to the future instead of dreading what each day might bring.

After we've paid the bill and walked halfway to the car, Antonia decides that she does after all need to go to the loo, despite earlier saying she didn't, and insists it's urgent. James pushes Wilfred back to the car in the pram while Antonia and I rush back to the restaurant to use the facilities. I mouth 'sorry' to the waitress who had served us as we head straight to the ladies.

On the way out, Antonia telling me she doesn't know if she preferred her own margherita or Daddy's pepperoni pizza is nearly drowned out by the noise from children sat at a long balloon-adorned table. I turn to see what the commotion is all about and come face to face with a shell-shocked looking woman staring straight at me.

It's Sophie. I haven't seen her since she sent me the infamous email.

I rip my gaze away, embarrassed by the awkward situation. She looks just the same, even her long, centre-parting hairstyle hasn't changed. Before I would have been delighted to see her and rushed to say hello. Now I can't wait to get out of the restaurant.

Antonia looks at Sophie quizzically. I can tell she recognises her a little but she was too young really to remember when Sophie tore herself out of our lives.

'Who is that lady, Mummy?'

I hesitate, not sure what to say. 'She's somebody Mummy used to know.'

I flick my eyes back for a split second. Sophie is still staring. I can't tell whether her gaze is hostile or conciliatory. She's on a table next to the children's party. Her partner Jack isn't there, if she's still with him that is, instead she's with a man I recognise as her brother, a dark-haired woman who I guess is her brother's partner, and a young boy of about three. That's it, I remember that her brother had a little boy. Although Sophie was happy for him it had upset her greatly at the time. Though not so greatly that she cut *him* out of her life. Her younger brother and his girlfriend hadn't been together long and their pregnancy was unplanned. She said, in her own inimitable way, that it was like life giving her a two-fingered salute.

I wonder whether to say anything. For a couple of long seconds I freeze. I know I should acknowledge her and be the better person. As my mum used to say, treat others like you wish to be treated yourself.

Yet there's an excruciating cavern between us. Seeing her overwhelms me with sadness and emotional pain. How could she have dropped me like she did? I'd longed for my pregnancy and Sophie knew the heartache I'd been through to have a family. Then I add guilt into the mix, stirring it up on a high speed with sadness and folding in regret. Was I smug about my pregnancy? Could I have handled the situation better? Did I hold off telling her for too long so as not to upset her, but causing the opposite? Or was she totally in the wrong for selfishly cutting ties with me? It's too much for me to think about right now, caught unawares.

I remember a conversation we had when Sophie was on her second round of IVF and I talked about dreaming of another child after Antonia had come to us through adoption. I knew how blessed and fortunate we are to have been picked to be her parents and never expected that luck to happen twice. Being without her is unthinkable and, with hindsight, my miscarriages before we applied to be adoptive parents led to us being gifted this wonderful little girl whom I never think of other than being one hundred per cent our own. The miscarriages were so hard, my fears once again coming true. To some it was just a clump of cells. To me it was our future, the lost potential of our longed-for baby, sadly mourned.

The advice from adoption services to James and I was to keep using contraception for at least a year after adopting Antonia so as to give her our sole attention. When I did come off the pill to our delight I fell pregnant five months later. We hadn't really been trying. We hadn't even had much sex because as new parents we were exhausted all the time.

I want to bolt out of the restaurant. All I can smell is a churning mix of pizza, perfume, sweaty children's bodies and sugar from the ice cream desserts. I start to gag like I want to be sick but my feet are rooted to the floor. Loud shouts and squeals from the children's party prompt Antonia to pull on my arm to go outside. On the back of my neck I can feel Sophie's eyes on me taking me back to her sobbing in my arms after a miscarriage at ten weeks. Another crushing disappointment for her.

The walls start to close in on me and I gulp for breath. A scream begins to form in my lungs, gathering in intensity like a twister ripping up everything in its way. Calm, try and be calm. I attempt to take a deep breath but I can't expand my lungs, all I can manage are short bursts of reverse hiccups, gasping to try and get more oxygen inside me. I have to get out. People are starting to stare. My feet begin to move. Holding tightly onto Antonia's hand I hurriedly move towards the door, head down and, like a horse with blinkers on, focus on the outside. Keep going I will myself. Onwards to the safe place of the car. A gust of wind hits my cheek like a slap around my face bringing me back to the here and now. Gravel is under my feet. There's the scent of petrol and chip fat in the air. In and out, in and out. My lungs begin to replenish themselves with oxygen.

'Mummy, who was that lady looking at us?' Antonia asks again as I lead her briskly, winding past parked vans and SUVs to get back to our car.

'Somebody I used to know. No one important.'

She's not interested enough to ask any more questions. James is by the car looking out for us and waves dramatically with both arms. Antonia waves back. There are no cars driving near us and I allow her to let go of my hand and skip towards Daddy where he envelops her tightly in a cuddle. Wilfred is already strapped in his car seat. James smiles at me as I approach.

'Everything OK?' he asks.

'I'll tell you when little ears aren't flapping,' I reply with a plastered-on smile for the children's sake. They don't need to know about my anxiety, nor about the stress I'm under with the stalker. I can't help my irrational fear that he is some kind of prophetic warning from the universe to me, that I'm not allowed to be happy and soon, just as Sophie cut herself out of my life, I'm going to lose those I love.

~ 11 ~

It's four days later, four long, angst-ridden days during which I tell James that I saw Sophie in the pizza restaurant, we didn't talk, the situation unnerved me but I'm fine.

Tina and I went to the book group and for a magical hour and a half my mind focussed on Daphne du Maurier's *Rebecca* instead of the ghosts haunting my own life. I even gave my opinion to the group. Tina said she was worried about speaking up in case she had totally got the wrong end of the stick in front of people she hadn't met before.

The clock hand moves to half past nine in the morning. After we walk Antonia to school I push Wilfred to the local shops to stock up on bread and milk, all the time anxiously looking round to see if there is anyone following. There isn't.

I turn the key in the lock of our front door and the hinge squeaks as I push it open with one hand and try to manoeuvre the pram in with another. There's a crunch under the wheels as I push the pram over the post that's scattered just inside the door. Bills probably, though we don't get as many as we used to since we tried to go green and opted for online notifications. Once I've unstrapped Wilfred and taken him out of his pram and settled him

114

in the playroom I begin to sort through the post. Indian takeaway flyer. Late birthday card for James. Letter from an electricity supplier we used to be with, no doubt wanting to regain our custom.

The paper of the last envelope feels different. It's smooth and shiny – expensive. Wilfred is playing with his soft toy carrot and babbling away to himself happily. One glimpse at the florid handwriting of my name and address tell me who it's from. Sophie. She's the only person I know, or knew, who still bothers writing letters, saying that they are far more personal than a text message. But why is she writing to me? Is she being conciliatory or antagonistic? I won't know until I open it but part of me worries about what she might have written – sometimes ignorance is bliss if it protects you from something you don't want to hear.

I wait until Wilfred goes down for his nap then bite the bullet, gently peeling back the envelope flap with shaky hands so as not to tear it.

Dear Audrey

I'm so sorry. I know these words are too late and I understand if you don't reply and never want to see me again. For a long time now I've regretted cutting you, James, Antonia and your new baby out of my life. It was selfish and wrong. Seeing you at the restaurant reminded me of how much I've missed you. Your friendship was so special and I threw it away. I cut my nose off to spite my face. If you can find it in your heart to forgive me then I'll make it up to you ten times over, but I know I don't deserve your forgiveness. I'll always cherish your friendship and support. We had such fun, didn't we?

    With love,

    Sophie xxx

It's only ink on paper but these words mean so much. A tear trickles down my cheek, quickly followed by many more as the pent-up frustration, worry and emotion that have built up over the past months seek release. It feels good to let them out, to not have anyone watching that I have to pretend I'm fine to. I sob silently so as not to wake Wilfred in the next room. Finally, like the ebb of the sea on the shore, my tears abate and I remain still, with a runny nose and a weight lifted from my heart. Sophie is sorry.

I wonder what she is doing in her life now, whether she still loves her TV soaps, whether she got that promotion at work and if she ever finished the evening fashion course she was taking. Is she still trying for a family?

I smile, thinking of her putting a chart music station on the radio and dancing round the kitchen when she thought we needed cheering up. I wonder whether a kitchen disco would be enough to mend our friendship. Can we go back? Do I want to go back? What steps should I take next? I think I'd like to see her but am nervous to do so. Perhaps I should take a leaf out of her book and write a letter back ensuring that I say exactly what I want to, that I forgive her and hope that we can find some way to be in each other's lives again. I'll compose a letter this coming weekend when James is looking after the children for half an hour. It won't be easy I know but the thought of potentially having my best friend back is wonderful.

My phone beeps. It's a text from Claire saying she can leave work early and wants to meet the three of us in a coffee shop after school. My heart starts to race with being overwhelmed with too much to think about. I know I'm being unfair but it feels as if Claire is putting me on the spot although she's only being friendly. There's just something that just doesn't feel quite right. I reply thanking her but explaining that we're busy today. Tina and I are going to a PTA meeting after school where there's a creche for the children whilst the adults talk about school business. I want to attend to see if anything's mentioned about the suspicious man spotted near the school gates.

Five seconds later there's another beep.

That's a shame. When are you free? X ☺

I like Claire, I do, but being older than her, with a family, I don't have the time that she does to make plans and socialise. I text back:

Life's really busy at the moment with the children. Sorry, maybe next week? I'll be in touch when I've got some time free. Hope all's well with you. x

The PTA meeting isn't very well attended. Alongside the next fundraising fête and whether money raised from the last should be spent on sports equipment or new books for the library, a key topic of discussion is if there have been any more sightings of the suspicious man hanging around the school gates. A mum of a Year 3 child says she may have seen him but she couldn't be sure because he only stayed for a couple of minutes and he didn't look very dodgy. One dad said he challenged a man he didn't recognise but it turned out he was a separated father who rarely picked his son up from school. None of us are reassured but we all agree to keep vigilant. Rob used to date a policeman and I make a mental note to ask his advice when he visits at the weekend.

When you're not working – well, I mean paid for work rather than 24/7 parenting work – Monday mornings and Friday evenings lose their significance in the weekly calendar, particularly if your child is pre-school age and Sunday night hasn't already become the time to ensure the school uniform is washed and ironed, school bag packed, and a stressed check of the parents' WhatsApp group to see if there are any requests such as show and tell day that you've forgotten about.

Friday night is still when James comes home and collapses, exhausted, after dinner in front of the TV in the knowledge he's got two days off, that's if he hasn't got to catch up on any work from home. I remember when, in our twenties, James and I used to get a thrilling 'schools out' flutter when we left the office on a Friday, usually for a trip to the pub with our younger colleagues and the older ones who wanted to delay returning home, then we two alone would head to a restaurant. Choosing Indian, Italian or French became the ritual that signified the beginning of our weekend. Two days of downtime with nothing we particularly had to do until Monday morning came around again from behind the clouds.

This Friday evening, however, I'm taking extra special care cleaning up the toys for Rob's visit. I sweep around the lounge and kitchen with a fluffy duster on a long handle before James vacuums. On top of the smaller sofa that turns into a bed I put fresh towels and pristinely clean bed linen to go on the pillow and duvet that James retrieved from the top of the wardrobe. It's 8 p.m. The children ate at their regular time and I had a couple of mouthfuls to finish their leftovers. My stomach grumbles, looking forward to the takeaway the three of us will order when Rob arrives. It's an hour and a half's drive for him to reach us but if the traffic's bad, who knows how much longer it will take.

A door creaks followed by the patter of two small feet into the lounge.

'Mummy, I'm not tired. I want to stay up and see Uncle Rob.' Antonia stands there in her pyjamas, her yawning and eyelid rubbing telling us a different tale to the one she's telling. We'd deliberately arranged Rob's arrival for after the children's bedtime. To no avail it appears.

'Back to bed sweetie, it's past your bedtime. Uncle Rob will be here when you get up in the morning,' James says, pulling her on his knee. She snuggles into him and shuts her eyes then remembers she's supposed to be wide awake and sits bolt upright.

'But I'm really not tired. I think I could stay up as late as a ten-year-old!'

I stifle a chuckle. In Antonia's mind ten is ancient, nearly as old as Mummy and Daddy.

James places a kiss on the top of her head. 'You can stay up as late as a ten-year-old when you are a ten-year-old but right now you're going back to bed.

Too late. There's the sound of a quiet engine pulling up

into the drive and then switching off, followed by a knock on the front door.

'Uncle Rob!'

'OK, you can say a quick hello but then it's straight to bed. Promise?'

'Pinky promise,' replies Antonia, and James carries her to the front door, turns the key and slides the bolt with one hand then opens the door to let Rob in.

'Uncle Rob!' she squeals and wriggles free of James to be picked up by Rob instead.

'Hello Doodle!' Antonia earned that nickname from Rob when she crayoned on the wall in his flat during the thirty or so seconds we weren't looking.

'Can you put me to bed please Uncle Rob and read me a story?'

'Of course!' He carries her in and James shuts and bolts the door behind him.

'She's already had one bedtime and story,' I say with a knowing look.

'Please…'

'Go on then, a quick story with Uncle Rob and if you're lucky he'll read you a longer one tomorrow.'

'Yes!!!'

'Usual for the takeaway Rob?' I ask.

He nods as he carries Antonia through to her bedroom, still not having taken off his jacket. James takes the sports bag Rob brought through to the lounge.

By the time Rob has settled Antonia then freshened up himself, the Indian takeaway has arrived. While we're munching away in the kitchen, where James has ordered his own curry and Rob and I share the same dishes we have done since university, I ask Rob if there was anyone out in the street when he arrived.

'To be honest I wasn't looking. I was glad to be here and out of the traffic. Are you still being watched?'

James looks at me as if to ask me to tell the story and takes a mouthful of beer from his glass. Rob, as usual, is drinking straight from the bottle. A barely touched white wine spritzer sits by my poppadoms on the table.

'The last time we saw him was quite a few days ago now but another parent has reported seeing a suspicious man hanging around the school gates.'

'The same man? With a dog?'

'No. No dog. But the man Claire saw outside my house didn't have a dog either. Perhaps he ditched the dog or perhaps there are two separate men.'

'Or maybe the suspicious man at the gates was actually legit?' interjects James.

I take a mouthful of my chicken tikka.

'Who's Claire?'

James laughs. 'Her new best friend. Took her out and got her plastered.'

'Ah, that Claire,' says Rob.

'Yes, I went out with her a few times last month. She's nice and I enjoyed getting out. What with everything going on though, I've wanted to spend more time at home recently. I missed James.'

'And I missed you too! But not the wino breath,' laughs James and reaches out over the tablecloth to hold my hand.

James tactfully goes to bed a little earlier than me to give me the chance to talk to Rob on my own. Rob tells me about his breakup with Kieran and that he's not in a hurry to go back on a dating app just yet although he did receive a text from a man he went on a date with about nine months ago but whose work then posted him to their office abroad for a temporary secondment and is now back.

'Are you going to meet up with him again?' I ask.

'I don't know if I want to just yet. I'll text him back and see what happens. What do you reckon?' Rob shows me a picture of the date on his phone. He looks vaguely familiar, about thirty maybe, receding hairline, squarish face, grey eyes.

'Not bad for you! Although he looks quite like the description of the man seen outside the school that I told you about. The art teacher drew a picture of what the parent said he looked like and emailed it to all the parents.' An involuntary shiver runs down my spine at the thought of those grey eyes watching me.

'Seriously? Well it's not him because he's been abroad.'

'I know. But he's got that kind of everyman white man look hasn't he? There's nothing really distinguishing about him. Do you think I'm overreacting about the dog walker?'

'No, not if you feel threatened. You're very down to earth Audrey, you're not a drama queen. And James saw him too. You're right to be careful but hopefully it's all over now.'

That night I pray that Rob, even though he doesn't know all of my fears, is right.

~ 12 ~

After a bracing trip to a National Trust house and gardens, where not once do I feel a sense of disquiet or that I'm being watched, we arrive home about 4.30 p.m. to get the children's dinner ready. Antonia is full of excitement and clings on to the cuddly black sheep Rob bought her in the gift shop. He bought Wilfred a white one and he's already dribbled over it and tried to bite its ear off.

James cooks his signature dish, spaghetti Bolognese with vegan mince, whilst Rob and I try to calm the children down. Wilfred is grumpy from missing a lot of his afternoon nap but I change him and try and keep him awake in the playroom until he's eaten so he won't be up all night. Antonia is busy daubing yellow and black face paint on Rob to turn him into a lion.

Amidst the chaos the doorbell rings. James turns down the hob and answers it. I hear a woman's voice and then into the playroom walks Claire. My heart sinks. I'm not used to casual visitors.

'I was nearby and thought I'd pop in and say hi. Your husband let me in. He said he's gone back into the kitchen to finish cooking.'

She flashes me a big smile but I can't help feeling it's an

inconvenient time to 'pop by'. I didn't realise people did that any more without calling first to see if you're in and free.

Nevertheless politeness kicks in. 'Hi! It's nice to see you. We're a bit busy at the moment though, we've come back from an afternoon out and are getting ready for the children's dinner.'

'Oh don't mind me, I won't get in the way,' Claire says, sitting herself down on a beanbag with a thump. The hint has evidently passed straight over her head.

'Everything OK?' Perhaps she's here to talk about something specific? A problem maybe?

'Yes, fine thanks.'

'What have you been up to today?'

'This and that, had a lie-in, did my washing and a bit of window shopping for clothes I can't possibly afford.' She laughs.

'Good!'

'Do you want me to amuse Wilfred for a bit?' She holds out her arms to take him.

'Um, well, we're having our dinner soon but I think we've got ten minutes. Can I get you a drink?' Offering refreshments is my reflex polite reaction to a visitor although I don't want to encourage her to hang around.

'A glass of water please. I've already had lots of caffeine today.'

I hand Wilfred over to Claire and go to the kitchen to fetch her a glass of filtered water from the fridge. 'It's Claire, my friend from the park. She's not staying long. I've told her we're having dinner soon,' I say to James who nods although I can tell from his mumbled reply that he's concentrating on his recipe and is only half listening.

When I get back to the playroom Antonia and Rob (whose yellow and black smudged face looks more like a bumblebee than a lion) are there. Antonia is chatting to Claire about running around the maze with Daddy at the National Trust house. I introduce Claire to Rob and, after taking a photo of Antonia's make-up artist work for posterity, suggest he might want to go and wash his face before dinner.

'I'm getting you back tomorrow. Want to be an elephant?' is his parting shot to Antonia before he leaves the room.

Ten minutes later James pops his head around the door. 'Dinner's ready!'

'Thanks for popping by Claire, it was lovely to see you,' I say. Rob picks up Wilfred to carry him through to the kitchen. Claire stays firmly still on the beanbag, not even moving a centimetre. Her brown ankle boots are strewn to the side of the chair like knocked over bowling pins. She's not reaching to put them back on.

'Our dinner's ready now,' I reiterate. Still no movement. Rob coughs pointedly.

'Oh that's OK, I can wait in here until you've finished. I don't mind.'

There's an embarrassed silence. Rob raises his eyebrows and mouths 'What?' without Claire seeing.

'Well, the thing is…' I start to say but am interrupted by James appearing at the playroom door again. 'Come on Antonia, I'm dishing up!'

He sees Claire still sitting on the sofa and looks confused. 'Is your friend joining us for dinner Audrey?'

'That would be lovely, thank you,' Claire says straight away before I can get a word in.

'Right, great.' James replies politely. 'If I chop up some more salad and butter some bread it should stretch to six.'

Claire follows him as he goes back into the kitchen, shuffling in her socks, and Antonia skips behind.

'Unbelievable!' says Rob, half laughing, half astonished at Claire's behaviour.

I shake my head in disbelief. I've not seen this side of her before.

After a dinner that passes affably enough Antonia reminds us that it's Rob's turn to put her to bed tonight and read a long story.

'That sounds lovely, can I join in?' pipes up Claire. 'I adore bedtime stories and can do a very good animal voice.'

'Which animal?'

'Ooh loads, dogs, cats, tigers, hippos...'

'Can you do a giraffe?' asks Antonia.

'Of course!' says Claire and proceeds to talk in a comically high voice.

To my gloom Antonia laughs and says to Claire that she can join in. Rob shoots me another look that I interpret as 'the cheek of the woman!' James, however, who has started to clear the table, appears oblivious.

I'd hoped I'd have some more time to talk to Rob on my own that evening yet still, even after Antonia is fast asleep, Claire is still here, not saying a great deal but drinking wine and making herself at home. At 10.30 p.m. I've had enough and try the exaggerated yawns trick and saying that it's getting late. No response. Now I'm fairly annoyed and bite the bullet.

'Well I think it's my bedtime now Claire. Can I call you a cab to get home?'

Please don't let her say she's fine sleeping on our sofa.

'No, I'll walk thanks, it's not that far.'

'Are you sure?' says James. 'Didn't you see a strange man outside the house last time you came?'

Claire goes quiet. 'Well, I didn't want to worry you but I saw a man walking his dog up and down the road today when I arrived. I lingered a bit until he went.'

My blood runs cold.

'In that case I'm definitely calling you a cab.' He takes his wallet out of his back chino pocket, pulls out a twenty-pound note and passes it to her

'I'd give you a lift but I've had a couple of beers. What's your address?'

Claire hesitates but takes the money. 'Thanks. You're probably right. I'll give the driver my address when they arrive.'

I make my excuses, feigning exhaustion, and go to bed before the cab arrives, leaving Rob and James to keep Claire company. I don't want them to see the tremble in my hands that her news has brought on or the fear on my face.

It's still happening. When will these strange men watching the house stop? Who the hell are they and why are they there? About half an hour later James crawls into bed beside me and I sense the comforting heat of his body against me. I pretend to be asleep, although the bliss of blank unconsciousness is something that eludes me until dawn when Wilfred cries out.

~ 13 ~

After brunch and a trip to the playground in the park Rob sets off home. There's no sign of the dog walker and although we don't call the police this time we add it to the list of sightings they told us to record. Once again I haven't had another chance to chat privately with Rob other than him making a comment about 'Clingy Claire' when James couldn't overhear.

I try to think the best of her behaviour but as hard as I try I cannot. Later on Sunday she sends a text to thank James and me for dinner and asks if we'd all like to meet her for lunch near the park next week. I reply breezily saying thank you but we're busy that weekend. What I don't say is that I'm annoyed with her and think it's best if we have a natural break from each other for a while.

She texts again two days later, suggesting I meet her for a drink. I reply with an explanation that money's tight and I'm prioritising family time at the moment but hope that she has someone else to go with. Her follow-up text, saying it wouldn't be as much fun with someone else, makes me feel guilty but I stick to my guns. Perhaps in a few weeks she might behave differently…

Those thoughts change to anger when I return home from a book group gathering with Tina only to find that

Claire had happened to visit during my absence – she knew I was in a book group and it wouldn't be hard for her to work out when the meeting was – or am I being unfair? Apparently she'd stayed an hour talking to James and once again had invited us all to meet up with her.

'I didn't agree to a plan, I said I'd let you sort something out,' James told me. I hid my anger, once again not wanting to be uncharitable.

'Thanks. I wouldn't have thought it would be your kind of thing.'

'It's not but it was kind of her to ask.'

I take deep breaths and try to unclench my shoulders.

'Don't you think it's a bit strange that she stayed that long? When I wasn't there?'

'Well she met me last Saturday I suppose, but I was starting to run out of conversation. I heard Wilfred cry on the baby monitor and said I needed to see to him so she left.'

My phone buzzes and I look to see who it is.

Unbelievable. It's another text from Claire.

Hi, I called by today but you weren't in. When's a good time for you?

I go to the loo to take time on my own to compose my answer.

Hi Claire, sorry I missed you. As I said before we're really busy right now and there's a lot going on for the next few weeks. Family life is hectic! Please don't drop by the house if we haven't made an arrangement. I'll call you when I'm free. Hope you are well.

I don't add a kiss on the end. For my standards the text is brutal but I hope she picks up the subtext and now gets the message.

She doesn't.

It's 2.45 p.m. the next day and I'm about to wake Wilfred up from his nap so we can get ready to go and pick Antonia up from school when the doorbell rings. I know it's not the postman because he came at midday.

With a deflated sigh I realise who it is before I open the front door. Claire.

'Hi!' she says brightly. 'I know you said to not come without calling but I was visiting some shops nearby and thought it would be rude to not say hello.'

This time my politeness is very strained. There's definitely something about Claire that's not quite right. Is she lonely? Can she not understand social signals? My usually calm hackles are rising.

'Claire, I'm busy. I've got to wake Wilfred up from his afternoon nap and then we are going out. I'm sorry I haven't got time to see you now. Like I said I'll call you when I have.'

Her face falls and for a couple of seconds I feel remorse. But on the third second my annoyance appears again.

'I could come with you if you like?'

'No. I don't think so. You're not at work then?'

'Afternoon off.'

'Well enjoy it. I've got to go now and see to Wilfred. Bye.'

I close the front door with an extra shove, lock it and slide the bolt for extra security. I don't like unexpected visitors breaking up mine and Wilfred's routine. Rather than a visit from a friend her knock on the door felt like an invasion. Rob was right, she has become clingy, almost like an extra child clamouring for my attention. Our friendship feels as if it has moved on too quickly for me. I've enjoyed her company but can't commit my time like a single twenty-something who hates to be on their own can. We've had fun, yes, but what do I really know about her? As an introvert I need my own space too as well as seeing others. Rob and Sophie always understood that.

Wilf is gurgling and smiling in his cot. Perhaps he's having a pleasant dream. Watching him sleep clams me down, slows my breathing and reminds me of what's most important to me: my family.

I gently wake him, get him ready and put him in the pram to go out to meet Antonia from school. This morning she had skipped off excitedly when I dropped her off at the gates. It was show and tell day in the classroom and she had chosen to take in a fossil that she found with Daddy on a beach on the Jurassic coast. Just a piece of rock really but to Antonia it means the world. I grin at the memory of my daughter sleeping with the fossil under her pillow to keep it safe in case the dinosaurs came back to get it when she was asleep. It's just like my daughter to choose a fossil and not a doll or sparkly unicorn to take to school. James is interested in natural history and Antonia loves whatever he does.

When I've put my coat on I start to feel like I've overreacted. The chastising voice in my head has a lot to say. 'You're being unkind Audrey.' 'You gave her your phone number in the first place.' 'Claire is alone in a new town.' 'She saved your son.' 'You have had some fun times with her.' 'She's lonely, no wonder she's acting needy.' 'Be kind.' 'Give her a break.'

But my practical side overrides it. I'm not Claire's mum or her big sister. I'm a wife and mother with responsibilities and can't be on call all the time or have the sort of intense, see you every day friendship that we usually leave behind once we've left school or college and embarked on proper adult life.

As I set off from home, the pram's wheels squeaking a little on the uneven pavement where I have to swerve to avoid the tree roots breaking through, a thought crosses my mind. I know so little about Claire or why she might be lonely and coming across as pushy. Could she be insecure? She's never appeared to be to me but perhaps she's good at masking. Maybe I haven't cut her enough slack.

My feet pound the pavement in rhythmic steps: left right, left right, lulling me into a meditative-type state where I mull over alternative possibilities. Could it be that what I'm sensing as pushy is actually Claire trying too hard? Am I being unfair? It's not easy to meet new people in a strange city. Has something happened in her life to leave her troubled? Where are her parents? I've never heard her talk about them. Is she close to them? Does she ever go and visit? Has she come out of a disastrous long-term relationship?

Maybe she lost touch with other friends when she moved here for work.

Come to think of it, I don't know where she works. She's never mentioned it to me or told me the company's name. She also seems to have a lot of free lunchtimes and late afternoons. Would an office assistant really be free those times in the day or be allowed all that time off? I don't know her home address and she's never invited me to visit. She says it's a shared house and very messy. I suppose that's why she likes coming to my house so much, it's an adult house, friendly, welcoming and (mostly) clean. Our bungalow isn't massive but the sofas are comfy and I like to think it's homely. It's a grown-up's house rather than a student's crash pad.

Maybe I overreacted. You'd think that once you graduate from the playground that friendship would be easy but turns out it's just as complicated as every other relationship in life.

I make it to the postbox just before the next collection and slide my reply to Sophie into its jaws. The letter is the eighth draft, written when the children were in bed. In it I say that I'd like to see her again and ask what she's doing now. I tell her about Antonia being at school and a little bit about Wilfred. I suggest that we meet in a coffee shop one day and that I'll come alone on a weekend if she'd prefer to see me without the children.

The only stationery in the house was an A4 lined pad and some thank you cards left over from Antonia's birthday last year when I wrote them to people who gave her a gift. For the letter to Sophie I bought some high-quality, watermarked cream writing paper with matching envelopes. I do want to see her again. Water has run under the bridge. We'll both be the same but different now. I hope we can build a new friendship stronger than the old.

To be honest, on the short distance to the school I half expect to see Claire appear around a corner or leap out from behind a bush in front of me. I've never had to break up with anyone before and have no experience of any of this. I had a couple of boyfriends before James but one relationship fizzled out naturally and the other ended it with me at university by text message.

I say hi to Tina at the gates and we listen to Jordan and Antonia chatter for five minutes when they come out of school. Antonia is brimming over with excitement to tell me about the fossil, now firmly packed away in her schoolbag. Jordan shows me his dad's shiny football trophy that he took in. The three of us arrive home feeling tired but happy.

James and I have decided that tonight is date night at home. With everything that's going on we want to spend a couple of hours focussing just on us.

I give the children their dinner a bit earlier than usual and have a quick slice of toast to keep me going until I eat with James later. He arrives home in time for the bath, story and bed routine with the children.

This date night it's his turn to cook. He's cheated a bit by picking up a ready-made lasagne, garlic bread, bottle of wine and bag of salad at the supermarket on the way home but I don't mind, he makes a delicious salad vinaigrette. We sneak a quick kiss whilst trying to settle Wilfred and then when the food is in the oven Antonia gets up for a glass of water and a cuddle, saying she had a bad dream that a witch flew on her broomstick and landed on our roof. Ten minutes of love and reassurance later she's fast asleep and finally, at last, date night begins.

The smell of the garlic bread sends my tummy rumbling. I clear the kitchen table of Wilfred's cuddly toy and Antonia's drawing pad and pencils and set the table. Besides the crockery I lay our special cream linen napkins and bring out two wedding present crystal champagne flutes from the cupboard even though tonight we're sticking to sparkling elderflower water with a slosh of white wine added.

James flings a tea-towel across his shoulder extravagantly. 'Madame! Our chef's special tonight is lasagne al forno with garlic bread and chef's special salad. Can I tempt you?'

'Absolutely monsieur!'

He brings the salad and garlic bread over to the table along with two pasta bowls containing steaming hot lasagne. It's delicious and a treat to eat together slowly, savouring our food, without feeding Wilfred, him throwing his food on the floor, or us having to coax Antonia to eat her vegetables whilst ours go cold.

Although we make a concerted effort not to have our mobiles near the table when we eat with the children, so as not to teach them bad habits, today James has his in his pocket because he's expecting a text from the cycling club and mine is on the kitchen counter from texting James earlier. A ring interrupts our meal.

It's mine.

I ignore it.

Two minutes later it rings again for thirty seconds.

James raises his eyebrows inquisitively. 'Not answering it then?'

'We're having dinner. I'm not going to interrupt our time together to answer the phone.'

'But it might be important? Do you want to see who it was?'

I go to the phone, half dreading what I'll see, and lo and behold, in the missed calls section, the most recent listing is 'Claire from park'.

I press the off button firmly and the screen goes blank.

'It was Claire. I'll call her back sometime.'

'I thought she was your best friend now?'

I decide against telling him that I'm finding Claire too pushy. It all seems trivial compared to the stalker business and I don't want him to think I'm being mean.

'We've had some fun times but I've missed you and the children. It's date night! I want to concentrate on us now. Remember that freelance accountancy work possibility I told you about? I'm meeting the business owner soon to discuss it.'

'That's brilliant!'

I smile. 'Yes, I'm looking forward to using my brain. What with everything going on and the book group and PTA and maybe seeing Sophie again, I haven't got time to go drinking with Claire.'

'She seemed alright to me and was good with the children. When's your meeting with the salon owner?'

'The seventeenth. Two days' time.'

James puts down his knife and fork, gently placing them vertically on his plate in the centre to ensure they don't clang against the china.

'Claire said something to me when she visited and you weren't here. About how you met in the park.'

My heart starts to race.

James carries on. 'She said that she met you when you saw Wilfred's pram roll into the pond in the park. Antonia had run off and the brake on the pram wasn't working properly. I'm not cross with you Audrey, I just wonder why you didn't tell me yourself? Auds?'

Annoyance rises in me. Did Claire come when she knew I wouldn't be there so she could tell him? But why would she? She didn't know I hadn't told him already.'I didn't, well, I didn't want you to worry. No harm was done. It was a split-second mistake. How did it come up in conversation?'

I spike my fork heavily into my food.

'She asked me how we got together and then told me how she was glad she was there in the park that day to help you when you first met. She looked embarrassed when it was obvious you hadn't told me about the pram.'

The lasagne that tasted so delicious before now threatens to choke me. I put my knife and fork down with a sigh. 'I'm not hungry any more.' A tear escapes from eye and I wipe it away.

'Auds? You alright? What is it?'

'I'll be fine. It's the stress I'm under with the stalker, or stalkers, I'm tense and on edge all the time. What if the men are after the children? I didn't tell you about the park because I don't want you thinking I'm a bad mother.'

James reaches across the table to hold my hand. 'I'm sorry, I know you're having a really hard time. I thought things were looking up for you what with going out more and the prospect of a job. I wish the police would catch the bastards who are watching you and the other women.'

I nod in agreement and squeeze his hand.

'I'd never think you are a bad mother. You're not. You're a brilliant one. A supermother. No other woman could love our children more. You made one easy mistake in the park. That's all. It could have happened to anybody. What about the time I was asleep with Antonia on the sofa when she was one and she rolled off? Or when it was my turn to pick her up from nursery when you were away at a work conference and I forgot?'

A half-smile creeps onto my face and reaches my eyes. 'That was rather atrocious of you.'

'But you forgave me. I felt terrible and I learned from it. I barricade Wilfred in on the sofa with cushions and I'll never again forget to pick up Antonia.'

'I know. You're a great dad.'

James points to his mobile phone and grins. 'Every time I've got a pick up or drop off I put it in my calendar and the phone rings to remind me!'

I laugh, my shoulders a little lighter now, and drink a few mouthfuls of wine. The little alcohol kick comes instantly.

'We're a team,' James goes on. 'You're a brilliant mother and I love you very much. No one else appreciates everything you and I have been through to get this far.'

I take another mouthful. 'I love you too. I've been finding it hard though being at home all the time with the children.'

'I know but to be honest I actually don't like missing out on the children growing up. My job is relentless. I envy you sometimes spending lots of time with them. I don't want to be one of those dads, like my own, who I only saw for half an hour at night and on a Sunday.'

'But we need your salary.'

James looks into my eyes and I can tell he's serious.

'I've been thinking about this for a week, ever since I went to a flexible working lunchtime seminar at work. The department's budget has been cut, as you know. What if I asked to work three days a week? I'd cost them less money and have two days at home with the children when you could do your freelance work.

'Would you? Do you think it could work?'

'I don't see why not. I can talk to HR at work and you've got your meeting with the salon boss soon. Why don't you get in touch with some old contacts and see if there's any more work going?'

I smile and nod. The future is suddenly looking much brighter. We finish our meal and most of the bottle of wine, with us both making sure we drink a pint of water before we go to bed. Before I close the curtains I look out of the front window at the street. The streetlamps illuminate the crooked pavement slabs and cars parked on the road just as they always do.

Our street is peaceful and sleeping. No one is lurking on the pavement. Everything is as it should be. Together in bed with James, after we've made enthusiastic love (although quietly so as not to wake the children), I'm hit with a strange sensation, something I haven't felt in a long time.

Joyful optimism for the future.

~ 14 ~

The kitchen is filled with the delicious smell of mushroom wellington cooking alongside roast potatoes in the oven. We're having a special Sunday lunch to celebrate me getting the freelance accountancy work contract, which will start in a month's time.

I'm happy to do the cooking today as it gives me the chance to listen to my kind of music on the radio and for James to have some one-to-one daddy time with Wilfred and Antonia. I smirk as I wonder whether, once he starts his two weekdays looking after them, he'll be as enthusiastic at 7 a.m.

I'm steaming the broccoli and carrots when my mobile rings. It's Rob. He skips over the pleasantries and cuts straight to the chase.

'I've been doing a bit of digging on Clingy Claire.'

'Really? Why? Have you found anything?' I'm balancing my phone between my shoulder and cheek to keep my hands free for cooking. The steam leaves a fine mist on my face.

'I thought there was something very odd about her, the way she turned up when I was visiting you and she wouldn't take the hint to leave.'

'She carried on not taking the hint for a few days

afterwards but I think she's finally got the message now. I think she's just lonely and a bit needy.'

'I felt it was more than that. There's something not quite right about her behaviour. You can be too nice Audrey. Some people in this world aren't. Her name is Claire Jones, right?'

'Yes.'

'That made it difficult from the start to track her. Handy for her isn't it that she's got two very common names. I went through pages and pages on Facebook and Twitter and didn't find anyone that could be her.'

'You've been searching for her on the internet? She might have tight privacy settings or not be on social media. A lot of twenty-somethings aren't on Facebook anyway.'

'I couldn't find her anywhere. How can you get to her age without a digital footprint? I also couldn't find any trace of her working at a local business. Where did she do her degree?'

'I'm not sure, somewhere in London I think. She definitely said she studied business but never said where.'

'I'll have a look at unis in London.'

'They're not going to give out her details though are they, confidentiality laws and all that. Aren't you going a bit far? What is it you're trying to find out?'

'Audrey, you're my best friend and Antonia is my god-daughter. I'm looking out for you. Something about Claire just doesn't feel right to me. That woman is weird. I don't want her causing you any trouble. What if she's got a background of psychiatric instability?'

At that I laugh. 'That had never occurred to me so thanks for giving me something extra to worry about. I think you're worrying about nothing there though. I might be finding her annoying but I don't think she's mentally ill, and if she is, it doesn't mean she'd cause me any problems. I think she's lonely.'

'She might be lonely but I still think her behaviour is odd. What's she like with James? Has she spent much time alone with him?'

I think back to her turning up at the house when I wasn't in. 'There was one time when I was with the book group people. She stayed for an hour James said. Claire told him how I met her, when she pulled Wilf's pram out of the pond.'

'Had you not told him?'

'No. We've talked about it since though.'

I hear Rob take a deep breath and can tell he's got something difficult to say. 'With hindsight, do you think she told him deliberately to discredit you?'

'It crossed my mind that she might have wanted to cause trouble but I don't think so. It's fair to say she must have assumed he knew already.'

Rob's voice takes on a more serious tone. 'Do you think she might be after James? That when you first became friends she liked your family life and now wants to keep in touch with you in order to get to him?'

I laugh. 'James? He wouldn't cheat on me, I've never worried about that. He wouldn't have an affair with her. He hasn't got the time. It's only me who doesn't think he's a bit boring, because I am too!'

'I'm not saying he would but that doesn't stop Claire trying to, does it. Do you know where she lives?'

'No. She lives in a shared house. She said it's not the sort of place you can invite friends to but didn't tell me the street or area.'

'She doesn't like giving out personal information, does she?'

'No, she doesn't. Look can I call you back this afternoon please? I'm in the middle of cooking Sunday lunch.'

'Of course. I've got a date. I'll tell you all about it.'

'You'd better! The man who moved abroad for a while?'

'Yes!'

The timer pings and I turn the oven and the hob off when I hear the doorbell. James is with the children in the playroom so I go to answer it.

I don't believe it. The front door opens to reveal Claire.

'Hi!' she says all smiley, her emotions being at a mismatch with mine.

'Claire, hello, I'm busy I'm afraid. I'm cooking.'

I only open the door a fraction so she can't invite herself in and stay the rest of the day.

'I was passing again and wanted to talk to you.'

I'm not usually one for confrontations but there's a first time for everything.

'Claire, I need to talk to you too but not here. Not in front of the children.' My hackles are rising quickly and I am gripped by a sudden feeling that I have to bring this odd friendship to a close right now.

'James I'm popping out for five minutes, I've turned the oven and hob off, won't be long!'

I wait until I hear an 'OK!' in response, step outside then pull the door not quite to so I can get back in.

'Follow me,' I say to Claire, marching ahead towards the park at the end of our road. The gates are open but it's surprisingly quiet for a Sunday. The only living creatures I see are butterflies fluttering around the faded wildflower borders the council planted to improve its environmental rating and cut back on mowing fees.

I stop in a secluded wooded area where no passers-by will hear us.

'Audrey, I came to say I'm sorry if you think I'm bothering you. I don't mean to,' pipes up Claire.

'But you still do, don't you? Bother me that is. I specifically asked you not to come round to my house and said to wait for me to call you.'

'I know but…'

I don't let her carry on and am quite taken aback with my new-found confidence.

'You've got to stop interfering in my life Claire. My family comes first and you're not one of them, OK?' I think about what Rob said. 'Have you been lying to me about something? What is it that you want? Why do you keep showing up when I've asked you not to so many times?'

'I just want to be friends that's all. I'm sorry I've upset you. I really am.'

'Ow!' I slap my neck instinctively when I feel a sharp prick. Was I stung? Is that a bee that flew away in the corner of my vision or some other biting insect?

My EpiPen is in my handbag.

My handbag is in the hall at home.

Trying not to panic I search my trouser pockets frantically in the vain hope that the EpiPen will magically appear.

'Are you after James, is that it? Do you want my husband, to slip into my shoes, have my house? My life?'

It's hard taking the moral high ground when I'm looking over a foot up to my adversary. Claire isn't saying anything. Her mouth is wide open as if she's going to shove a gobstopper into it.

I run my hand over my neck trying to feel if there's a bump there and try not to panic. I'm not far from the house. This won't take long.

'James isn't interested in you, he's *my* husband. Please, back off.'

'I'm not—'

I cut Claire off mid-flow, not wanting to hear any of her excuses. 'Just stay away. I'm sorry, I don't have time now to carry on being friends and I have to go back home because I'm about to serve up Sunday lunch. I don't want to upset you but I need time and space with my family. And you're not in it. I haven't said anything to James. I don't want to embarrass you any further.'

My heart starts to beat faster and a sheen of sweat covers my palms.

'Are you OK?' Claire asks.

'I think I've been stung.' I try to take slow breaths and search again with my fingertips to see if the bee's sting is still in my neck.

'I'm allergic. My EpiPen – it's in my handbag back at the house. My phone and keys are in there too.' My welling panic takes over as I remember ten years ago when I was stung before. I used the EpiPen straight away as per doctor's orders but felt faint and wheezy for a while and it took a day for the symptoms to go after I sought medical help. Anaphylactic shock works quickly on me.

'Sit down,' Claire says, although she probably hasn't a clue what to do in this situation.

I wipe the perspiration off my brow with the back of my hand and my top clings to my moist underarms.

'I can't sit down, I need to go and get my EpiPen. Have you got your mobile on you?'

'I only came out with my keys in my jeans pocket. Really, I think you should sit down, you've gone a funny colour.'

'I have to get home. I can't believe I came out without my handbag, I never do that. Please find someone with a phone and call James and tell him to run here with my EpiPen.'

My heart is beating in a frenzy, is it the sting, panic or both? My knees start to shake. I flop down on the slightly damp grass, feeling the remnants of early morning rain through the seat of my jeans. I try to take a deep breath but can't seem to inhale enough oxygen. I look up. Claire is standing there, looking at me, her mouth slightly agape. I try to call out for help but haven't the breath to shout.

'Go, Claire, find someone, please, it's urgent.' I whisper.

She bends down and squeezes my hand. Her grip feels clammy.

'What's James's mobile number?'

'I can't remember, it's saved into my phone. Just run and find someone and call an ambulance. Tell them to hurry, it's anaphylactic shock.'

Dizziness overtakes me. I lie down on the grass, curled up in the foetal position as I do to sleep, when James usually spoons me, his warm arms wrapped around my chest, holding me tight for the night. Now, instead of arms, it feels like there's a vice around my chest, slowly squeezing the air out of me. I hold onto the picture of James, Antonia and Wilfred in my head. They are all that I care about. I must breathe for them, hold on until the ambulance comes.

Part Two

Claire

~ 15 ~

I never meant to do this. I never meant for things to go this far. Please believe me, oh God, if you exist, please believe me.

I'm frozen, staring at Audrey lying grey-faced on the grass, my brain not taking in what is happening. What's going on? How can people get so ill from a bee sting? I don't know what to do, my brain is befuddled, then Audrey tells me to go and call James and tell him to bring her EpiPen, whatever that is. Time seems to slow down to a millisecond, the tableau of horror fixed before my eyes. 'Go!' she says, she needs her handbag, which she left at home in her hurry to accuse me and push me out of her family after she'd welcomed me in with cake, a latte and a declaration of not knowing how she could ever thank me.

I've never seen someone so poorly before. When Audrey mentioned her allergy once in the past I thought she was hamming it up like rich people do about milk, gluten and wheat. All that jazz about how they are so special that they have to eat differently from everyone else, make a fuss and buy posh food because they'll simply die if they don't.

Shit, I think that's actually happening to her. She looks so tiny, vulnerable and child-like on the grass.

There's no one around. Audrey obviously likes to bin

someone off in private and she's brought me to a secluded part of the park in the wooded area where kids like to smoke weed and leave used condoms instead of carrying them to the rubbish bin at the park entrance. I must scream and get help. I ought to go and get help. Her lips are turning a pale shade of blue now. My muscles start to respond to my brain's call for action and I bend down, take Audrey's outstretched fingers and squeeze them. They're still warm. 'Don't worry, I'll get help. I'll get an ambulance,' I say to reassure her and I mean it. I turn on my heels and run. What Audrey can't see is that I'm running in the opposite direction from the main path.

You see, I need a second to think about what to do.

Audrey has a kind heart. I like her. She's cossetted, yes, but that's what you get from being born middle class and never having to want for anything. When I think this I feel a pang of sympathy for her as I remember the difficulties she's been through being born with restricted growth; I've seen with my own eyes the way that some people judge her, stare, mutter to each other when she's walked past.

Yet she's still unfairly got what I want, and I want it so badly. No, I never meant it to go this far but I didn't sting her, did I? I didn't tell her to go out without her EpiPen and leave her mobile phone at home.

'You're not my family,' she said to me.

We've been friends. I'm not an animal. I need to get help for her. I can't leave her on the damp grass struggling to breathe. I'm deeper into the wooded area now, the tree's canopy shielding me from the clouded sun and any prying eyes. I touch my back jeans pocket and feel the familiar hard, thin rectangle of my knock off pay-as-you-go smartphone tucked in there. In my panic I'd forgotten that, although I hadn't brought a handbag on my walk over to Audrey's house, I have my phone with me. My shaking fingers dial the wrong access code. I get it right on the third clumsy attempt and then jab the nine button once. Twice.

I'm about to press it the third time when I stop. A picture of what I have to lose comes into my head. It can't happen a second time. But am I really prepared to do what it takes to stop it? My head bypasses my heart and decides to run the show. My hands are like a robot's obeying instructions, working to the rhythm of the blood pounding in my veins. I switch the phone off. About five metres away I bury it under some stones and bracken, then count to fifty. Slowly.

When park-goers see me a couple of minutes later I'm running towards the entrance shouting for help. In the distance, too far away to hear me, is a man walking a dog. Turning a corner I come across a dad with a couple of teenage children. He stops to ask me what's wrong and I'm panicking now, trying to get my breath. I don't need to act – my fear and worry are real, just not quite for what he thinks they are for. I'm telling him to ring for an ambulance, saying my friend has been stung. She's collapsed and doesn't have her EpiPen.

The man, whom I later find out is called Jon, takes control. He calls 999 then tells his boy and girl to wait by the entrance for the ambulance whilst I show him where Audrey is. I'm inhaling lungfuls of air so quickly that I feel dizzy and nearly collapse. Through the ringing in my ears I hear Jon telling me to copy him breathing in and out and focus on that, in, out, in, out, until my fluttering heart calms down and I can pull myself together to show him where I left Audrey.

We enter the woods, Jon following in my footsteps, telling me the ambulance is on its way and everything will be OK, as if I were a child who still believes in the tooth fairy, not that the tooth fairy ever visited my house. Suddenly we turn a corner and there Audrey is, lying in the same position I left her in but with vomit coming out of her mouth.

Jon kneels down next to her. 'She's not breathing.' He must have been on some sort of first aid course because he feels for a pulse then rolls Audrey onto her back, pokes his fingers in her mouth to clear it of sick and then starts pressing on her chest like they do on hospital TV programmes when someone has had a heart attack.

She looks so limp under Jon's large body, so tiny. My heart kicks my head into submission and I retch then start to cry, the situation and my part in it really hitting me. Let her live I pray. Let her sit up and breathe and everything be alright.

I'm holding my breath, willing it to work as Jon pumps away at Audrey's chest and blows air into her mouth. He keeps doing this until the ambulance crew arrive and they take over. They inject her with something and carry on pressing on her breastbone, her small body jumping in rhythm, responding to each pressure. I don't want to see it any more and turn away to look at the trees, tuning out the medics' voices.

There's a small bird on a tree looking down at what's going on. It is brown. I know nothing about types of birds, that's not the sort of knowledge you pick up when you grew up in an inner-city concrete jungle that nature avoids just as those loaded enough to get out of there do. It's fluttering its wings but not flying away, just watching, sizing up whether we're a threat. Perhaps it has a nest of chicks up there it's protecting. Do birds lay eggs all year round or is there a season to it? Do they have a choice whether to mate and when their eggs hatch? Do they love their babies or is it simply that they're genetically pre-programmed to protect them to keep the species going?

I'm so deep into my thoughts that I jump when I feel a tap on my shoulder. I turn around to see one of the paramedics ask me if I'm OK. I stare at him not knowing what to say. He wraps a blanket around my shoulders and says something about shock. He's treating me like a victim.

When I look back at the trees the brown bird has flown away. In its place is a blackbird sitting still. Staring right at me. Accusing me with its jet-black eyes.

~ 16 ~

The house I share is empty when I get back. When the paramedic said I was OK to leave, a policewoman offered to drop me home. The last thing I wanted to do was get in the back of a police car and I said I wanted the walk, the fresh air. To clear my head. Before I set off she asked if there was anyone she could call for me. I didn't say there's no one she could call, and I didn't ask if Audrey is dead and whether James had been told what has happened either. She can't still be alive, can she? They whisked her away quickly enough into the ambulance. Did the paramedics manage to find a pulse in the end?

The policewoman wanted my phone number to keep in touch. I explained that we don't have a landline in the shared house, that I've lost my mobile and have been meaning to buy a new one. She gave me her business card with her contact details on and told me to call her as soon as I do.

Inside the house is quiet. The others must be out at work and RJ, one of the others who pays for a room here, is probably shut up in his room as always. I've only ever seen him come out once. That's the only reason I know he actually exists and there isn't some anonymous person paying his share of the rent.

I go to my bedroom in the downstairs front room and shut the door firmly behind me, turning the key to lock the world out. The smell of damp hits my nostrils as I dive under my duvet, face down, and press the pillow against my nose and mouth as if to muffle a silent scream. Yet I don't cry out or shout. I feel numb. I've shut down to dodge the guilt hammering my head with a pickaxe.

You must have realised why I did it, why I lingered in calling for help for Audrey. I did it all for Lily, or Antonia as James and Audrey called her.

The social worker explained to me that Lily's adoptive parents were allowed to change her first name as long as they kept the one I gave her as a middle name on her new birth certificate, which wiped every other trace of me out of existence. Only once did Audrey and James mention to me in conversation that Antonia had a middle name but they never said what it was. They probably want to forget it. It's a reminder that Antonia isn't truly theirs and never can be.

Yes, Lily is the name I chose for my daughter. I named her after the beautiful, heavily scented flower because I wanted her to, unlike me, have the kind of life where she is special, desired, looked after and protected from anything that could tarnish her. Except it's me, not Audrey, that is supposed to be keeping her safe.

I said none of this to the police officer when she arrived at the park and asked me what happened. My knees gave way mid-interview – shock, the paramedic said, but I knew it was also partly due to fear. Fear that they'd work out what I did and cart me straight off to jail. Fear that I was capable of such actions in order to be with my daughter. Fear that if Audrey survives and is successful in banishing me from her life I will never see Lily again, unless she tries to find me when she's over eighteen.

Lily, I did what I did for you. Your sweet face flashed into my mind when Audrey's eyes looked imploringly up at me from the ground. She said she didn't want me as a friend any more, didn't want me in her life, and that means I wouldn't be in yours. Those snatched minutes I spend with you whenever I can are all I live for, despite never being able to tell you who I really am and always having to let your adoptive mother take the lead, seem to know best and make decisions for you. Surely Audrey must have realised how strong the motherly bond is and has felt it herself with Wilfred. But my bond with Lily is stronger than hers because I'm the one who grew her in my womb, I'm the one who gave her life, she has my genes and that can never be taken away from us.

I see in Lily's face the penetrative eyes of her father. Her hair is the colour mine was at her age, but the colour is now long changed by dye to alter my appearance. When she falls over I feel her pain, when I hold her hand to walk her across the road I know that there's love in the squeeze from her little fingers. I adore her. She needs me.

I shouldn't have been so persistent with Audrey, should have played it cooler. I called too many times. I kept telling myself to hang back but I missed seeing Lily so forcefully that I couldn't bear not to hear about her or see her much longer.

After my darling daughter was taken away from me I found the strength I wish I'd summoned before to leave *him* and where I was living. A women's refuge run by the

Salvation Army took me in and helped, through fits and starts, leak the poison from my veins that I'd injected in. They believed in me. Viv, the support worker, and Ashlee who'd not long since been clean herself, taught me what real friendship and love were, not like my dad who buggered off when I was a toddler or my mother who always saw me as a liability with *his ugly face* and left me alone in our two-bed council flat, which I had no way of continuing to pay for, not long before my GCSEs started so she could fuck off to Spain with the latest love of her life who owned a bar there.

'It's my last chance of happiness,' she whined. 'Surely even you can be pleased for me.' Obviously I, the bastard daughter she'd only wanted so her boyfriend would stay with her and who inconveniently didn't take me with him when he left, didn't make her happy.

I can picture her now in her bedroom. She bought a new suitcase so large that you could fit the sodding kitchen sink in it. I found out later she'd spent the rent money on bikinis and dresses, earrings and anything else to turn her into the adorable partner she thought this latest man wanted. Of course he wouldn't want her for herself. Don't get me wrong, she wasn't bad looking for forty-ish despite the pack of fags she smoked every day and the lines round her eyes that showed it. She could doll herself up well if she tried but it was all fabric and war paint. Inside she's got a mean streak, always the victim, always badly done to, always looking for someone to change her life and unable to see that life has thrown her shit because she deserves it for the way she behaves. I don't think she knew how to love really, but I used to wish she did.

My Lily deserves so much better.

The excuse for Mum not taking me with her was my exams, though she never took them herself or showed any interest in my schoolwork. I think she only ever went to one parents' evening and that was when her boyfriend at the time said she ought to.

Mum told me I had to stay in our flat until the summer and that Jan, our elderly next-door neighbour whom I'd known all my life, would keep an eye on me. When she was settled and working in the bar she'd save up and send me the airfare to come over.

Yeah, right, and I might marry a prince.

Charlie, the man she'd not long since met, might do me a favour she said and give me work as a barmaid as long as I didn't scare off the punters with my sour face. She sent me a couple of texts after she left, one to say she'd arrived and the other a pouting selfie of her on the beach, then nothing. Radio silence. The bills went unpaid.

I didn't have any money other than the child benefit which she'd arranged to be paid to Jan and who faithfully passed it to me. That barely covered food. The electricity was disconnected for non-payment. Jan had a stroke and was taken into hospital. I told no one at school, I only had a few friends anyway. No way was I going to invite anyone back to the flat. I hid when there was a knock on the front door. I didn't want to be taken into care but in the end I sat in the dark, with the curtains open so I could see a tiny bit with the light from the security lamps outside, eating packets of biscuits I'd nicked from the corner shop.

That's where Grimey came in. He got his nickname,

apparently, because he was an expert in grime music. He wanted to be a star and dressed for success with his designer gear and bling. Behind that though, he seemed kind. He was three years ahead of me at school and, even though he'd long since left, sometimes he'd hang around the gates at leaving time to talk to his mates and sort out 'business'.

Looking back I was a naïve cow. Desperate. When he saw me start to walk home one day after a revision session (I went for the free school meal and electricity), my jumper tied round my waist and holes beginning to break through the weave in the cuffs, he stopped me to introduce himself. I thought he was another one of those boys masquerading as men who only wanted a lay and would say anything to get it. My mum's experiences had taught me to steer well clear of them. Yet when he said I looked hungry and could he buy me a chicken dinner, no pressure whatsoever, there seemed to be real concern in his eyes. He told me his business was DJing and raising cash to promote his own music. What I didn't see, until a lot later on, was that 'raising cash' involved selling drugs to the schoolkids, a few of whom he employed as mules to deliver his products to other customers. But that's a story for later.

By then I was in love with him. He's the only one, apart from Jan, who ever cared where I'd been, who I'd been with, whether I'd eaten properly and was safe. After he saw where I lived he moved me into his shared house, gave me a roof over my head and didn't ask for any money. He bought me clothes when I needed them and gave me cash for delivering packages to his friends' houses. DVDs, money he owed, trainers, he said. The packages were sealed. I never thought to look. Perhaps I didn't want to look because I knew I wouldn't like what was inside. Ignorance is bliss when you don't have any other option.

I went back to college, retook some GCSEs and started A levels. The social didn't bother me. I heard they repossessed mum's flat. Jan moved into a care home and I visited her once a week until she died a couple of months later. The only person who cared about me, apart from Grimey, was now gone. No one thought to check up on me. College was a different place from my previous school and it was easy to blend anonymously into the background. It's a skill that was to come in handy in the future.

Then one evening I came back early to the house Grimey and me shared with his mate Dom. Grimey liked to know where I was, what I was doing, he wanted to make sure his girl was safe he said. Not that I had many places to go to. I'd drifted away from the few school mates I used to have, the ones with the happy families and four-bedroom houses, and wasn't interested in making any new ones at college. I didn't need anyone else other than Grimey and his crew and certainly didn't want anyone 'official' poking their nose in. My routine was college in the weekdays and on Saturdays I worked in a clothes shop for some cash in hand. Grimey said I didn't need to, he would give me everything I needed, but I wanted some money of my own to buy tampons and girl stuff, plus I was saving up to buy him designer trainers for his birthday. My way of saying thank you for him giving a damn sight more of a shit than my mother did about me.

That Tuesday afternoon and evening I'd planned on staying late at the library with a girl called Suze. Our history teacher had paired us up to work on a presentation about power in Henry VIII's Tudor court. We only had a couple of days left to prepare and it was a lot easier to concentrate at the library rather than at home with Grimey's music constantly playing. Trouble was Suze left after a quarter of an hour saying she had a migraine and would finish her section at home. I stayed another half hour to complete my part then, instead of hanging around in the library on my own, decided to head home, stopping off at the corner shop to buy ingredients to cook a chilli. I'd seen a chef on the TV make it the night before. Proper food, not another pizza or Indian takeaway.

I should have known something was up when I saw the front stripy curtains were drawn. What first caught my eye was that the left one was bunched up behind the right and I wanted to shake it out to make it look nice. Then I wondered why they were drawn at five o'clock on a sunny afternoon.

No one could have heard me turn the key in the lock over the music playing in the lounge. The door was ajar and I could smell dope – Mum used to smoke it now and then saying it calmed her nerves. I dropped the food off in the kitchen and didn't know whether to go straight upstairs or say hello. Instead I decided to stand by the door and say hi.

'You're back early!' Dom replied loudly. I hesitated on the threshold until Grimey gave me permission to come in.

They were both sitting on the sofa and I noticed a couple of joint ends on a saucer sitting on a side table. Grimey's eyes were large and strange. He seemed to have trouble focusing on me. Dom was lolling back on the sofa, laughing although no one had made a joke.

'I'll leave you two to it,' I said, wanting to get out of the way. My mum used to smoke it but I had never wanted to. I didn't want to be like her.

'No, come here gorgeous. Come and join us.' I walked in and he pulled me into his arms causing me to fall on him on the sofa. There was a funny smell in the room, one I didn't recognise. That's when I saw the needle on the floor and the tourniquet.

'We're trying out the new gear, checking its street quality like. Want to help?' He kissed me fully on the lips and, unlike other times, I wanted to pull away. His breath stank.

'No you're alright, I've got stuff to do.'

'More important than helping out the family business?' Dom said, laughing again. Nothing was funny to me.

'You must have realised how we make our money. We need it to pay for the music. You know I want to start my own record label. I ain't rich, how else am I going to save up? How else could I afford to keep my beautiful girl? I don't claim anything from the social. I earn my money. Our family business, like Dom says.'

Grimey strokes my hair the way he knows I like it, the way Mum occasionally used to do when I was little.

'I'm not sure. What is it?'

'Skag. New batch. Got to make sure it's as good as my source says it is. Don't want to go selling an inferior product, I'd lose all my customers. Reputation is everything in this business.'

'I'll go first,' Dom said. Grimey held me tight next to

him as Dom pulled out a spoon from a bag, put some white powder from a wrap onto it, drew up some water with a syringe from a glass then added it to the spoon and mixed it with the blunt end of the syringe. I wanted to look away but part of me was fascinated. I'd never seen Mum take Class As.

Dom drew up the solution in the syringe then flicked it and pushed up the end a little. 'Got to get rid of the bubbles babe,' Grimey said. 'They could kill you.' I thought that the drugs were more likely to do that but kept quiet.

I took a deep breath and scrunched my eyelids together squeamishly as Dom wrapped the tourniquet around his arm and pulled it tight. He then injected himself, took the tourniquet off and laid back again on the sofa with a smile. 'Good skag Grimey, good skag.'

'My turn now.' Grimey reached for a new syringe. 'Got to be clean babe. Hygiene is cool.' Dom started laughing to himself whilst Grimey repeated Dom's previous moves on himself. After the needle had gone in he let out a sigh and undid the tourniquet on his arm.

'Want to try? Just a little for your first time. I promise you, you'll love it.'

I hesitated. I didn't really want to but neither did I want to look like a child either.

'Does it hurt?'

'Nah, just like having a vaccination at the docs.'

My stomach squirmed.

'Yeah?' he said. 'Just a bit. I won't give you much.' He took another syringe from the bag. Dom started lightly snoring. I considered bolting out of the door but Grimey looked at me with love. 'You'll enjoy it.'

I held out my arm as he put the tourniquet on. My hand began to go numb. I closed my eyes.

'In we go.'

The needle went in. I felt the liquid go into my veins.

And that's how I became addicted to heroin.

~ 17 ~

I keep to my bedroom all night and the following day in the shared house. There's washing hanging on the radiator and dirty plates and cups I haven't tidied up. I don't want to leave these four walls. In here I feel safe. No one can see me. The curtains are closed, the window is locked as is my bedroom door. I've put myself into prison before the authorities can do it themselves. None of the others knock on my door to see how I am. It's not that kind of house. I could die in my bed and they wouldn't notice until my rotting corpse stank the whole place out.

I have lost track of time. I don't look at my watch and the only way to tell if it's night or day is by the fading light at the window. They're going to come for me, aren't they? Surely it was obvious to the first responder, the police officer, even Jon, what I did. I'm not that good an actress. I've seen crime shows on TV. They're waiting for me to tie myself in knots, make a mistake, or perhaps break down and confess. Maybe I should. What if she's dead? They'll say that if I'd have called an ambulance sooner I could have saved her. If anyone saw me burying my phone I'm done for. Is burying a phone illegal? I certainly wouldn't be able to explain why I did it. I don't even know why myself. I panicked and thought that if

I was found with a phone on me when I had told Audrey I hadn't got it then I'd look guilty. Perhaps of murder.

My heart pumps loudly as I hear a siren go by. In this part of town they're a regular occurrence, not like the leafy streets where Lily lives. My daughter. The reason for all this. My love for her hits me again like a wrecking ball careering into a condemned building. What if Audrey has died? Without her Lily will think she's lost her mum. I imagine her struggling to understand, crying for Audrey, and Wilf joining in with the tears. My first thought had been to keep myself in Lily's life and not the grief my daughter would feel about losing the woman she called Mummy.

Selfish, selfish, selfish.

What kind of monster am I?

I peek out of the curtains to see the small, weed and bin-covered patch of land that creeps up to the public pavement. An empty crisp packet is fluttering in the wind, dancing to its own tune. There's no police car outside, no journalists, no stern-faced plain clothes police officers waiting with handcuffs to take me away. It should be a relief but my stomach contracts with revulsion at what I've done. Is deliberately taking time to get medical help a crime? If Audrey dies would it be murder? Or is it manslaughter? I didn't lay a hand on her, didn't shoot or strangle her. How could anyone else know that at that moment when she kicked me out of hers and the children's lives, that I wished her dead?

For the first time I consider the possibility that no one is coming for me. That the statement the police took was all they needed. That I may be called as a witness at an inquest if she's dead (the thought of which makes me feel faint). But perhaps, that's it. All I'd have to do would be to confirm the facts. That Audrey was stung, she didn't have her EpiPen, there wasn't anyone else around, I went to find help and by the time Jon and I reached her she was very poorly. An everyday tragedy. I don't look like a murderer. People who don't know me would think I'm an ordinary, respectably turned-out, rather bland young woman.

What's done is done. What matters now is Lily. My darling Lily. It's because of me that the woman you think was your mum is gone. You'll need me in your life even more now. Your proper mother. I can't hide in this fetid, junk of a room for ever. I've got to carry on.

With that thought a part of my soul scorches black, lost to me for ever. I've chosen my path and there's no turning back. In for a penny, in for a grand. I will my daughter's face into my mind's eye. Lily, this is all for you.

Sitting on my bed, wrapping the single duvet around me so tightly it becomes a cocoon, I try and think back clearly. Audrey – I can barely bring myself to think her name – had told me she didn't want to be friends any more but had she told James? I don't think so, there was something she said in the park, what was it? Ah yes, 'I haven't said anything to James. I don't want to embarrass you any further,' that was it. When I met him those couple of times, James seemed to like me. Audrey didn't want to make a fuss about turning on me, probably didn't want her husband to think her unkind: dropping the nice, younger girl whose only crime was to be lonely and over-eager.

That's the scenario I'll paint. The grieving friend. I *am* grieving, it's true. I liked Audrey. If only she had been someone else, not the woman who had stolen my child. But of course I won't tell James that. If I want to be part of Lily's life I'm going to have to go and see him, tell him how sorry I am that she was stung, use a bit of reverse psychology and say I'll understand if he doesn't want to see me again, but hope he takes the bait. As Audrey's friend and the person she spent her last minutes with it's only natural that I'd want to see James and find out what happened. Leaving it too long would look suspicious but a day or so is an appropriate amount of time before I show up, isn't it? I'll offer my help in the future with childcare if she's incapacitated. If she's dead, Lily and Wilf need a woman around to help take them to school, to the park, play with them, make fish fingers and chips for tea. A woman's touch. Without James's agreement I have no legitimate place in their lives. It's all down to his goodwill. I can't see him managing on his own. He's not exactly a go-getter.

I'll subtly weave in an alternative to Lily's posh name. Antonia no more, Toni will do fine. And who calls their son Wilfred?? All I can think of is a dead World War One soldier whose poems we studied in English lessons. Wilf though is part ironic, part hipster. I've got to play the long game again. Start slow, not be too eager and hope to reap the rewards in the future.

But what if Audrey is still alive and has told James everything? It's something I'll have to risk. If she has, she won't see me again anyway. In a way I've got nothing to lose. My plan is forming in my mind and, once again, I tiptoe to the window to peek out of the curtains. Still nothing, only an ordinary street view of cars, litter and an old woman on a mobility scooter walking her dog.

It's time to be brave and go and see James.

There's no one in the hall when I step out onto the unvacuumed flowery carpet. Someone has come back to the house though. There's an unusually faint rhythm of bass coming from the upstairs back room and a foul smell of burnt curry coming from the kitchen.

I close the bedroom door and feel a sharp twinge in my hand. Looking down I see a ruby red drop of blood begin to swell on my skin. Instinctively I wipe it away with my left forefinger but another appears, eager to replace it. There's another tiny wood splinter at the side of my palm. I nip it out with the forefinger and thumb nails on my other hand but that doesn't stop another orb falling to the carpet, adding to the multi-coloured splotches.

Funny how so little blood can stain something irrevocably.

~ 18 ~

I didn't use heroin every day at first. I stayed off it on a school day, well, alright, every now and then if I'd had a difficult day and there wasn't any homework to be done I'd have some. Grimey didn't take it that often, he usually stuck to the dope and he said he only used skag when a new batch came in. I felt uncomfortable asking for it when he didn't offer it so I took to using my wages from my Saturday job to buy wraps from Dom. He had no scruples, it was all business to him, a family business with me included.

My marks at college began to get worse. I got spotty and had huge black bags under my eyes thirty years too soon. I never wore short-sleeved T-shirts and I grew thinner, that was until I noticed that the only part of me getting bigger was my stomach.

Due to wanting to stay under the radar I didn't register with the GP to go on the pill. We used condoms, but as the sexual health campaigns tell you, they're not one hundred per cent effective. I got pregnant. I wasn't sure how Grimey would take it but he smiled when I told him and took me in his arms promising to take care of me. 'The family business is going to have an heir!' he said. He gave me a present of a Babygro with 'I love Mummy' printed on it and then produced another one printed with 'I love Daddy'.

I stopped taking the skag of course. God it was hard but I knew that it wasn't about me any more, it was about the baby too. I skipped college whilst I went through withdrawal. Hitch, one of Grimey's gang, brought me vitamin smoothies and folic acid tablets and left them outside our bedroom door. Grimey soaked my forehead with a wet flannel and brought me food in bed. He said he wouldn't let me out of the house until we both knew I wouldn't be tempted any more. You gave me the determination to get through it, Lily. The thought of you the size of a grape, an apple and then even larger. I read all the baby information I could find on the internet. We were going to be a family of three. From the moment I got through cold turkey I knew I loved you more fiercely than anyone in my life.

At college I went to see the pastoral care worker and she got me an appointment at a health clinic. By then I was seventeen and when I gave my address there weren't any questions asked about who I was living with. Grimey came with me to the scans and we pinned the scan photo of Lily up in the kitchen. I didn't want to know whether she was a boy or a girl. I wanted it to be a surprise.

Everything seemed to be coming together by the time I was ready to give birth a week late. We'd turned a spare bedroom into a nursery. Grimey and Dom built a white cot, wardrobe and changing table from flatpack kits and I painted over the faded wallpaper with bright yellow paint and hung up a huge animal mobile. I wanted only sunshine for our baby and stuck posters over the parts of the wall where you could still see hints of the wallpaper pattern.

I'd arranged with college that I'd take a few months out.

My grades had started to improve since I stopped using. The red marks on my arms faded to a soft pink, although still I only ever wore tops with long sleeves. I told Grimey I wanted him to find a different way to earn a living and he smiled at me saying, 'Yes babe'. I believed him.

Lily's birth was long and difficult. The umbilical cord was wrapped around her neck and it was an emergency to get her out safely. When she took her first breath and I saw her little scrunched-up face I saw it as a sign that she was special. She was a survivor and she was mine. Little did I know that six months later Lily would be forcibly taken away from me and I would be bereft, in a women's shelter, struggling to find a reason to stay alive.

The shelter was supposed to be my new start. At my lowest I was faced with a choice: an overdose or a leaflet given to me by a social worker about the shelter. I spent a long dark night counting the paracetamols I'd bought from five different chemists and wondering whether I could go on. I clutched the photo of the baby scan close to my heart until it finally struck me that as long as Lily was in the world I owed it to her to be here too.

Although the shelter was run by the Salvation Army it didn't shove God down your throat. The women running it were kind, didn't judge me, and advised me to focus on my future rather than my past. As well as emotional support from them and the other women there (I didn't tell them why Lily was taken away, I was too ashamed and didn't want them to hate me) there was practical stuff too like benefits advice, registering for housing, and support in going back to college. They ended up finding me a bedsit but whilst I was at the hostel my sanctuary was a small single bedroom with a wardrobe, chest of drawers and a desk. I'd brought all I owned in two plastic bin bags on the bus. Some clothes and shoes, my college books, a few toiletries and little else. Apart from the scan I didn't have a printed-out photo of Lily. They were all on my phone and I'd greedily scroll through them every day, wondering how she had changed and what I'd missed. Grieving for her. Longing to smell her again and hold her so tightly that no one could ever prise her out of my arms.

There was rarely a moment I didn't think of her and when there was, because I was having a laugh with Ashlee or watching something funny on YouTube, my heart contracted and I wanted to bang my head against the wall for not keeping my daughter safe. A head injury would be my punishment but it was a lot less than I felt I deserved. Then I'd switch and rail against the government, the social and the injustice of it all.

The shelter also organised healthcare and it was whilst I was there that I went to see a female GP about period pain. A scan found a gynaecological problem resulting from the birth that needed an operation. She told me it was unlikely I would be able to have any more children and if I wanted to I'd have to seek medical advice and look into things like IVF. Once again I went to every pharmacy I could find to buy paracetamol and then back to my single room with a bottle of vodka. I took one but then I swear blind I heard Lily's laugh and gurgle. It gave me the courage I needed to carry on. If I died she'd be left without her birth mother. She still needed me, I knew. No one else could love her like

175

her mother. I poured the vodka down the sink, much to the disgruntlement of Ashlee who said she'd have drunk it before hugging me for a few seconds too long. She'd guessed what I'd bought it for. She'd been there herself.

I moved to the bedsit and went back to college, a different one in a different town, away from Grimey and my previous life. I didn't know anyone there. Ashlee moved to live near her granny and we kept in touch by text. She's the only person from my past life I still text from time to time although I never say anything that would identify my new name, life or where I live.

In fact Ashlee was the first person I contacted when Lily's adoption went through despite my desperate opposition and hopes that my pleas for a second chance would be heeded. A few weeks later Lily's social worker sent me a photo and letter from the adoptive parents.

It was then that, with the realisation that I had no legal route back to Lily, I came up with a plan. I changed my name by deed poll from Cheryl to Claire (there's a lot of them around) and picked an equally common surname – Jones. After doing better than I expected in my A levels I was offered a university scholarship and moved 150 miles away, where no one would know me, to study for a degree in Business Administration and broke off all contact with social services. At weekends I worked on the till in a supermarket. Cheryl Lavardi, the old me, was finally dead and buried. I became Claire Jones for good.

Whilst doing my degree, keeping myself to myself, not getting too close to any man or friends, I tortured myself by imagining what Lily was doing, what she looked like now and how much like her father or I she was. Going AWOL from the social worker meant that I no longer had a yearly update on Lily's progress, but I knew that in the long run it was the best strategy to make the rest of my plan fall into place.

The next stage, in my final year of my degree, was to find out where Lily lived. As I knew her adoptive parents' names it didn't take the intelligence of a brain surgeon for me to find them on Instagram thanks to James's lack of privacy settings (Audrey wasn't on there). All I had to do was set up a fake account and lurk. James didn't post pics of Lily but I found out who he and Audrey were and what they looked like, where they went at the weekend and what they liked to watch on TV. He mentioned the Tour de France a lot. Gradually, as I stitched on my new identity as a man who liked cycling and followed world-class competitors, posting my opinions on the latest event (which I copied and changed around from other people's) I picked up snippets of James's life. To my amusement I had to pick up quite a lot of knowledge about a sport that I'd usually rather eat my own toenails than watch. After a couple of weeks he took the bait and followed me. I was in the inner sanctum. He invited me to join a WhatsApp group for cycling supporters. Banter on there, using my pay-as-you-go mobile with a throwaway SIM card, brought me more information on James and Audrey. It's amazing what people will let slip to a stranger. He even started telling me about how he didn't get out to cycle as much now, not as much as he'd like to anyway, because he was spending family time with his daughter instead. It seems it never occurred to him that his sporty thirty-five-year-old computer programmer mate was actually a twentysomething woman with an agenda.

177

After my finals my Instagram character announced he was joining in with the getting authentic movement and ditching social media. 'Good luck with that mate, still keep in touch on WhatsApp though yeah? You up for the group meet-up at the Tour de Yorkshire?' messaged James. I exited the WhatsApp group with a smile, cut up my phone's SIM card and bought another one.

I got a job, a dull office assistant job that paid the rent in my cheapish house share (cheap because nearly every other renter had expectations of higher standards in accommodation – even students didn't want to live there), in James and Audrey's hometown. The rest of the plan was sketchy, I only knew I wanted to see my daughter, be near her, check that she was happy and well looked after. But how? Legally there was no going back from Lily's adoption. No second chances. It had been well over three years since I'd last seen my daughter. How cruel, how barbaric to part a mother from her child and legally ban me from her side. Surely though it's not against the law for me to view her from a distance? A look, a glance won't hurt?

So that's what I did. The trouble was, like the first hit of heroin I took back when I was sixteen, once was never enough. After I found James on Instagram it was easy to follow the trail to work out which area they lived in, the school Lily went to and the local swings she played on.

Following each sighting of her coming out of the school gates holding Audrey's hand or riding on James's shoulders on the way to the park I wanted more. I *needed* more. It was out of my control; the blood pull was too strong. A mother's love will out. Whilst I was glad that Lily looked happy and healthy, oh how I resented that the law had taken her away from me and not given me another chance. When I gave birth to her I was little more than a child myself, a teenager you'd now called disadvantaged and groomed. Yet instead of helping me, the judge handed over my daughter to two people who had the wealth and power that I did not, as if she were a dog at a rescue shelter touted around to the highest bidder.

Of course I already knew what my daughter looked like now after all those times I'd followed them in the park at a distance, stood near the school gates in the morning and at home time, worked out Audrey's routine and the little things like the hairstyles she put Lily's hair in: plaits or bunches. I was very careful not to get caught, always near enough to the school to see but never close enough to arouse suspicion. I wore different coats, plain ones that wouldn't stand out, and jabbed at my phone, sometimes pretending to speak on it when people walked by. Mind you, a young woman near a school, what's there to be suspicious about? If asked I planned to say I was helping out a friend who couldn't make the pick-up. It's not like I'm an old man in a dirty mac who looks like he's wanking off watching young kids.

The first time I saw Audrey with a pram I wondered if the baby was adopted too. I suppose I thought that she and James adopted my daughter because they couldn't have their own. When I pretended to take selfies in the park on my mobile, whilst really zooming in on Lily and Audrey, I realised he must be genetically hers. Looking at his face you can tell the similarity in their looks, the same oval eyes, thin lips and ruddy complexion. My Lily is a lot fairer than James and Audrey but Wilf has their darker hair. Then it hit me, having two children meant she had half the time to devote to Lily. Another reason my daughter would need me in her life even more.

For weeks I forced myself to steer clear and keep my distance – long, agonizing weeks when I played it safe and worked out a plan. Could I try and get a job as a teaching assistant at Lily's school? How else could I slot into their family life? Could I befriend Audrey? She'd be suspicious if I homed in on James instead.

What I needed was a good reason to introduce myself. I only had one chance to get it right and if I blew it there wouldn't be another one because I'd end up looking like some kind of stalker, which I suppose I was. That's when I had the idea that I needed her to be grateful to me. I'd do something to gain her trust. But what? Audrey was a creature of clockwork habits, visiting the park at the same time every weekday in school term time unless the weather was shitting down seven bells. Once mid-morning with the baby in the posh pram and then after school with the baby and Lily. One day when I was following them I saw a little girl on her tricycle roll towards the pond and get stuck, screaming, in the shallow waters. It gave me the idea of what to do. It'd be very risky and it took two weeks of subtly hanging round the park watching them from behind trees, rotating the three cheap coats and woolly hats I bought to vary my appearance, until my luck was in.

I had been following at a distance as usual and just as I was pondering going home, Lily ran off and Audrey turned her back on the pram to go after her. No one else was in sight. I rushed to the pram, took the brake off, gave it a little push in the right direction, then jumped behind a nearby tree and counted quickly to ten. Next I ran back to the pram as soon as I heard the splash. The baby was never in any danger. 'It's OK! I've got the baby!' I shouted and fell to my knees in the pond seemingly to dislodge the wheels from the stones but really to get as wet as possible.

My friendship with Audrey cunningly began from there.

~ 19 ~

On the way to Audrey's house I stop off at a cheap phone shop and buy a refurbished pay-as-you-go mobile and a SIM card. No one quizzes me or asks why I don't have a phone already. The shop assistant is chatting about stock control to another employee all the time I'm being served. Behind his head is a CCTV camera. There'll be a record of my visit if the police come looking. Yet I told the police officer I'd lost my mobile and that I'd buy a new one. Despite the fact that everything looks above board I'm glad to be out of the shop and into the fresh air, where I don't have to try and act 'normal'.

My first call is to the police officer to give her my phone number.

'I'm sorry to inform you that Audrey is in a critical condition. She is in coma,' the officer says after I've introduced myself. 'Be prepared, it's touch and go.'

My head rushes. So Audrey is alive but she's unconscious and may not survive. I don't know whether to smile or cry. There are no more questions from the police officer. It's almost too easy. My thoughts whirl around my mind, and I wonder whether I should leave town now in case Audrey wakes up. If I do that there's no coming back to Lily. Audrey didn't know I took too long to get help but she could still tell James that she wants me out of their lives.

No, I'll stick to the plan. For now Audrey is unconscious. I must go to see James.

The walk to Audrey's house doesn't take too long in sunshine that's fighting a losing battle not to be overtaken by a huge grey cloud. When I turn the corner into their road, the sun loses and a shadow darkens the pavement.

It's an ordinary day. The only thing that marks it out as any different are the two bouquets of supermarket flowers, still in their plastic wrapping, left at the end of the driveway. Some people must think Audrey is dead already. I don't know whether to take them with me or leave them where they are, but I don't want James to think that I brought some cheap, half-dead flowers so I leave them to their fate.

I summon my courage and knock on the door, the sound of my knuckles rapping against the wood breaking the silence of the sleepy afternoon. An older lady with blonde bobbed hair and Botox (you're not telling me that a woman of that age naturally has a smooth forehead) answers. Lily is standing behind her clutching a stuffed toy and trying to see who it is.

When I saw Lily close up for the first time since she'd been a snuggly baby in my arms I struggled to hold it together. Back then in the park Lily shook my hand with her mittened one and it took all my strength to batten down the hatches on my emotions and stop myself from scooping her up in my arms and never letting her go again. Now my hands twitch, wanting to do the same thing.

'Yes?' the woman asks. I can't tell the expression she's trying to pull, if any. The blank forehead makes it difficult.

'Claire!' cries Lily and runs up to me, her little face smiling.

'Claire? Audrey's friend? You were with her in the park?'

'Yes. I came to see James. I'm so, so sorry about Audrey.' I struggle to think of the right words to say and instead of talking more I bend down and pick Lily up in my arms. The woman shoots me a look, and whispers, 'She doesn't know.'

'Hello Antonia, what are you playing today?' I make sure my hug is affectionate but not stifling.

'Grandma and Grandad have come to visit. Mummy's poorly and is with the doctor. I'm playing doctors and Wilfred is my patient but he keeps crying when I try to see if he's got chickenpox. Will you come and play?'

'Claire might be busy darling,' says the woman to Lily before turning to me. I notice she's tried to cover up the red around her eyes with concealer.

'I'm Susan, James's mother. My husband is with him in the kitchen. I'm watching the children in the playroom.' I wonder if she is going to offer a hand to shake, she seems that kind of woman, but she doesn't. We have an awkward moment where I nod instead and then Lily breaks it by piping up, 'Come on Claire! You can be the nurse. Or another patient. Have you got a sore throat? I can look in your mouth. Mummy looks in mine if it hurts to see if it's swollen.'

Susan and I flinch when Lily mentions her mummy. I wonder when they're going to tell her the truth. She's a clever girl, it won't take her long to realise that something is very wrong and her grandparents aren't on a regular weekend visit.

'I can stay a little while if you'd like me to Susan.'

'Yes, well, it's good of you to visit. If you'd be so kind as to entertain Antonia and Wilfred in the playroom I'll see if James is up for visitors. Run along Antonia, Claire will join you in a minute.'

'Promise?' Her little dark eyes look up seriously at me. How could I refuse her anything?

'I promise.'

Antonia turns on her heel and skips back to the playroom where I can hear Wilfred start to babble away. Susan places her left hand, laced with gold rings, onto my forearm and leaves it there for a few seconds.

'I'd like to talk to you too. Thank you for calling for help for Audrey. It must have been a horrible thing for you to go through. She's your friend and I hope you don't blame yourself. God knows life is cruel. She's only young, for this to happen after everything she's been through...' A little sob escapes her lips before she takes a deep breath, pulls her shoulders back and the mask reappears.

'How is she?' I ask.

Susan shakes her head and lowers her voice. 'She's still in a coma. Her chances of recovery are slim and if even if she does she may have some sort of brain damage.'

I lower my eyes respectfully. To James I'm still the new best friend who added a bit of pizzazz to Audrey's dull, stay-at-home life. Thank goodness for that.

'I haven't known her that long but we are good friends. I can't believe this has happened to her. I wish there was something more I could have done.' Perhaps I'm over-egging the pudding a bit but Susan doesn't seem to notice, it's what she wants to hear. And it's actually true, just not in the way Susan might think.

'Poor James is broken. He's not ready to tell Antonia the whole story yet. I'll go and see if he's up to seeing you. Don't take offence if he isn't, he barely slept last night. Can I get you a drink of anything whilst I'm in the kitchen? Tea? Coffee?'

I shake my head. 'I'm fine thanks.'

'Between you and me I could do with something stronger,' Susan says and heads off to the kitchen. I walk into the lounge through the half-open door. It's as it usually is except a bit less tidy. Wilfred is on a playmat on the floor and Lily – I really ought to start thinking of her as Antonia or I'll give the game away – is asking him where it hurts and pretending to speak for him.

I kneel down and look concerned. 'What's the diagnosis doctor?'

Antonia lifts Wilfred towards her for a cuddle, which he grizzles against and then relaxes in to.

'He hasn't got chickenpox and now I need to see if he has got the measles. My friend at school had them and he had lots of pink spots but Wilfred doesn't have any spots. Unless I draw some on him with a crayon.'

'Well spotted doctor, but no need to draw any spots on him. How about you look down my throat to see if it's sore?'

Antonia puts Wilfred back down on floor and he reaches out for her again, pulling himself along the playmat on his tummy. She stands up and tells me to open my mouth.

'Say aah.'

I open my mouth widely and obey. 'Aah.' She peers in and I feel the urge to laugh, thinking of the image of a mouse getting close to a crocodile's jaws.

'It looks very sore. I might have to take your throat out. Either that or give you lots of medicine.'

'Medicine would be better.'

Antonia goes to a plastic box full of toys and picks out a small plastic mug. 'Here you go. You have to drink it all or you won't get better.'

I play along and feign taking a long, deep gulp. 'Thanks Toni. I feel much better now.'

'Toni? I'm Antonia!' She looks puzzled.

'Toni is a short version of your name. Like a pet name. A special name for me to call you.'

'Isn't Toni a boy's name?'

'It can be either. What do you think?'

She chews her bottom lip and thinks hard. 'If you call me Toni, what special name can I call you?'

'I don't know, what would you like to call me?'

I can tell by the look on her face that she's thinking. 'Does your mummy have a pet name for you?'

Ha. When she wanted something from me Mum would call me Princess. The rest of the time I was plain Cheryl. Jan next door though used to call me Boo. For years I didn't know why and when I finally asked she said it's the pet name her much-missed grandmother used to call her.

'Boo. My pet name was Boo.'

'That's a funny name. If I call you, you might think I'm trying to scare you!' I giggle along with her.

'I'll call you Toni and you can call me Boo. Our special names for each other.'

'What about Wilfred? We could call him Smelly Poo. That rhymes with Boo.'

'Hmm, that's not a very nice name though, is it? What about Wilf? Short for Wilfred like Toni is short for Antonia.'

'Wilf! Wilf! Do you like that Wilf?' Wilf laughs as his sister tickles him.

'I think he does,' I say. 'Toni and Wilf, two special names for two very special kids.'

Susan pops her head round the door and says I can go in the kitchen and say hello to James and she'll stay with the children. 'Want to watch some CBBC Antonia?'

'Mummy doesn't let me in the afternoon.'

Susan picks up the TV remote and turns her head away from Antonia. 'I don't think she'll mind, just this once.'

'I'll be back in a minute,' I say to Toni and then head for the kitchen with a shaky but excited step.

This stage of the plan is coming together rather nicely.

~ 20 ~

I knock, then enter the kitchen. James has his back to me. He is sitting down and leaning on the table holding his head in his hands as it if would topple off unless he gripped it tight. I'm not sure what to do, what to say, but then an older, fatter, balder and more red-faced version of James, breaks the ice.

'You must be Claire, I'm Alan, James's father. Thank you for coming, do sit down.'

I avoid the seat Audrey always sat on, the one with a white seat pad on, and choose the chair to the right. It means I'm sitting opposite James who is still rigidly staring at the kitchen table. The squeak of the chair legs on the floor as I sit down makes me jump but he doesn't flinch.

'Hello Alan. James.'

'Can I get you a cup of coffee? There's a some freshly made in the cafetière.'

'Yes please. Thanks.' My mouth quickly dries up when I catch sight of James, albeit only his head, which sports a slightly thinning patch on top. There's an air of brokenness about him, as though Audrey has snapped off his side leaving a jagged bone that once held them together.

It wasn't my fault I tell myself. How could I have known it would be too late when I got help for her? Audrey had a

189

serious allergic reaction. She didn't have her EpiPen on her. If only she'd wanted to remain friends... I repeat this on a loop in my head so many times that I'm a millimetre way from believing it.

Alan reaches into a cupboard and pulls out a mug. He's begins to pour in coffee when he suddenly stops and puts the mug down on the work surface with a clank. I look over. The mug is yellow with a pink flower on and the words 'World's Best Mum'. Putting down the cafetière on the work surface he hides the mug in the dishwasher and chooses a plain red mug from out of the cupboard. Coffee pouring resumes.

The coffee is slightly tepid and I wish I'd been offered sugar. Alan sips water from a pink beaker that was upside down on the draining board and he fills from the tap. I've seen Lily drink from it before. Bought in a charity shop Audrey said; because it had been around for years she didn't feel guilty about encouraging the use of plastic. Glass tumblers are a danger to the children if one smashes.

A memory comes back to me with a jolt. I was about seven and washing up when a glass slipped through my soapy fingers and smashed against the metal sink. I tried to pick up the pieces until I felt a sharp pain in my finger and the water swirled with a stream of red. Instead of being cross with me, Mum washed my finger under the tap, patted it dry with a tea-towel and wrapped a plaster over it, soothing my tears. She made me a hot chocolate, for her brave little soldier, then hugged me tight. It was one of the few times in my childhood I ever felt loved, so much so that a month later I deliberately did it again. It took a few goes to break the glass and I held my breath as I clutched a sharp shard. This time though Mum told me I was stupid for not learning my lesson, handed me a box of plasters and told me to get on with it.

I bite the bullet. 'James, I'm so sorry about Audrey. Your mum told me the latest news. I don't know what to say. I'm so, so sorry that I couldn't get help to her sooner. It might have made a difference.' He doesn't look up. I hear a sniff and look away to give him his privacy. A hand is thrust towards me over the table. It's James's. I take it and he squeezes mine tightly, then nods, still not raising his head enough to look at me.

'We know it's not your fault,' says Alan. 'No one knew she would be stung. She'd said to James she was only popping out for five minutes. A tragedy. So bloody unfair.' He squeezes James's shoulder with his hand and we made a funny sort of human chain of mourning. Tears well up in me. I don't know whether they come from guilt or grief. The absence of Audrey in the kitchen, which was her domain, is overwhelming. A part of me expects her to walk through the door. Will she ever come back?

'If there's anything I can do. Babysitting, something like that? I'd like to help.'

Another nod and hand squeeze. Alan clears his throat. 'Thanks for coming Claire, we really appreciate it. Susan and I will be staying here for a while and we'll keep in touch.' He passes me a pad of paper and biro that were stuck with magnets to the fridge. 'Can you write down your phone number please?'

I pull out the piece of cardboard with my new number on and write it down. 'Call me anytime,' I say.

'James said the children get on well with you.'

'They're lovely kids. Who wouldn't get on well with them?' Grandparents always like their grandchildren to be praised and the smile that creeps onto Alan's face shows he's no exception.

'Quite. I'll show you out.' I haven't finished my coffee yet but the sniffing noises coming from James are getting louder and I guess Alan wants to guard his son's privacy.

In the hallway Susan pops her head out of the playroom door to say goodbye. I'm dying to say goodbye to Lily but don't get the chance because Alan opens the front door and politely sweeps his arm to beckon me to walk through it.

'Thanks again for coming Claire,' he says, sombre-faced, and shuts the door behind me. I hear the click of a bolt, the one Audrey told me she had fitted after being watched by the man and his dog. I'd told her I'd seen him too, but of course I hadn't. I thought she was confusing the time when she actually did see someone follow her – me – with an honest dog walker who has a night-time walking habit. The poor dog probably needed a shit.

She nearly caught me that time I lurked near the school gates, watching as she went to pick Lily up. I craved another sighting of my daughter and had bunked off work saying I had a dentist appointment. It's a temp job. I was sacked from the other one for poor timekeeping. They got wind that when I was supposed to be on the post run or stocking up on snacks for a meeting I took too long. One time I went to get my Lily coming out of school fix and returned to the office empty handed, completely forgetting the errand I'd been sent out to do. It happened one time too many.

I cringe at the memory of me jumping behind a tree when

Audrey looked in my direction and then I bolted through the side gate of a house so she wouldn't see me. I've no idea who lives there. I hid at the end of a side path that runs to the back garden. There was nobody in it. When Audrey's and another woman's voice faded into the distance I held my head up high and walked out of the drive as if I owned the place. That's one thing I've learned during my time trying to be incognito. Look like you belong and no one will give you a second glance.

That's what I'm doing now as I cross the short distance to the park. It's not very busy today and the council must have been there recently because the empty cans, crisp packets and plastic bags that usually litter the entrance have gone.

I don't walk directly to where I buried the phone. I wander around a bit first, down various paths looking for cameras. I can't see any, the only visible one is by the gate entrance.

Here's the spot. It's embedded in my memory. I brush the leaves aside with my palm and dig with my fingers, brown earth collecting under my fingernails, two of which split with the effort. The rock I put it underneath has gone. I dig a bit further, cursing as I jab at the soil with a plastic biro that's neither use nor ornament.

I crouch down and put my spinning head between my knees, gasping for breath. I know I left my phone here. Could I be confused? Have I got it wrong? No. I don't get things wrong. The burial site is empty.

Someone has been and taken it.

~ 21 ~

After giving birth to Lily I stayed in hospital a couple of nights due to having lost so much blood. Looking back, the exultation at holding her in my arms, this tiny, precious, adorable creature who was so small it seemed a miracle that she could exist, is mingled with the cries of the other women's babies (I was the youngest on the maternity ward by at least ten years), sleeplessness, pain, hormones and a cup of tea never before tasting so glorious. Grimey was with me at the birth and returned later with a huge bunch of new baby balloons and a pink teddy bear that was bigger than Lily.

Back at home the gang stayed away on Grimey's orders and we looked after Lily together. She didn't take to breastfeeding and the health visitor suggested I bottle feed instead. Grimey and I would take it in turns to feed her, he shared the nappy-changing duties and took Lily into another room a couple of times to care for her when I was chronically sleep-deprived. Those days were the best I can remember. We were a family. The three of us fitted together.

It didn't last long.

After a few weeks Grimey was itching to get out and about again. We took Lily out to the park on his suggestion where Dom and Jimbo just happened coincidentally to arrive. He and I had decided to get a pizza delivery together that evening once Lily went to sleep but the lads said they had some urgent business they needed Grimey for and he didn't come home with us.

By and by the gang started coming to the house more often and I could tell the 'family business' was still going strong. It led to a big row between us where he shouted at me to not tell him what to do because he was the one who paid for the roof over mine and Lily's heads. I was exhausted all the time and when Grimey disappeared in the day for 'business' I found it hard to look after Lily all on my own. One evening, after staying out all night, Grimey came back and took over from me bathing her and putting her down in her cot.

'Cheryl, I've got something to tell you,' he said. I knew it wasn't good by his tone of voice and hangdog expression. 'I'm sorry I shouted.'

I waited for the next part.

'I spent the night in a cell. I was arrested. Suspicion of drug dealing. I'm out on bail,' he said.

My world caved in and I started to cry, partly in fear and partly in anger.

'I'm sorry Cheryl, I really am. I'm sorry. I can't bear the thought of leaving you and going to prison. You and Lily are my world. My solicitor says he thinks he can get me off. The police are trying to scare me. They don't have enough evidence and the so-called witnesses will know better than to stand up against me in court.'

I was so relieved that he still loved me and wanted us that I didn't think of the consequences of his arrest.

He'd been so stressed he said, he needed something to take the edge off it. When I asked him what would help he said skag. Just a little bit. Just enough to help him sleep. No, I said, we'd both stopped doing that. There was a baby in the house. He cried in my arms and said he was finding it difficult to cope. Just this once to calm him down. He'd done it before. He could stop. So he took it. And, blindsided by my love for him, exhausted, emotional and desperate for some sleep and with Lily out of sight in her room, quiet as a mouse, so did I. Just a little bit. Just this once. Just to help me sleep. Not enough that I wouldn't hear the baby. Not enough for me to get addicted again.

More fool me. It is the biggest regret of my life.

Days pass and still no news from the hospital. Audrey is still alive but remains in a coma with no signs of regaining consciousness. Each day that passes apparently lessens her chances of a full recovery. There's barely a moment when I'm not running on adrenaline, every sense geared up in hyper mode waiting for a ferocious attack. In the supermarket I expect a police car to be waiting for me outside. In bed I jump at every sound, thinking that the police might come for me in the middle of the night and break the door down. At work, the little I've shown up there, I hold my breath when the boss gets a phone call or looks in my direction. It's as if I have a flashing neon pink sign over my head saying 'guilty'. Trying to act normal takes every ounce of my energy.

It's Lily who gives me the will to carry on. James's mum calls me to ask me to babysit the children a couple of times while the adults go to the hospital together. When Susan and Alan go back home for a couple of days to check on their house and collect fresh clothes I volunteer to keep James company at his house. He says very little but Lily makes up for it, not fully understanding that her mummy can't come home from hospital. Where is it? Can Daddy take her in the car? Does Mummy want to have her cuddly rabbit to keep her company? James decides that seeing her mum tethered to so many machines would frighten her and it's best at the moment for her not to visit.

Over the next few weeks, once James's parents have returned home, we settle into some sort of routine. He does the school drop-off and pick-ups, being on compassionate leave, and I turn up after work to help with tea-time and the kids' bedtime routine. Once they're asleep I put the washing on and encourage James to eat, concerned at how his cheekbones are now jutting out and his new, stark and gaunt appearance. Sometimes he asks me to keep him company whilst he talks about Audrey or sits silently watching a boring documentary on TV.

After a month I'm a regular visitor. There are others, yes, but few of them. I don't think James is very sociable. He and Audrey seemed to keep themselves to themselves. Work colleagues, other parents from school and guys from his cycling group turn up once or twice with flowers or beer and a look on their face that says they want to hurry home again, far away from here where they don't know what to say.

Then Susan and Alan come back again to stay for a couple of days and James asks me to go with him to see Audrey at the hospital whilst they look after the children. I'd rather not and offer to babysit instead but Susan and Alan think they're doing me a kindness enabling me to go and see my 'best friend'. What if the sound of my voice wakes Audrey up?

As we walk into the critical care ward my stomach starts to lurch and my knees shake. I'm wearing my most anonymous beige coat but with the hospital's high heating I don't need it. I don't like hospitals; their disinfectant smell makes me feel sick. Sweat gathers on my forehead and under my arms. At the nurses' station a young male nurse turns to me.

'It's OK to be nervous, it's daunting when you've never been here before,' he says in a professional manner. 'Talk to Audrey, it all helps. She might be able to hear you.'

I really hope not.

I feel the blood drain from my face when I stand at the end of Audrey's bed. Two machines are beeping, I don't know why, and there are wires attached to her and a tube coming out of her right nostril. She looks tiny lying there, eyes shut, tucked under a white regulation blanket.

James sits down and takes her hand. I grip the end of the bed firmly until my knuckles turn white. I did this. It's my fault she's here. The whole situation doesn't feel real. It's as if I've walked onto the set of a hospital drama, someone will shout 'Cut!' and Audrey will sit up and grin, then chase me down the corridor.

'How are you today darling? The children send their love. Mum and Dad do too. They're babysitting. I've come with Claire who wants to see how you are.'

I flinch and stare at Audrey. She doesn't move. Her eyelids don't flutter. Nothing. I exhale.

'Hi Audrey. I've been thinking of you,' I say, which is at least true.

James carries on talking, forcing his voice to be happy and breezy. He repeats to Audrey how much he and the children love her.

I'm about to offer to go on a tea run when the male nurse approaches with two more people. One, a stocky man on the smallish side, I recognise. It's Audrey's friend Rob, but he's grown a goatee. The other, a woman with beautiful curly black hair tied back in a ponytail, I don't recognise. Neither of them look pleased to see me and they scowl at me before greeting James. I think about sneaking off but decide that looks suspicious.

'Only two visitors by the bed at a time I'm afraid,' the nurse says.

Thank God. 'I was going to the café anyway,' I reply, glad to escape the suddenly hostile environment.

'I'll join you then,' Rob says to my dismay. 'Coffee or tea?'

The woman who is introduced to me as Tina and James both ask for tea, one black with sugar and the other white with no sugar. We agree to bring the drinks back for the pair and then James and I will leave. He'll come back on his own later.

There's no hint of warmth on Rob's face as he walks right by my side down the corridor as if he wants to frogmarch me.

'So Claire. You like turning up when you're not expected, don't you?' he says.

'James asked me to come with him.'

'You two seem very pally.'

'I've been helping out with the kids.'

'I don't think Audrey would have wanted that, would she? She was fed up of you bothering her all the time. Is that what you were doing in the park when she was stung? Bothering her again?' Rob isn't mincing his words and my stomach is knotted with apprehension.

'We went there for a chat. It wasn't long before her Sunday lunch. I didn't want to intrude on another family meal.'

'So why did you go to her house?'

200

'Girl stuff.' My mind clutches at straws. 'I'd seen the same man again, the one I saw before hanging around the house. I came to tell her about it.'

'Right. Did you also tell the police?'

'No. After everything that happened it slipped my mind.'

We've reached the lift and the button is nearest to me. I press it with a firm push. We wait until the doors open then step in and join a couple of others.

'Why didn't Audrey take her EpiPen with her? She never went anywhere without it.'

'I don't know. She wanted to talk away from the kids so they wouldn't hear. I guess she forgot.'

I can feel the force of his disapproval without seeing his face.

'What I don't understand is why Audrey didn't talk to you in the house. You could have done so privately in the kitchen or any room Antonia and Wilfred weren't in. Why go to the park?'

'I don't know. She suggested it. Perhaps she wanted some fresh air.'

Rob snorts. The lift doors open on the café floor and we step out. I head to the snack stand and pick up a muffin for a sugar rush. By the time I'm at the drinks queue I'm two people behind Rob. 'I think I'll stay here to eat my cake and drink my drink. Are you OK taking the teas back to the ward Rob please? You can tell James I'll meet him here when he's ready to go.'

'Not wanting to see Audrey again then? Not going to say goodbye to your best friend?' he replies with more than a hint of sarcasm.

'I'll give her and James their privacy.'

Rob reaches the front of the queue, pays for three drinks, puts them in a carrier then leaves without a word.

I buy my own coffee.

~ 23 ~

Months pass with no change in Audrey's condition. James eventually has to go back to work full time and offers me work as Wilf and Toni's nanny. He can't afford to pay me a great deal and I tell him I can't afford to take the job and keep on my room in the shared house (I could but I'd rather see the back of it). The result is him buying a sofa bed for the playroom and it becoming my bedroom, which the kids still love invading even though James now keeps their toys in the lounge.

It goes without saying that I love my new job. Living with Lily is seventh heaven and I have to keep reminding myself to call her Toni. She still cries for Audrey but it's lessening now. When she wants something and James isn't there she comes running to me, her Boo. I've also become attached to Wilf. When he turned one we had a family birthday party without inviting Rob – I'd told James of Rob's hostility towards me but stressed I didn't want him to say anything and cause a fuss and his response was to limit the party to his relatives and me, the nanny. Rob never knew it was happening.

Wilf can say 'Claire' now and hold out his chubby little arms for me to pick him up. If I shut my eyes I can almost believe that they are both my children. Except legally, neither is. They are the children of Audrey who lies in her hospital bed whilst James sleeps in the marital bed and me on the sofa bed in the makeshift bedroom. That's my place in the hierarchy.

Every day I am on tenterhooks, expecting a call to say that Audrey has regained consciousness. James tries to visit the hospital daily, even if it's only for ten minutes. I hold my breath when he returns but it's always the same news. No change.

It's a sunny day as I do the school run, my fake-designer sunglasses perched on top of my newly highlighted hair. I've gone for the red tones over the brown. I can afford to go to a hairdresser now rather than dye it myself out of a packet. I don't want to do that at James's house. He thinks I'm a brunette. I have to ensure my blonde roots don't show through. I've a can of spray-on brown tint hidden in a shoebox in case of emergencies.

I'm beginning to be accepted at the school gates too. Today I've picked up Laura's son and Samira's daughter from their homes too because they both have to head off to work early. Doing them a favour earns me lots of brownie points now I'm in with what they call the Hot Mum Gang. The WhatsApp group leader, Em, added me a couple of months ago. It's invitation only, separate from the class one where it's all about PTA fundraising, which kids have got nits and when it's show and tell day. Getting in the Hot Mum Gang is like an invite to the Oscars. I can't say I like them particularly, though Laura can be a good laugh and spills a lot of gossip when she's a few glasses of Merlot down. But I need allies at the school and Tina sure isn't going to be one of them. I catch her watching me at school and when I drop Lily off for play dates with Jordan. She rarely makes chit chat and certainly no overtures of friendship.

'Audrey's a good friend of mine,' she said the first time I picked Lily up from her house. 'And she still will be when she wakes up.'

When Tina asks me what I'm doing I feel like it's an interrogation with her wanting to know how close I am to James. I guess a few people assume we're shagging, but we're not. He has never looked at me in that way.

Because Samira lives a couple of miles away I've used the car for the school run, Lily in the front in her car seat and the other three squashed in the back in theirs. I manage to find a space a couple of streets away from the school. With me pushing Wilf in his buggy I walk alongside the other three to the playground where I drop them off in the crush of hyperactive children (no kiss from Lily when her friends are around) before going inside to give some money for Lily's school trip to the school secretary. Miss Walsh gives me a big grin when she sees me. Every now and then I bring in cakes for the staff, listen to her moaning about other parents and tell her what a brilliant job she's doing.

'Thank you Claire, you're always prompt with paying. You'd be surprised how many parents I have to chase after the deadline and it's not the ones who can't afford it – they manage to drop their children off in their 4x4s – though obviously I can't tell you who. I'll make sure you get a heads-up on the ballet trip the head's organising. Antonia would like that, she's such a little performer, and there are only twenty places. I'll keep one free for her.' With that Miss Walsh, or Irene as she asked me to call her when other parents aren't around, taps her forefinger to her nose, then coughs as another mum approaches. I thank her with a conspiratorial smile.

On the way out there are a few last-minuters rushing to the gates with their kids dashing beside them. Jen is talking to Connor, aka the Hot Dad and honorary Hot Mums member, and breaks off as I approach.

'Claire! How're things? Connor and I were just talking about a rounders playdate at the park on Saturday afternoon. Wear the kids out before tea-time so the parents can have a free evening. You in?'

Lily would be, I knew, but I couldn't think of anything more tedious. Still it would give James chance to go to the hospital and I can entertain Wilf.

'Sounds great. I see it's the same faces only just making it before gate closing time.'

Jen rolls her eyes and Connor laughs. Jen and Connor don't have day jobs, although she occasionally does some freelance PR for local businesses and he tutors A level students in the evenings. The 'to work or not to work' issue now and then rears its ugly head with Laura, Samira and another Hot Mum slogging full-time and praising the benefits of staying true to themselves. Personally I think they're lucky they don't have to be cleaners or work in a supermarket to pay the debt collector like my mum. Me being a nanny is never mentioned because no one wants to talk about sick people.

'You'd think they could get the kids up five minutes earlier, wouldn't you?' says Jen.

'Perhaps it's them who aren't getting up, too much working at home at night. This is the age when kids need a routine, to be organised. Set a pattern and they'll follow it,' replies Connor. With a straight face. I stifle my laughter, thinking of him scheduling in sex at 8 p.m. on a Saturday night with his wife. One minute past eight? Too late, she's lost her slot. He might be good looking in the American style, tall with a square, chiselled jaw, dark eyes and cropped tawny hair that's just starting to go salt and pepper around his ears, but he can't half be dull. Not that I'd tell him so. I'm aiming for top rating in the mum points scoreboard so no one can ever doubt my parenting abilities. They may not know I'm Lily's genetic mother but I want them, and James, to think I'm as good as. Better, even, than Audrey.

But what if Audrey doesn't regain consciousness? What if she dies? Legally I'm on a sticky wicket. As a nanny I have no rights to see the children whatsoever. It hinges on James's goodwill. If Audrey does die then James will be free to marry again, and who better than me? Perhaps I could even legally adopt the children. Yet I can't do that with my current birth certificate that still says Cheryl Lavardi. I'd need one that says Claire Jones like my passport. If James sees my real birth certificate my cover will be blown out of the water. He's sure to remember the name of Antonia's birth mother. I'd be out on my ear and in legal boiling water too. What I need is someone who can source me a genuine-looking fake birth certificate but I haven't known anyone who might know how to do that since A levels.

The Hot Mums have asked me why I'm not dating. Again I think that they reckon I'm secretly banging James or at least want to. The truth is that the kids' love is enough for me and I haven't got the time or the inclination to find a boyfriend.

My life is complicated enough as it is. I haven't loved anyone since I fell head first for Grimey. So I stay in and keep James company with a bottle of wine and a film on the TV. They help me push thoughts of Audrey's words in the park as far back as possible in my mind.

The bell goes and the children line up to go inside. We three smile at each other, all thinking that ours are the best of the lot. When they've slithered into their classrooms in a snake formation we adults say goodbye to each other and head our separate ways home. Connor and Jen turn left to their houses and I turn right to retrieve my car. On the way out I spot Tina, talking to a man with curly black hair that needs a decent cut. I freeze on the spot. It's Rob, my nemesis, the chink in my armour. What's he talking to her for? Is this an Audrey's best mates reunion? I haven't seen him since the hospital. James says Rob's been to see Audrey often since then but I make sure, the few times I go, that I'm never there when he is. I'm about to swivel and walk in the opposite direction when Rob and Tina break their conversation and he stares at me, as if his eyes are lasers that try to suck the secrets out of my soul. I wonder whether Tina's hearing aids have some sort of super microphone in so she can hear what I'm saying at a thousand paces away. I'm having none of it. I plaster a smile on my face and try to look like I'm pleased to see them. I'm probably fooling no one.

'Rob, what a surprise! What are you doing here?'

Tina turns round to look at me as well. I can tell by the guilty look on her face, like a child caught with its hand in the biscuit tin, that they were talking about me. Silly cow.

'Tina, how's Jordan getting on with the Egypt project?

Toni's adamant she want's black kohl under her eyes to look like Cleopatra. It's not happening though – I've hidden my make-up bag and even she knows not try with a black felt-tip pen!'

No one laughs. Tina regains her composure and says straight to my face that Jordan's doing really well. Rob just stares at me until he says, 'An Egypt project? I could help *Antonia* with that. It has been a long time since I've seen my god-daughter. Shame you never return my calls. I'm around until this evening – how about I take Antonia and Wilfred out for tea after school? I'm sure you could do with a break.'

I note that I'm not included in the invitation. I need a break my arse, he wants to quiz them about how I'm doing, find something to criticise about me to James and his parents, or dig up some dirt that I'm really the devil incarnate. The last time Rob 'raised his concerns' about my background, James said I'd proved I am a great friend and help to the family. James is not the sort of man to issue a threat or cause a scene. Everything's got to be nicey nicey, dull and middle of the road. It drives me crackers sometimes. If James was the sort to throw a punch then I'd probably like Rob to have another go in order to get rid of him for good. After all, I say to James, he might be Toni's godfather but it was Audrey he was friends with and not James. One night after a rare few beers James admitted that he doubts he'd have been friends with Rob if it wasn't for Audrey because they didn't have much in common and sometimes he used to resent the close friendship they had that had taken root before he and Audrey met.

'That would be lovely but she has her piano lesson after school. Some other time?' I say to Rob.

He snorts and doesn't even try to hide his contempt. Tina says she needs to go and check in on her partner's mum who is recovering from an operation and will look in on Audrey at the same time. I say goodbye to her as if she were my best friend. 'And do give my best to your partner's mum!' She hurries off along the cracked pavement. Rob still stands there. He folds his arms across his chest, the sleeves of his jacket riding up his arms.

I still have the stock smile plastered on my face. My cheek muscles are beginning to ache.

'Well I'm in a rush too and must be getting off. Nice to see you again Rob. I'll give your love to Toni.'

'Antonia,' he corrects me with a sour face. 'Audrey never called her Toni. You've changed her name.'

Ha! It's Audrey and James who did that to my Lily. I ignore the jibe but my smile starts to flicker.

'Bye then Rob.' I start to walk past him when he puts his hand on my arm to stop me.

'Wait, aren't you going to ask me why I'm here?'

In my impatience I pull my arm away with a little too much force.

'What, loitering by the school gates?'

'I have to come to the school gates to try and see Antonia seeing as you're always seemingly too busy.'

'Go on then Rob, tell me, why are you here.'

'I've got a work meeting at eleven and I've arranged to stay here all day. This meeting is with a client who has become a friend. He's from Bristol. Perhaps you know him? He can't be that much older than you.'

'Half a million people live in Bristol. It's very unlikely.'

'Which school did you say you went to again? It might have been the same one.'

'I didn't.'

'Funny that. Can't you remember? Did you really live in Bristol?'

He gives me another death stare. This one, and his truth, hits close to home. My smile is hanging by a thread.

'I don't see that the name of my old school is any of your business, is it? Anyway it changed its name after I left. They're all academies now. What's with your interest Rob? Shall I ring James and tell him about it?'

At that he takes a step back. I notice that the six months haven't been kind to him. Despite its length his hair has receded, his trouser waistband is slightly too tight and there are dark shadows under his eyes. 'Perhaps instead of being interested in me you should be interested in your latest boyfriend. Or is he another one that didn't work out?'

Bingo. His shoulders slump down and just for a second I spot a flash of pain in his expression.

'My love life is none of your business.'

'It is if you're seeing Toni and bringing a partner along. James and I certainly wouldn't be happy with her spending time with a stranger.'

Check. I raise my eyebrows in victory and start to walk away until his words stop me in my tracks.

'Interesting chat I had with Tina by the way. She told me ages ago what I knew already, that Audrey had tried to get rid of you before she was stung. You weren't the best friends you've been saying you were. So why are you lying about it? What else are you lying about? I don't think your name is even Claire. I've got a contact who is going to help me prove it. It's just a matter of time, *Claire*, just a matter of time. Still, if you've nothing to hide then you won't be worried, will you?'

I carry on walking down the street and turn the nearest corner so he can't see me. In the car I catch a glimpse of my face in the rear-view mirror. It's ashen. Checkmate to Rob.

~ 24 ~

When Audrey said she thought she was being watched by a dog walker I assumed she was paranoid. When she told me that a parent had reported a suspicious person lurking around the school gates I thought it was me until she added that the person was male. An over-active imagination I reckoned. Parents are so scared of stalkers and perverts they conjure their own fears up before their eyes.

That was until a couple of times on the school run I had a sense that someone was looking at me. I looked round but nobody appeared to be glancing in my direction. I thought that maybe it's my guilt and uncertainty in my position manifesting themselves into a bogeyman. I feel that someone *should* be following me therefore I imagine it happening. I need to get a grip.

But today, a couple of tense days after bumping into Rob, the hairs on the back of my neck prickle. I turn to see if someone is behind me or if Rob is ready to pounce again but there is only the usual school crowd there. My eyes flick between faces to see if there's anyone I don't recognise. I've already dropped off Lily and plan to take Wilf to the under-threes story time at the library, which is why I've come in the car. Well Audrey's car really, that James is letting me use.

She had hand controls that a man at the garage took off for me.

The slam of a car door interrupts my search. Which car is it? There are lots parked down the road, as near to the school gates as they can possibly get away with without getting a parking ticket. I whirl around, my senses on high alert, hearing the clump of feet on pavements and a half-heard one-sided conversation of a woman talking on her mobile phone.

There it is. A car is pulling out of a space in a hurry. It's a grey saloon car, the sort that business people get as a work perk, a car as boring as they are. All I can make out behind the wheel is the back of a head over the top of the driver's seat. I think it's a man. Was he following me? I know the tricks. I've done it myself all those times to Audrey, merging into crowds, heading into doorways and standing behind trees.

'Hey! Stop!' I shout and push the buggy towards the car as fast as I can. The car brakes to avoid an older lady with one of those three-wheeled walking frames crossing the road. As soon as she's far enough over the car swerves around her and I run to catch up, trying to see who is behind the wheel. Yes, it is a short-haired man. A nondescript-looking bloke, with light brownish hair; he could be an old-looking twenty-five or a fit fifty-year-old, but I don't get a good look, he doesn't turn his face to look at me. The tyres squeal on the tarmac as the car heads off, surely going faster than the twenty mph speed limit enforced around the school.

I stop running and take a moment to regain my breath. Wilf giggles with the excitement of going so fast. Damn, I forgot to take down the car registration number. I think it began with a B. But what could I do if I had memorised it? It's not as if I can report the car to the police, give my name and address and ask them to investigate. They'd want to know all about me first, that's if they believed me in the first place that I'm being followed. I have no proof. I've given up all my rights to justice. Who could it be? No one knows who I was, I've made a good job of that. But then who took my mobile from the park? Was it kids messing around or an animal digging it up as I'd reassured myself? Or had someone been watching me back then too?

I'm running on autopilot for the story time session and lunch with other mums. In the afternoon I take Wilf to the park to feed the ducks then later pick Lily up from school. My mind isn't on it, instead I'm still on high alert, kickstarted by adrenaline to keep me safe. I keep looking around to see if there's anyone out of the ordinary. Is someone doing the same to me as I did to Audrey? Following me from a distance? But if they are I know they won't look out of the ordinary. They'll look bland, nondescript and fade into the background. That is as long as they don't make a mistake…

James misses dinner and putting the kids to bed because he goes to the hospital to see Audrey. She's had a slight infection that they've treated with antibiotics but apart from that there's no change he tells me wearily, hanging up his jacket on the family coat rack on his return. I heat up the rest of a casserole for him. He goes straight to the cupboard, picks out a bottle of beer, opens the bottle and pours it into a pint glass.

'Not like you to drink on a weeknight,' I say. The sausage casserole is warming up nicely in the pan and I give it a stir, remembering how good it tasted when I ate my portion with the kids earlier.

'I can't bear carrying on seeing her like that,' he replies, then gulps down about a quarter of the glass.

I genuinely don't know what to say.

'I can't imagine how you must be feeling,' is the best I can come up with.

'Every day she lies there not moving. I talk and she doesn't answer back. I hold her hand and she can't squeeze it back. I've tried everything, playing her favourite music, reminiscing about how we met, our wedding, telling her how Antonia and Wilfred are… Today I put my phone to her ear so she could listen to a message that Antonia recorded for her. Antonia said she loves her very much and wants her to wake up and come home. But still nothing. I can't bear any more nothing!'

There's a glug as he drains most of the glass.

I dish up the casserole into a pasta bowl and carry it over to the table. 'Have the doctors said any more?'

'Wait and see they say. Well I can't wait any longer. I need my wife. The children need their mum. I feel like shaking her until she opens her eyes but that won't do anything, will it? There'll still be nothing.'

I grab a beer myself and drink it straight out of the bottle. I also take the top off another bottle for James and he tops up his glass.

A piece of cut sausage dangles on the end of his fork, spiked next to a carrot dripping with gravy and a circle of onion. He's barely taken a bite.

There's a clink as he sets the fork down on the edge of the plate. 'When I was sitting by her today an awful thought came to me.' He looks at me, white-faced. The black circles under his eyes have become crevices.

'It might have been better if she had died. What if she never comes round and spends the rest of her life lying in that hospital bed waiting for something else to kill her, a superbug or something? Does she know what's happening? Life can't move on – for her or for me either. Antonia has stopped asking when Mummy is coming home. Would Wilfred even remember her now? He's changed so much since it happened.'

'I don't know. It's cruel, and unfair.' As soon as the words come out of my mouth a sense of shame creeps over me. James doesn't know what I did. He can never know what I did.

He abandons the food and carries on with the beer. I've never seen him drink much before. I always got the impression that he is very strait-laced.

'Do you want to go and watch some TV in the lounge?' I ask. He shrugs his shoulders then nods.

I walk through to the lounge and kick the toys all into one corner. There's a vibration in the back pocket of my jeans. A text. I pull the phone out, flop down on the sofa with one leg under me, then take a swig of beer with the bottle in one hand and my phone in the other. I click to open the text.

I know what uve done

My thoughts curdle with panic. The number is blocked. Knows I've done what? The only people who have this number are James, the police, the Hot Mums, the GP and the kids' school. Mum doesn't have it, I haven't been in contact with her in years. I don't know if she still has the same mobile number herself. Then there's Ashlee, I text her occasionally but never give any details that would give away where I am. Could it be her? Is she trying to freak me out? But why? I look back at my phone. The last text from her was six months ago telling me that she's moved in with her new boyfriend and sending me a selfie of them.

With a shaking thumb I quickly delete the text, switch the phone off and push it under the sofa cushion, as if that will protect me from any more coming in. I reach for the TV controller, press the on button and flick through channels aimlessly until I come across some old drama.

James comes in with his glass and sits on the other end of the sofa to me, leaving a respectful gap as he always does. We watch the box in silence although he seems to be lost in his own thoughts rather than following the plot.

Unexpectedly in the middle of a scene he blurts out, 'I miss her so much. I don't know how I'm going to carry on coping without her.' Instinctively I shuffle closer to him and place a comforting hand on his shoulder.

'I know.'

'Thanks. You've been very good to us.'

He puts his hand on top of mine and pats it twice before taking it away.

What if Audrey doesn't wake up? James will need me to carry on around the house, won't he? Yet I'm only an employee. He could kick me out at any time. But what if I were more than that? What if he felt he owed it to me stay? What if I wasn't just his paid nanny?

James's glass is nearly empty, as is my bottle.

'I'll get you a top-up,' I say and carry his glass through to the kitchen. There I look in the cupboard for another of his artisan beers. They're all different brands, some I've never heard of. I choose one at random because I like the label on the bottle and use a bottle opener to get the top off. I rinse out James's glass and am about to pour the beer into it when I suddenly stop and look back into the cupboard again. Inside there's a half-full bottle of vodka. I glance towards the kitchen door to check it's still shut and then surreptitiously pour a couple of inches of it into the glass. I pour some tap water in the vodka bottle to bring it up to the previous level then give it a shake. Once it settles you'd never guess. I fill up the beer glass with the new beer from the bottle and down the leftover myself. A quick stir with a spoon later, which I wash straight up and put back in the drawer, and I'm ready to go back through to the lounge.

'Thanks,' says James as I pass him the glass. He takes a few mouthfuls.

'That's a strong one,' he says, squinting at the drink he's holding.

'Oh, sorry, I forgot to wash out the last of the old beer before I put the new one in. Is it OK?'

'Yes it's fine. Thank you.'

He carries on drinking for another quarter of an hour. I inch that little bit closer to him until our thighs are nearly touching. The scene on the TV drama changes. The hero and heroine dash to a hotel room and kiss passionately, tugging at each other's clothes with gusto.

My fingers are right next to his leg. I put my hand on his

knee and leave it there to see how James reacts. He doesn't move. I slide my hand higher and caress the top of his thigh. On screen the couple are now naked, sliding together skin on skin.

A bulge rises in James's trousers. My hand covers it, teasing him until I hear a groan come from his lips.

'Claire, you shouldn't…'

'Ssh, it's alright James. It'll make you feel better. Trust me.'

I open his flies and release him, stroking up and down the way Grimey used to like it. James's body responds. He tips his head back and closes his eyes. Quickly I undo my jeans and pull them and my knickers down, tossing them into the middle of the room. I straddle James, easing him into me, then hold onto his shoulders and move my hips rhythmically, bucking him until he lets out a shout and goes limp underneath me.

Softly I kiss him on the lips then stand up. He looks away. 'I, I, um, you…' he slurs.

'Don't worry, I won't stay in your bed tonight. We wouldn't want the kids to find out. I'd probably best go to my room now. I'll get them up in the morning and listen out for Wilf tonight. Goodnight.'

I pick up my clothes then go to the bathroom to freshen up. When I come out James has turned the TV and the lounge light off. His bedroom door is shut.

Looks like the gossips are right now about me and James. Something *has* gone on. Surely now, the gentleman that he is, I'm more deeply connected to his life and the kids than ever?

It's only when I'm tucked up on the lumpy sofa bed that I

remember I left my mobile under the cushion in the lounge. I tiptoe through to retrieve it but don't look to see if there are any more texts.

Tonight nothing is going to spoil my mood.

My mind is all over the place and I hear the crunch before I realise what I've done. The parking space I'm in is tight and, when reversing back before turning the wheel and pulling out, I hit the car behind's bumper and something else by the sound of it. In my agitation I'd reversed too quickly. Curtains flicker in a house across the road and by the time I've taken a few deep breaths to calm my burgeoning panic an elderly woman appears on the pavement.

I undo my seatbelt and get out of the car. What I really want to do is curse, kick the tyre then slump to the tarmac and burst into tears. That's what Cheryl would do but Claire has much better manners. Life has been tense since the TV night. James hasn't mentioned it but is being awkwardly extra polite. In the evenings he either brings work home or goes to his room after the kids are in bed. Sometimes Lily comes to me first when she wakes up instead of her dad. She'll creep into the playroom and jump on me, asking for a story or saying she can't sleep and wants a cuddle. If only it could be like this all the time, just the two of us.

Conscious of the approaching woman I make a big show of inspecting the damage. There's a small scratch on my bumper but I've smashed a headlight on the black VW

Golf that had the audacity to park behind me. It wasn't there when I arrived. There would have been lots of room for me to pull out if that bastard hadn't parked there whilst I was at the school and blocked me in. But of course, because I hit him, it's my fault and my insurance (or rather James's) that has to pay up.

I take a notebook out of my handbag, write down the VW's registration number, take some photos with my phone and then begin to compose a note to put under the windscreen. If I thought I could have gotten away with it I'd have done a runner but there's CCTV on these streets and, of course, lots of neighbours.

The woman, dressed in jeans and an oversized jumper with dogs on, starts to talk to me. Well I assume it's to me because there's no one else in the street.

'That's the second time this week.'

'Excuse me?'

'A parking smash. I see them all out of my window I do. The parents park here when they drop their children off to school because it's the nearest street that hasn't got parking permits. Is that why you parked here?'

'Yes, but there was a lot of space behind me when I parked.'

'That black car often parks there but it's not owned by any of us in the street. I say to Bryn next door I don't mind people parking here when they're visiting us, or even the odd time if they're dropping off kiddies at the school as long as it's not regular, but when we come home and can't park our own cars because of all the outsiders here well, then it's just not on.'

'I'm leaving a note with my contact details and insurance.' I momentarily wonder if she's going to call the police.

'Yes, that's the right thing to do but to be honest pet, I think that car kind of deserves it. If you drove off without leaving your details I wouldn't say a word.' She smiles conspiratorially and all at once my tears start to come, unbunged by her unexpected kindness.

'Oh don't cry, it's only a bit of metal. Not worth shedding tears over, eh?' She walks nearer to me, sprightly for the age I reckon she is, about eighty, and pats me on the arm.

'I know. It's not just that,' I sniff.

'Do you want to come in for a cup of tea? A hot drink with lots of sugar is what you need for the shock. Maybe a tot of whisky too, eh? My late husband used to swear by it.'

'No, thank you. That's very kind of you, though.'

'What's upsetting you pet? Sometimes it helps telling a stranger.'

If only she knew the half of it.

'It's my daughter. I think this man, er my ex, wants to take her away from me. He's fishing to find reasons to say I'm an unfit mum, but I'm not. She's my world. I'd never do anything to harm her.'

It's simpler for the story to call Rob an ex. I haven't seen him since he was the outside the school gates with Tina but is he the one getting someone to follow me? Maybe a private detective? The thought makes me want to throw up.

'Well don't you let him. Men? Most of them cause more trouble than good. I was lucky with mine, I'm not saying he was perfect mind but he always treated me and our girls right and never played away. My three daughters are my world too, they still are even though they're over fifty and one's a grandmother herself. They'll always be my children. I'll never, ever let anyone harm them.'

'But what can I do if he tries to twist things? He knows people in authority. People with power.' I start to open my heart to this woman just a tiny bit, opening the scar wound with tiny tweezers.

'You are her mother. Nothing can change that. Nothing can sever the bond between a woman and her child. So if he threatens you, fight back. If he thinks you've got a bit of muck in your closet, well what about his? Chances are he's no saint. Everyone has dirty laundry tucked away.'

She's right. A memory comes to light, a conversation I found dead boring at the time but pretended to be engrossed in. Audrey was telling me about Rob having to go to court for some professional business, I think his company was being sued, and she was worried for him. I try to remember what she said. She used the word 'again', which made me think it wasn't the first time it had happened to him, that it may also have occurred at a previous company. That's something I can certainly look into. Has he gone solo because he was sacked? Does his professional body know? I bet his new clients don't.

This time the smile on my face is genuine. 'Thank you so much,' I say. 'You're right. I need to fight back. Anything for my girl, anything.'

I've not come this far to fall at the next hurdle. I'm a different person from the timid woman who was content with a glimpse of Lily in the park or at the school gates. I've been coasting, too focused on the day-to-day rather than the long game. What I need is a plan to put Rob in his place, cut him out of our lives and get a birth certificate in the name of Claire Jones. Tina? I can deal with her: one word to the Hot Mums will see to that. They love me because I agree with them, am deferential without being challenging, am attractive enough to be seen with but not enough for them to feel threatened by, and because I'm a nanny I'm usually available for ad-hoc childcare requests. If she tries then Tina will soon discover that it's not done to tell tales about me. Two can play at that game. I heard from Laura that Tina's partner Kofi had to be carried home from the pub the other night by another dad. How will she like a rumour going around school that Jordan's dad is an alcoholic who is putting his son at risk?

Back at home I'm thankful that the bungalow has a drive, though I wish I could move away from here with Lily and put all this behind us. Tonight I'm cooking a special meal for the four of us to eat together to show James how good I am with the kids. Pasta Bolognese but with turkey mince instead because James has given up red meat for his cholesterol (yawn). The washing needs doing and I want to pop to the shops for a few bits and bobs we've run out of. I decide to do the chores before finalising my plan and pop the radio on in the background for a bit of motivation. I'm sorting out the whites from the coloureds before I shove them in the washer, singing along to a song in the charts until the news comes on.

I'm slamming the washing machine door shut when the newsreader announces the headlines and when a name catches my attention I cry out in pain as I hit my fingers, still clutching on to the rim of the drum. Wayne Macey. That's the name mentioned by the newsreader in the second headline. Wayne Macey. I start to retch but there's nothing to come up.

Instantly I can smell the acrid scent of drugs all around me, choking the fresh air out of the room. I'm holding on to baby Lily so tightly, not wanting the social worker to take her from me. 'Let her go baby, let her go. They've got a warrant. You can't stop them,' Wayne says, not even trying to fight them for me or have one final cuddle with his daughter. He avoids looking at her, saying it's too painful. 'You've got me. We've still got each other babe.' I want him, I want him, but I want her too. They have to prise Lily from me, I'm crying and shouting, hissing and clawing, but they hold me back, Wayne watching with his head hanging low, until the social worker has left with Lily and her toy giraffe she always sleeps with.

Wayne Macey. Grimey.

'In Birmingham a man has been arrested on charges of drug dealing and trafficking as part of a successful government initiative. Ade Abebe reports.

'West Midlands Police announced today that they have arrested a man as part of Operation Unicorn, a nationwide government drive to crack down on drug smuggling and dealing. Wayne Macey, from Selly Oak, was charged with drug dealing, supplying and trafficking and selling Class A and B drugs including crack cocaine, heroin, amphetamines and cannabis to minors. Chief Inspector Sally Irwin praised her officers' diligence and said that Mason had been a person of interest for a long time, adding that it was a sign to all citizens of Birmingham that drugs offences will not be tolerated. Mason is due to appear in court next week.'

I never wanted to hear from him, or about him again. Changing my identity made sure he couldn't find me. I'd loved him so much I didn't think I could function in the world without him. Despite what the social worker had said I didn't believe they'd take Lily away from us. I didn't think he'd let them. The day I was at my lowest ebb, that rainy day I looked at the leaflet about the refuge and turned up, shell-like, barely hanging on to life by a thread, was the day I ripped myself apart from him. He hadn't hit me, no, but he had made me believe I couldn't survive without him. He chose drugs over his daughter and me. I didn't put her first then. From then on, I vowed, I was going to.

The radio goes back to playing dance music. I stab the off button with my finger until it obeys. The room is quiet but the flashbacks in my head scream out: Lily's cries, Grimey's reassurances that he wouldn't get caught. That cocoon of safety I slipped into when I first took the skag.

The reality of the situation dawns. Grimey has been arrested. The police are investigating him. What if they delve into Grimey's past and his previous crimes looking for witnesses? It sounds like he's been on their radar for a long time. Of course he has. When I was with him he was only charged with possession. 'They can't pin any more on me,' he'd said with a wink, his green eyes looking at me in the way he knew I couldn't resist.

The police would know he had a daughter who was taken into care. Lily. For all I know he's had more children since. He could have got married. I burn with anger at the thought of him having another child in the world who lives with its mum and him. What if the police try and find me for evidence, as a witness? Despite me trying not to leave a trail they could find out about my name change and then, even though I'm not on the electoral register, they will track me down. Everything will come out. James will know. I'll lose Lily. Grimey's got to not say anything. He owes me. I won't let him drag me down again to where I was before.

Think Cheryl, think. Perhaps this is a chance to kill two birds with one stone. I need to get a message to him to leave me out of it and I also want a fake birth certificate for myself in case I have to run. Lily has her own passport. Worst case scenario if things come to a head is I take her and fly abroad somewhere where they can't find us. Since James has been paying me I've been saving money in an old tin hidden in my room. There's enough to get us to Spain.

Grimey's gang are the only people I've ever known who could get hold of fake documents. When I left him I severed connections with all of them. They weren't my friends, they were part of that old life I never wanted to think about again. There was one of them, however, who was quieter than the others, more thoughtful. He was the driver but didn't want to get involved in anything else even though he must have known where all that money was coming from. Perhaps, like me, he pretended not to know to make life easier for his conscience. Hitch they called him. I think it was short for his surname. I was rarely with him on my own, Grimey wasn't happy me being alone with other men without him there to 'protect' me, but on the few occasions I was he called himself Daz instead of Hitch. The name Hitch, I guess, was just for the boys. Perhaps he didn't even like it.

The last time I heard from him was after Lily was taken away. I spent days in the house crying, not eating, sleeping, washing or living. He popped his head round the kitchen door and said how sorry he was, how I deserved better, how

Grimey was wrong for involving us in the drugs. It was the first time I'd ever heard one of Grimey's mates criticise him. The social had gone on and on about Grimey being an unsuitable father and how I should leave him for the sake of myself and the baby but it hadn't got through my thick skull. I had nobody else, no money, no job, nowhere to live, and I loved him, believed that all would be well and that Grimey was right – they were just rattling their sabres trying to frighten me. But when Hitch said it too, the scales that were already dislodged began to fall from my eyes.

Hitch had said to go to him if I needed anything. Well I do now. It's another risk, a big one, but doing nothing is an even bigger one. I won't lose my child again. I'll do anything to prevent that happening. I need to hold on until the day she turns eighteen and then everything will be OK. No one can separate us then.

Suddenly my phone beeps and I look at the text. It's another one from an anonymous number.

Leave now for good. I know what u did

I take a sharp breath. My skin is clammy under my T-shirt although I feel hot and my heart is pounding with adrenaline. I need to calm myself down and prepare a plan. I open the back door and stick my head out to take a big gulp. The breeze is rising, whipping a few stray twigs into the air. It'll be too windy to hang the washing out this morning.

Suddenly I hear the second crash of the morning. I jerk my head round to see what it is. On the floor lying on its front is a photo frame. I shut the door, walk over and pick it up. It's one of Audrey and the kids that has lived on the windowsill ever since I moved in. Toni is smiling at her and Wilf is looking at the photographer.

Audrey is staring right at me, eyes boring into me, bold as brass.

~26~

It's not too difficult to track Hitch down. A quick internet search of his real name, Daniel Hitchinbotham (there aren't many of those around) reveals he's cut his hair, put on a suit and some weight and is now is the manager of a stupidly expensive sound and vision store about twenty miles away from where we used to live. His shop is the type that sells TVs for twenty grand – my soundbar is bigger than your soundbar and all that willy-waving jazz.

James tells me it's a great idea when a fortnight later I say I want to go shopping with a friend on Saturday afternoon. In fact his eyes light up and he says he's glad I'm getting out and that he'll take the kids to visit his parents overnight. Now and again I catch a pained look on his face and I know his wounded heart won't heal. It's festering and covered in pus. The sex still hasn't been mentioned and I'm surer than ever that he's not going to want me as an Audrey replacement.

I buy a cheap short bobbed redhead wig in a shop near where Daz works and put it on, along with some thick make-up, in the loo at a fast food restaurant. When I go in the shop another assistant approaches but I ask to talk to Darren. She beckons him over.

'Yes madam, how can I help?' I want to laugh at the change in him, all posh and corporate.

'Daz?'

'Yes?'

'It's Cheryl. I need your help. Can I talk to you somewhere private please?'

I watch as recognition sweeps over his eyes.

'Cheryl? Cheryl Lavardi?' He grins. 'Great to see you mate! Stacey? I've got to go out for a short while, watch the store will you? Phone me if you have a problem.' The assistant nods and Daz leads me to a pub a few doors down where we find a quiet seat at the back and he buys a round.

Without giving away anything about where I'm living now or what I'm doing I ask him to get a message to Grimey to leave me out of it. I've nothing to do with him any more and want it to stay that way.

Daz sips his Coke through a paper straw. 'I don't have much to do with him any more either but I'll visit him and tell him. He owes you a lot. He went to pieces when you left, when he realised that he'd lost both you and the baby. Didn't stop him selling drugs though, did it? I had to get away from all that too so I left the gang, did an evening college course and got a traineeship in retail. I love it, worked my way up to being store manager. And it's all legit.'

I raise my glass of lemonade up to him. 'There's another thing and please, don't tell anyone. Definitely not Grimey. I need a birth certificate in the name of Claire Jones. No questions asked. Can you get me one?'

He looks ruffled. 'I'm not in that business any more. Haven't seen those people for years. Why do you need it?'

'I can't say. It's to keep me safe. I don't have much money but I can pay. I've got a P.O. Box where you can leave me messages and send me the certificate. I wouldn't ask if it wasn't urgent.'

Across the table I slide him a piece of paper with the P.O. Box details. He picks it up, glances at it then puts it in his jacket pocket.

'OK. I'll see what I can do. Just this once. I still know a good forger. Only use the birth certificate though if it's desperate because if the police check the historical records they won't find a copy and the game will be up.'

My hand shakes involuntarily at the thought of getting caught. Still, it's a risk I'm prepared to take.

'And of course nothing comes back to me.'

I nod in agreement. He smiles.

'You look well Cheryl. Are things alright with you now?'

'Yes, but I need to make sure they stay that way.'

He raises his eyebrows. 'I won't ask. I've got to get back to the shop. I'll ask around and then send you a message. Good to see you. He did you wrong. I'm sorry I didn't do more for you.'

I shrug my shoulders. 'I'm sorry I didn't do more for myself.'

I stay out for a while mooching around the shops and then eat dinner at a little cheap pasta café. There's no hurry – the house will be empty when I get home. Surprisingly my train is right on time and after another bus ride I walk back to the house.

There's a familiar-looking car parked outside. I rush past it, getting my key out of my bag to make a quick entrance into the bungalow. I'm not quick enough. The car door slams behind me.

'Claire? We'd like a word.'

I turn round, key half in the lock and my stomach flops. It's Rob with a woman I haven't met before, the type that's probably quite plain but makes herself look striking with bright clothes and a quirky hairstyle.

'They've gone to James's parents and I'm busy,' I say.

'We know. James told Tina. You're not going to let us in?' he asks. I stand with my back to the door.

'No. I'm busy. I doubt you've got anything pleasant to say anyway.'

I hold my keyring in my right hand with the door key sticking out like a weapon. Just in case.

They don't leave and the woman steps forward.

'Coincidence wasn't it that you were with Audrey when she was stung?' she says.

'What business is it of yours?' My fingers clench the keyring harder.

'I'm Sophie. Audrey's best friend.'

'Best friend?' I snort, remembering what Audrey told me about her. 'Didn't you dump her because she got pregnant?'

For a second a faint flush appears on Sophie's cheeks but it's hard to tell underneath the blusher. 'We made up before she was stung. Funny how you were the one with her when it happened.'

'What are you implying, that I trained a bee to sting her?'

Sophie's expression is hard. 'I'm saying that you're not the friend James thinks you are. We've been looking into you.'

'Who's we?' I say, stalling for time as I already know the answer.

235

'Tina, Sophie and me,' replies Rob. 'We found out where you worked and that you were sacked for poor timekeeping. We know where you went to university too and it wasn't Bristol. Before that there's nothing. We can't find anything about you in any public records. Don't you think that's odd?'

'I don't have time for this. Please leave.' I start to turn the key in the lock and stick my foot out to prevent them nipping in past me.

'Oh we will. We're going to do more research on who you actually are and what you want. Your name isn't Claire Jones, is it? It won't take us long to find out what it really is. Tina's partner works in IT and gets paid to do this sort of thing. He's on the case and she's helping him. So are we. The clock's ticking *Claire*.'

I open the door just wide enough to let me though. When I slam it shut the letterbox opens from the other side.

'Tick tock,' says the woman's voice. 'Tick tock.'

I wrench the door back open and face them. 'Oh yes? It's ticking on you three as well. Rob, I could give your professional association a call. Do your clients know you've been sued in court? Tina's partner is a drunk, I'm sure the school safeguarding team would like to hear about that. And as for you Sophie, who will believe a word you say when you cruelly dropped Audrey just because she got pregnant and you were jealous? Best friend, my arse.'

With that I shut the door, push the bolt firmly across and don't wait to see if they reply. Instead I go into Lily's bedroom, hug her cuddly toys in my arms, taking in the comforting scent of her, and collapse into a heap.

I barely sleep that night and feel sick with worry. When it gets to 5 a.m. I give up trying and switch the light on to do the only thing I can think of. Be practical. I now have two cheap suitcases, which I used to bring my things over from the shared house. In one I pack everything I will need for a quick escape: documents, money, Lily's Babygro I kept after she was taken from me, a few changes of clothes and a necklace Jan gave me when I was eight. James has a housekeeping pot of money in the kitchen for anything that can't be paid for by card. He tells me to help myself when I shop for food. I've counted it and last time there was a couple of hundred quid in there. I can always take that with me too.

One suitcase, that's all my life comes down to. Two if I take some more clothes and shoes and a couple of knick-knacks. I may have faced up to Rob and Sophie but inside I'm trembling, terrified I'm going to lose everything I've worked so hard for the past few years.

But if I run now it'll play right into their hands. I could become Cheryl again somewhere new, start fresh, but that will mean I have no chance of seeing Lily again until she becomes an adult and then how can I explain to her that I gave up? She's already lost one mum. If I take her with me

I've got to time it right. There's precious little time when we're alone. If she's not at school then the three or four of us are at home. Maybe I could ask one of the Hot Mums to take care of Wilf for the day and instead of taking Lily to school we'll go to the airport. Her passport is in a drawer in the kitchen dresser alongside James and Audrey's. Apparently before Audrey got pregnant with Wilf the three of them had a summer holiday in Greece. They haven't got round to applying for a passport for Wilf yet. I'd love to take him with me too but it's impossible. It'll be hard enough me earning enough money to look after Lily. Besides, I have no claim on Wilf, he is James's biological son whereas Lily is mine. All mine.

Running will take planning. I decide to hold on for a few days longer and call Rob, Tina and Sophie's bluff. In the morning I research flights and destinations on my phone. I put a chicken in the oven to roast, ready for when James and the kids get home. For now I'll hold my own.

The chicken cooks and I turn the oven off. The potatoes I've prepared to microwave sit on a plate next to a brightly covered salad. Time passes. The front door opens at 5 p.m., and the quiet inside the bungalow is immediately shattered. Lily comes skipping in singing away to herself whilst Wilf is wailing in his dad's arms.

'Hi,' says James. 'Something smells nice. I hope you weren't waiting for us to get back.'

I smile brightly. 'No, I roasted a chicken just in case you were all hungry.'

'I need a wee!' shouts Lily, jumping theatrically from one leg to another.

'You'd better have one then, you know where the loo is,' says James.

'Do you want help taking your coat off?' I ask, but she shakes her head and runs to the bathroom.

James shushes Wilf and he quietens down.

'He's tired. He got lots of attention from his grandma and grandad. We had Sunday lunch there actually but a chicken sandwich or something would be great. I can make it myself and mash some up for Wilf.'

He's still skirting politely round me.

'It's no trouble. Why don't you see to the kids and I'll see to the food.'

'Are you sure?'

'Yes, you must be tired after all that driving.'

'I am. I'll have an early night tonight. Work in the morning and I want to visit Audrey tomorrow evening if you don't mind giving the children their dinner and putting them to bed. It's the first time I haven't seen her for two days but right now all I want is a bath then bed.'

'No problem. It's what you pay me for.'

At that he flinches. No doubt he's thinking about what he didn't pay me for.

'Yes, well. Thank you.'

He sticks to his word. After he's put the kids to bed, which he says he's fine doing alone although I long to read Lily a story and catch up alone on what she's been doing, he spends twenty minutes in the bathroom then disappears into his bedroom for the night. I wonder whether he thinks I'm going to knock on the door. No, that would be too much. If anything happens next he's got to come to me and I doubt that's what he wants. He'd rather forget about our shag on the sofa.

Every day I check the P.O. Box to see if there's a message from Daz. The only one is a letter to say he's going to see Grimey and is on the case about 'the other thing'.

At school Tina ignores me. Jordan and Lily are still best buddies but I ensure that whenever she asks if she can play with him after school that I have something else planned for her.

I stick with the Hot Mums and Dad, organising playdates, swimming trips and a cinema visit with their kids for Lily. James works late or brings work home to do straight after Lily and Wilf's bedtime.

I hold out and stay put, hoping that my threats have put Rob, Tina and Sophie in their place. If they don't know my old name then they have no chance of digging anything up from my past, have they? I almost begin to believe it.

Three weeks later I'm giving the kids their dinner after school when James rushes in early and sweeps the children into his arms. He looks like a child who has found out Father Christmas has been. My heart sinks.

I push my chair back and stand up. 'What is it?'

Tears are rolling down James's face. A queasiness clenches my stomach.

'She's waking up.'

'What?'

He smiles at the kids. 'Your mummy is waking up. She's blinked her eyelids and squeezed my hand. The hospital rang me at work and I went straight over. Your mummy is waking up. Oh thank God, thank God.'

Lily bursts straight into tears and nestles into James's arms. He breaks away briefly to lift Wilf out of his highchair and put him on this knee then the three of them embrace like a sodding nativity tableau.

I force a smile on my face. 'That's wonderful news! Is she awake now? Is she talking?'

'No not yet. The doctor says it's a gradual process and it may take a few days for her to be fully awake. We'll know then if her brain is poorly. But she's waking up. She's coming back to us.'

'That's fabulous, wonderful news. I'm so pleased for you.' I stand in the kitchen like a spare part. This is a scene I don't have a place in.

'Erm, do you mind if I pop out for a short while now you're home? There's something I've got to get from the supermarket.'

'Sure,' replies James but his attention is not on me. He and Lily are crying, laughing and hugging Wilf who sits beaming at all the excitement.

I put on my boots by the front door and grab my coat and the car keys. Audrey's car keys. They won't be mine for much longer. This house won't be my home for much longer. The walls are closing in on me. I need to think. I have to check the P.O. Box to see if Daz has finally come up with what I need.

In the car I don't look to see if there's anyone watching. I head straight for the small office with lock-up boxes. It's always open until 10 p.m. and after that you can't get in. Occasionally I've seen an old man checking in and adding post, cleaning the floor and once locking up early.

I need a plan and I need it fast. There's a parking space

in the parade of shops and I pull up straddling two spaces. I don't care, I won't be here long. The light flickers on when I press the keypad and open the front door. No one else is there. I go to my box, put the key in and cross my fingers that there's something inside.

There is. A thick letter.

I lock the box and go back to the car to read it, ripping the side open in my haste to see what's inside. It's a computer printed note from Daz. There are two pages and another envelope. I tear that one open and find a birth certificate for Claire Jones.

I bash the steering wheel three times in celebration. Daz has come up trumps. My options are wider. I put it on the passenger seat and turn to the letter. He says that he managed to get me the birth certificate and for me not to worry about paying him but he won't be able to do it again. He tells me that he visited Grimey who has promised to say nothing about me and, if asked, he'll deny that I knew anything about the family business.

I fall back in my seat in relief. That means I have a little more time. Audrey won't fully wake for a couple of days and even then all she can say is that she told me to get help. The worst she can do is tell James that she'd told me she didn't want to be friends with me any more. It's James, after all, who asked me to be the kids' nanny and invited me to stay in their home.

Two days, enough for me to buy plane tickets and plan mine and Lily's getaway. I'll tell her we're going on a girls' adventure and when we get there I'll explain who I really am and that we were meant to be together. We can go to Spain, maybe near Mum, and I can get work in the daytime when Lily is at school. She'll have to change her name back so they can't track her down. I'll become Cheryl again.

Suddenly there's a bang on the windscreen. I look up. A middle-aged woman gesticulates at me to wind the window down. I do so by an inch.

'Can you move your car please? You're taking up two spaces and there's nowhere else for me to park.' I turn my head and see a 4x4 blocking some other cars in.

Silly cow. 'I'm just leaving,' I say and put the letter and the birth certificate back in the big envelope.

She stares as I reverse out and then beckons the driver of the 4x4 to take the space. As I drive away I stick two fingers up at her out of the window.

Back at the bungalow I walk in and hear lots of voices chattering away. 'Claire, is that you? Come and join us!' The voice comes from the lounge.

My heart wants me to bolt but I hold my head up and walk into the room with trepidation. Inside are James, Rob, Sophie and Tina, all drinking fizz from wine glasses. Lily sticks her arm that's holding her glass of juice in the air and says, 'Cheers!' They all laugh, even Wilf who James is holding in his arms.

There's nowhere to sit down. 'Brilliant news, isn't it *Claire*,' says Rob. Tina and Sophie smirk but the intonation seems to go over James's head.

I smile. 'Yes, wonderful.'

'Glass of champagne Claire? These three brought it with them. I called them from the hospital to tell them the news. Mum and Dad are driving here tomorrow. We can't all see

Audrey at once but we can stagger our visits. The doctors say different voices might help her come to.'

'I'll get you a glass,' says Rob who walks to the kitchen and comes back with a plastic beaker. 'Sorry, it's all I could find.' He pours the last of the bottle into it. Sophie reaches into a huge bag beside her and pulls out another bottle. 'I always come prepared!' she laughs and the others join in.

'It'll be so good to have Audrey back,' says Tina, offering her glass for a top up whilst Sophie uncorks the bottle. Tina catches the bubbles that spill out with it.

'I've missed her so much.'

'We all have,' agrees Rob.

James sounds a note of caution. 'The doctors have got to see how she is first when she's fully awake. She might need more help in hospital before she comes home.'

I'm aware he's choosing his words carefully in front of Lily. What he really means is that she might have brain damage and never return to her old self.

'We'll all be around to help when we can. I took tomorrow off as last-minute leave when I got your call James. Let me know if there's anything I can do,' Rob says.

'Same here, I can look after these two when you're at the hospital,' Tina adds to James.

Out of the corner of my eye I see Sophie patting her stomach. Maybe there's a reason she's wearing a baggy A-line dress. 'Me too. I'm going to need the practice!' She smiles smugly. I want to throw up.

'Have you thought about where you are going to go next Claire? Looks like your services won't be needed much longer.' Rob smirks at me. James lowers his gaze and says nothing.

'I've got lots of options,' I reply and swig the rest of my champagne down. It leaves a sharp, metallic taste in my mouth. 'Thanks for the drink. If you don't mind I'll leave you all to it. I'm very tired and it's a school day tomorrow.'

'I've got the day off, I'll take Antonia to school then I'll go on to the hospital,' says James. I turn to leave so they won't see my face fall.

'Great. Goodnight.' With that I leave the room and shut the door quietly behind me. In my room I hear hustle and bustle, doors opening and closing and I assume it's bedtime for the kids. The voices from the lounge don't stop afterwards. The celebrations continue. I lie face down on the sofa bed and curl my pillow around my ears to shut out the noise.

Behind the bed my zipped and padlocked suitcase lies ready and waiting.

~28~

I dream of being strapped into a strait jacket in a dark and damp cell. I open my mouth as wide as I can to scream, stretching the skin to tearing point, but as hard as I try no sound comes out. No one can hear me. No one comes to help.

When I wake a little sunshine is peeping through the curtains and I find I've wrapped the duvet all around me, trapping my arms until I wriggle free. My watch reads 7.30 a.m. It's unlike me to sleep in and I know the others will be up already. I stay in the playroom for over an hour until I hear the front door click shut and the bungalow is quiet again. James and Wilf have taken Lily to school. Lily didn't knock on my door to say good morning or goodbye. James probably said I was resting and told her not to.

My first port of call is the kitchen where I open the paper-filled drawer and search through for what I'm looking for. Lily, or rather Antonia's, passport is still there. I take it and go back to my room, securing it in my locked suitcase. I also pack the housekeeping money from the tin.

Whilst I was waiting in the playroom for them to leave I thought my plan through logically. I need to go today or tomorrow before the police come knocking on the door for me. If Audrey wakes up she's going to tell James her concerns about me and maybe the police too. At the very least James will kick me out. The walls are closing in. I've hardly any time left to leave with Lily when I'm alone with her. James will probably want to pick her up from school today and do the same tomorrow, keeping Wilf and his buggy with him at the hospital.

Then I remember that James's parents are arriving today. That makes my situation more urgent. They'll be around to look after the children and I might not get an opportunity to be with Lily on my own. The thought causes a wave of nausea to wash over me. How can I carry on for another twelve years without seeing her?

We've got to leave today. I can pick Lily up from school at lunchtime saying she's got a doctor's appointment. I dress quickly in jeans, a T-shirt and jumper then eat leftovers from the fridge for breakfast. With any luck my next meal will be at the airport.

On my phone I search for flights to Spain from the nearest airport, which is about twenty miles away. There's a flight that goes to Malaga at 4 p.m. I do the maths in my head. If I pick Lily up as soon as her lunch break starts we'll have time to drive to the airport and check in. I book two seats on my debit card using my overdraft.

Lily's room is messy when I go in, something it never was when Audrey was in charge. There are clothes strewn on the floor and her bed hasn't been made. I lovingly plump and straighten her pillow then smooth out her duvet so it looks perfect. Not that she'll need it tonight.

In my second suitcase I pack her essential clothes to take

with us and squeeze in a few toys along with her favourite storybooks. A thought hits me: I should take a first aid kit and some toiletries. Putting on my coat and boots I head out to the local pharmacy for things like plasters, toothbrushes, toothpaste, shampoo, paracetamol and a thermometer. James will need his for Wilf. Something nags at the back of my mind. I hesitate then throw another item in the basket.

My mission is all I can think about when I march back to the bungalow carrying my plastic bag. With a fumbling hand I hurriedly let myself in through the front door and head straight for the bathroom. Could my hunch be right? I open the rectangular cardboard box. There's no need for me to drink a glass of water because with my nerves I'm ready to wee straight away. Afterwards I wrap the stick in some loo roll and wait, counting the grey tiles on the wall to pass the three minutes that seem longer than eternity.

The second the time is up I sneak a peek.

There are two lines on the display. I'm pregnant.

How can it be? The doctor told me it was unlikely it would happen. And after one poor shag? I wee on the other plastic stick to be sure. Same two lines. Same result.

I'm pregnant. I'm going to have a baby. James's baby. And he doesn't know. He must *never* know. If he finds out, he'll want to be involved. For a split second I imagine him as a doting dad and the six of us as a blended family all happily spending Christmas together. But no. That would never happen. James will want custody.

No baby should be separated from its mother.

This is *my* baby and mine alone, never to be taken away from me. My new start. Lily, the baby and me, we'll be a proper little family in Spain. I can't stop smiling at the thought, imagining us all playing on a sunny beach with not a care in the world.

Suddenly another thought crashes into my mind. If I take Lily to Spain with me James is bound to come looking for her, and Audrey too if she wakes up. The police too. They'll find out about the baby. It'll come out that James is the father.

I throw up in the sink and stash the sticks wrapped in loo roll in my jeans pocket. They're too big and stick out. I take them to my room and push them to the bottom of my suitcase, tears of joy and sorrow rolling down my cheeks.

How can a mother choose between two children? Do I stay and tell Lily the truth and fight to stay in her life, whatever the police may do, or leave and keep this baby, the one that's still a small clump of cells in my womb?

I have to make a choice and there's hardly any time left to do it. The seconds on my watch are ticking by. Five, four, three, two, one.

There's only one choice I can make if I want to remain a free woman. I go to the study, snatch a piece of paper from the printer and run into Lily's room. With her purple crayon I hastily scribble a note.

I love you and Wilf very much but I have to go. I hope I'll see you when you're all grown up. I'll be looking out for you. Be happy xxx

There's no point telling her that I'm her real mum. The police will have a field day at what I've already done, breaking the law by not staying away as the adoption order said I had to. James and Audrey, if she wakes up, will throw the book at me. When she's eighteen I'll find her and tell her, then she can move to Spain to be with her real family. I'll save up and buy a little house by the beach with enough room for her to join us.

I place my palm on my flat stomach and think of the clump of cells, of life, growing inside me, the second baby I thought I'd never have. A solitary tear falls on the paper and smudges the kisses I wrote.

I slip the paper under Antonia's pillow for her to find and read before James does. Turning to leave, something on the top of her chest of drawers catches my eye: a drawing she's done of stick people. There are three figures on the paper, a woman with a triangular skirt, a smaller girl with a big grin, and a baby in a pram. Maybe I'm the woman, not Audrey. Perhaps it's Lily's drawing of the three of us. I fold it carefully and put it in my jeans pocket to remember her by. I know I'll treasure it always.

The suitcase! I'd packed it with Lily's things. I empty it, put her passport back in the kitchen drawer, and quickly fill the case back up with what's left of my clothes. There's hardly anything I'm leaving behind. Nothing to mark that I was ever here. I carry the two suitcases outside the front door, lock it behind me, slide the key off the keyring and post it through the letterbox. I don't do the same with the car keys, I need them to travel to the airport on time. I quickly scribble a note on the back of a receipt in my purse saying that I've borrowed Audrey's car and James can pick it up from the airport car park. He owes me that much, surely.

My eyes fill up again as I walk to the car and I sniff loudly. Suddenly I hear a screech of tyres and the car similar to the one I saw near the school the other week, the grey saloon, pulls up half on the kerb. I hurry to the car but am slowed down by the suitcases. Where's the car key? I put the suitcases down on the pavement and fumble in my jeans pocket to fish it out. Something's not right. My body is on high alert. I hear a car door slam and then footsteps behind me. The key, where is it, which pocket did I put it in?

I'm just about to turn around when I gag as a hand from behind clamps over my mouth and nose.

'Get in the car. I need to talk to you,' a man's voice says. It's a smoker's voice, slightly husky but with the accent of home.

With his other hand he pins my wrists behind my back. In my terror I don't struggle. The car key I could have used as a weapon is still in my jeans pocket.

'Don't struggle, I won't hurt you. Just get in the car. It's for your own good.'

I can't scream. All I can hear is his heavy breathing by my ear and the sound of another car pulling up as he tries to pull me away from Audrey's car.

A horn beeps, sending a surge of adrenaline through my body. I take my chance, raise my knee and stamp hard where I think my attacker's foot must be.

'Aaagh!' He releases his grip and I swivel on one foot then swiftly knee him in the groin.

'You bitch!' He folds over, obscuring his face.

'Claire, are you OK? What's going on?' James comes running over. I turn my head and see the car that must have arrived. Tina is getting out of the front seat.

I nod. The burst of energy I had has now seeped away and I start to shake. I rub my wrists and see the pink finger marks the man has left behind. I can still feel his sweaty palm on my face.

'I'm calling the police.' James takes his mobile out and presses a key.

'Whoa, no mate, don't do that, I can explain,' the man says, standing upright again.

I see his face for the first time and my jaw drops in recognition.

It's Dom.

'Yeah, explain to the police. I saw you attacking Claire,' replies James but I notice he doesn't tap on his phone again.

'Claire? This is Cheryl,' Dom says.

'Don't listen to him James. Just let him go. He's someone I used to know.'

'Cheryl? Claire, I don't understand. What's going on?' James's brow knits in incomprehension.

Tina has now joined us on the pavement. 'Claire? Cheryl? Who are you?'

'I…' I don't know what to say. My brain scrambles for a plausible explanation. I hold my head up and walk towards the suitcases. 'I'm putting these in the car. You don't mind if I borrow it for a day do you James? Now that Audrey's on the mend you won't need me around any more.'

I can feel them staring at me but no one moves to stop me as I finally pull the car key from my pocket, open the boot, put the suitcases in, then close it. My handbag with the tickets in is firmly on my shoulder.

'Any news on Audrey?' I plan on distracting James by talking about her whilst I get into the car.

James hesitates but he can't stop his mouth turning up into a smile. 'Fantastic news. She's waking up. She said hello and asked for a glass of water this morning. She wanted a

252

few bits from home which is why we've come back. Rob's staying with her in the hospital. But what's going on? Who is this man? Where are you going? I won't lend you my car until you've told me.'

Tina steps in front of me to block my way getting to the driver's seat. Ha, didn't she see me knee Dom in the balls?

'Isn't it good news about Audrey, Claire/Cheryl/whoever you are?' she says, raising an eyebrow suspiciously.

James pulls his phone out of his back pocket. 'I really should call the police.'

Dom lifts up both his palms in a peace gesture. 'It needn't come to that. Look, why don't we go inside and I'll tell you why I'm here.' I shoot him the dirtiest look I can muster.

James's finger wavers on the nine button then he puts his phone back in his pocket. 'OK, we'll all go inside. If you try and hurt her again though, I *will* call the police.'

Tina takes my arm to lead me down the drive and into the house. I've no choice but to go with her. As soon as I can I'll run out to the car and head off. Time is running out for me to catch my flight.

James opens the door and we all traipse into the hall and then the lounge. No one sits down. Dom tries to catch my eye but I fix my eyes firmly on the carpet instead.

James breaks the silence. 'So, what's going on?' He looks at Dom. Why are you here and what is this about Cheryl?'

It's crunch time. My body starts to shake so badly that I have to sit down on the sofa to disguise it.

Dom looks at me. 'I hear Hitch paid a visit to Grimey for you. You don't want to be involved in the court case that's coming up.'

'What court case?' asks James.

'Her ex, Grimey.'

'The trial is nothing to do with me. I don't want to be dragged into it. How do you know?'

Dom still has the same sticky out ears, buzzcut and beady grey eyes. He addresses me directly. 'Grimey told me. We're still mates.'

'What court case?' James asks him in a mixture of anger and bewilderment.

'Didn't you get my texts, Cheryl? I've been watching you. You didn't cover your tracks as well as you thought you did when you changed your name and went to university. It was easy to find out that you'd moved here. I thought I'd better start keeping tighter tabs on you.'

My mind flashes back to the incident near the school. It must have been him.

'That was you in the car then following me the other week?'

His pale lips break into a grin. 'Course it was. You nearly got me there. Thought I'd have to run over the old bird to get away.'

Tina butts in, 'Why were you following her? Who is she really?'

Dom still talks to me as if the others weren't in the room. 'I came to talk to Cheryl.'

'Why is Cheryl calling herself Claire?' James butts in. 'Just get to the point!'

Once again Dom's eyes pierce mine. 'Do you want to tell them or shall I?' He winks as if it's a game but then I see him briefly cross his fingers and wonder whether that's a sign meant for me or if he's actually enjoying this. Did Grimey send him?

I take a deep breath.

'I'm Claire Jones. I changed my name by deed poll. I used to be called Cheryl Lavardi. I knew Dom around the time I got pregnant.'

The room freezes. James's eyes widen in recognition, then his face falls as if he's been punched.

'No! All this time you've been pretending? No!' He raises a fist. Momentarily I wonder if he's going to hit me but then he pummels the arm of the sofa.

Tina looks puzzled. 'Who is Cheryl Lavardi? Do you know her James?'

Dom reaches out and squeezes my wrist.

James voice sounds strangled. 'She's Antonia's birth mother.'

'Lily,' I correct him. 'Her name is Lily.'

Tina looks at me as if I'm something nasty she's brought in on her shoe. 'So that's why you wanted to be friends with Audrey. She wasn't so keen on being your friend after a while though, was she? You've got to call the police, James.'

She shakes her head in condemnation and then leaves the room.

James spews out lots of sentences that I can't bear to listen to. The words and phrases mingle together; liar, breaking the law, drug addict, monster...

Dom squeezes my wrist again and cuts James short. 'Look, I know Cheryl is completely in the wrong here, and she shouldn't have done what she did, but she's never harmed the kids, has she?

James falters for a couple of seconds, then speaks up again. 'That's true but if Audrey and I knew who she was we would never have let her anywhere near our children.' He paces the room before turning to face me.

'You weaselled your way into this family by lying and cheating. You even moved in! You used us. You broke the adoption law. I have to inform social services at the least.'

My panic is rising now but I need to be strong. I need to fight. For Lily.

Dom faces James square on. 'Look, man to man, I know where you're coming from but I knew Cheryl way back and she's had a tough time, a tough life. Grimey got her into drugs. I could have helped her more. It hit her so hard when the social took Lily away. Cheryl was barely a kid herself when she had her. Can't you understand her wanting to see her daughter? When she happened to bump into Audrey and the kids it was too tempting for her to resist.'

That's not quite how it went but I don't correct him. Might James soften a little? A spark of hope flickers in my heart.

'She has never told Antonia who she really is, has she? Never done anything but love her? Audrey was her friend, you were gutted when Audrey went into hospital, right Cheryl?'

I nod enthusiastically. 'She really was my friend James. We had fun. Didn't she tell you that?'

James looks unsure. 'Well, yes she did…'

'And Cheryl is really sorry for what she did. She knows it was wrong and was going to leave but that's when we arrived.' I don't know why Dom's laying it on so thick for me but I'm not going to stop him.

James's jaw relaxes, softening his expression. 'Are you?'

'Yes, I really am. I went too far, so far I didn't know how to back out. You needed help with Toni and Wilf, I didn't want to let you down. But it's true, I was going to leave today. Audrey is getting better and I need to get out of your life.'

For a moment I think Dom's managed to get me off the hook but then James turns to him. 'If you think she's so great then how come you were trying to drag her into your car?'

'Oh that, just my little joke. I didn't think she would want to talk to me because I could have helped her when she had the baby, could have tried to get her off the drugs, but I didn't. I wanted her to get in the car just to talk to me, you know, I figured out that if she's had to visit our mutual mate, she might need some help.'

The sound of the toilet flushing and water pipes creaking interrupts Dom. I look at him, trying to read from his face why he, who sold me drugs and assaulted me a quarter of an hour ago, is now being so nice.

James's phone rings. I hope he'll leave the room to answer it so I can talk to Dom alone but just as he does Tina comes back.

'How could you lie to Audrey for that long? Rob will be thrilled to know who you really are,' she says. 'He says he knew from the start that there was something fishy about you. He'll throw the book at you. You haven't told us everything though, have you?'

I look at Dom. What does she mean? Does she know about me burying my mobile phone in the woods? Did the person who took it tell her? Could it have been to do with Grimey?

I'm not going to give her any satisfaction and make sure my voice doesn't wobble.

'I don't know what you mean.'

'This.' She pulls out of her handbag a cardboard box, the one the pregnancy kit came in and I'd put in the bathroom bin. Shit, I should have packed it in my case. How could I have been so stupid?

'So, whose baby are you having now?'

'Oh Cheryl, that's brilliant news!' Dom piped up and pulled me into a hug. 'I know we've been on and off but I'll stand by you.' Thankfully Tina can't see my dumbstruck face as it's hidden by Dom's shoulder that has a more than a hint of BO under it.

'It's your baby? You two have been seeing each other?'

I turn around and to carry on the pretence grab Dom's hand. 'Just a few times recently. We had a big row, I wouldn't talk to him and that's why he came round today, isn't it Dom?'

'Of course. You wouldn't answer my calls or texts.' He frowns. He's getting quite good at this acting game.

'I took the test today after deciding I was going to leave anyway. I was sick a few times.'

'Oh baby. I'm so pleased I'm going to be a dad.' Once again he pulls me into an embrace. Is that a tear I see inch down his cheek?

I turn to Tina. 'I promise I'll get out of your lives for ever but please, don't tell social services. This baby is my new start, my chance for my own family.' She doesn't reply, just sits down heavily, on a side chair.

James comes back into the room with a grin on his face.

'That was Rob, Audrey's feeling much better and wants me to bring Antonia in after school. I left Wilfred with him and he and Audrey have been having a cuddle! Rob says it was a beautiful sight and told me another couple of things she wants me to bring to the hospital. I'd better get cracking.'

He stops talking and I see that his eyes are looking at the cardboard box on Tina's knee.

'What's that?'

'Turns out Claire's pregnant after a quick fling with Dom,' answers Tina, rolling her eyes.

'But…' His face falls and his eyes widen like a frightened rabbit's. 'Tina, will you go and put the kettle on please? I don't know about you but I'm thirsty.'

Tina looks at us and then back to James. 'You OK on your own with them?'

'Of course.'

'Right, tea OK for everyone?'

Dom says yes. I don't care but nod anyway.

As soon as she's gone James shuts the lounge door with a loud click and turns to Dom.

'You said that you haven't seen Claire for years. You're not the father are you? It's just another lie! To think I was about to let you two go!'

I stand up, fighting for my freedom, for my unborn baby.

'You will let me go James. Or do you want me to tell Audrey that you're a cheat and you slept with me whilst she was lying in a coma?'

'I'm the father?' His face drains of colour.

'If you call the police or the social services I swear I'll tell anyone who'll listen, I'll sell my story to the papers and let everyone know what an unfaithful piece of shit you are, and a crap shag at that.'

'No, it'll break Audrey and she's only just come out of the coma. I didn't even want to have sex with you.'

'Ah, there you go, you admit it happened! Dom you're a witness. And James you didn't exactly push me off did you? Didn't get up and walk out of the room?'

'But… I was drunk…'

He's flailing now, drowning in his guilt and its potential consequences.

'If the news doesn't cause a relapse, Audrey will leave you, take the kids with her and you'll be one of those dads who only sees them once a week on a Sunday afternoon.'

'No! You can't do that.'

I fold my arms and stand up straight. 'It's your choice. Let me leave, carrying this baby and I'll stay out of your life; or if you keep me here, or call the police or social services I'll bring your happy family crashing down right on your cheating head.'

The door opens and Tina pops her head around. 'I forgot to ask if you want milk or sugar?'

Dom walks to my side and links his arm through mine. 'No need now Tina, we're about to leave.'

She turns eyes wide to James. 'Is that true? You're not letting them go?'

He nods and adds wearily, 'This is just between us Tina – not Rob or Sophie, certainly not Audrey. She's fragile right now, we don't know how the shock would affect her. All she needs to know is that Claire has moved away.'

'Surely she has a right to know?'

I'm surprised to hear James raise his voice. 'No! This is family business, Tina. I know what's best for my wife and as her good friend I trust you'll understand it's what is best for her too and not say a word.'

Dom nudges me to go. 'You can pick the car up at the airport car park. I'll ring and leave a message telling you which spot it is in. You have another car key, don't you? I'll leave the one I'm taking under the bonnet,' I say.

'Just go. Get out of my house please.'

We walk briskly to the front door, which James opens, and Dom and I walk out. Tina doesn't stop us. A couple of steps down the path I turn around.

'Say bye to the kids and Audrey for me. She really was my friend you know. I liked her. That was real.'

With that I stride towards the car, open the door and get into the driver's seat. Dom gets in the passenger seat, slams the door and puts his seatbelt on with a loud click.

'What are you doing?'

'We need to talk. I'll pick my car up later.'

I point towards the pavement. 'Out'. He slowly shakes his head and folds his arms emphatically.

There's no time for me to argue with him. I take a quick backward glance, pining for Lily, and then drive off.

~29~

There's not that much time to spare before I need to get to the airport. I head towards the A road that leads to the motorway and take a deep breath, hardly believing that I managed to get away. I check the rear-view mirror but there are no police cars racing towards me. No sirens coming in my direction.

'You owe me one now,' says Dom, twiddling the heating knob on the dashboard back and forth.

'Thanks. Where do you want dropping off?' I stop at a red traffic light and put the handbrake on.

'Maybe I'll come with you. Where are you going?'

'That's my business.'

The lights change and I set off again following the snaking traffic.

'Come on Cheryl, like I said, you owe me one. I'll stay in the car.'

'Why did you really come, Dom? Did Grimey get you to spy on me? You never liked me. The thought of us having an affair is laughable.'

'Ouch!' he says. 'Can't you guess why I'm here?'

I don't answer and keep my eyes on the road, putting my foot on the brake at a pedestrian crossing. Two teenagers that look like they're bunking off school walk over. My foot moves to the accelerator.

'Go on then, tell me.' I sigh impatiently.

'Oh, come on Cheryl. Why do you think? To protect my daughter.'

I catch my breath in horror.

The suspicion in the back of my mind that I'd always pushed away, the way Lily tilts her head sometimes and wears her hair down to cover her ears, they all flood back and roar in my head. Those three times I needed drugs so badly but I'd spent all my money and Grimey wouldn't give me more; the whisper in my ear from Dom that he'd help me, the quick sex in the bathroom up against the sink, my bare feet cold against the tiles as I tried to stop myself slipping whilst he pushed himself inside me.

'Never told him, did you? Never said he's not Lily's dad. Sorry, *Antonia's* dad. I had my suspicions when I saw her after she was born. Grimey told me he was surprised you got pregnant because you used condoms. He thought so much of you that it never occurred to him you might have slept with someone else. Then when the social took her away I followed the case and like you, tracked James and Audrey down. When I saw Antonia at the school gates, I knew straight away I was right. The spitting image of my sister at that age. I knew you were up to something by lying your way into her life. When someone reported me hanging round the school gates I asked my sister to go instead. She fancies herself as an amateur actress.'

I'm stunned into silence.

'Want a toffee?' he asks, pulling two out of his trouser

pocket. I shake my head. He unwraps one and pops it into his mouth, rolling it with his tongue. The other one goes back into his pocket. He crinkles the wrapper between his fingers at a volume that makes me want to scream.

'I've got another friend I pay to help me. A friend with a dog. He's been keeping an eye on Audrey's house, checking you're not up to no good. When he got a tip-off that you went there that Sunday he followed you to the park. You know, the day Audrey was stung and went into a coma?'

Sickness starts to well up from my gut. I turn onto the A road and put my foot down to the maximum speed limit.

'He was quite far away when you and Audrey were talking but with his telephoto lens he saw you burying your mobile phone. Strange thing to do that, isn't it? So I told him to take it for safekeeping.'

Vomit rises in my throat. It's Dom who has had my mobile phone all along.

'He took pictures of you burying it. They're date and time stamped.'

'Why?'

'A better question is why did you do that? You got rid of your phone and delayed calling for help on purpose. What sort of person doesn't call 999 straight away?'

'I was in shock.'

An old car in front of me is going at a paltry fifty miles per hour. It's not a dual carriageway. I want to beep my horn in annoyance but instead drive as close to their boot as possible.

'Look, I know you've not had it easy and it was me and Grimey who got you into the skag, that's our fault. But you didn't have to start taking it again after Antonia was born.'

'She's not Antonia, she's Lily.'

'No, that's my point. She's not Lily any more, she's Antonia. She has a home and a family. You also wanted a fake birth certificate from Hitch, didn't you? As soon as I heard that Audrey was pulling through I guessed you would try to abduct Antonia. She's my daughter too and you aren't fit to be in charge of her, not after what you did in the park.'

My heckles rise and I want to open the passenger door and push him out onto the verge. The car in front of me turns off at the next junction and once again I go as fast as I think I can get away with.

'If you knew about the phone in the park ages ago why did you wait so long?'

'I texted you, didn't I? I warned you.'

The anonymous texts. I'd forgotten about them.

'I wanted to give you the benefit of the doubt. Then it all ran out.' Out of the corner of my eye I see him flick his left hand as if throwing something away.

Another signpost appears in front of me. The next junction is the turn-off to a nature reserve. I take it.

'What is it you want from me Dom? Money? I haven't got any. Drugs? I haven't got any of those either. I have nothing, Dom, nothing. Just two suitcases in the boot. So leave me alone. We'll call you helping me out payback for getting me on the drugs in the first place. If you hadn't taken them yourself or you had stopped Grimey when he wanted me to take them, then Lily wouldn't have been taken away.'

He laughs and reaches for the radio, switching it on. Agonising minutes pass as he flicks through radio stations listening to adverts and parts of songs until he finds a channel to stay with.

There's another sign for the nature reserve, half a mile down the road on the right.

'Where are you going?'

'Somewhere to stop. We need to talk. I can't concentrate whilst I'm driving.'

'If you like.'

Chart music pounds out of the car speakers as I drive a bit further then turn into the car park and turn off the engine. There are only a few other cars there.

'Right, let's go for a walk.'

'Really? You want to go bird spotting? I thought you had a plane to catch?'

'We'll only be five minutes.'

We get out the car and he follows me down the wooded path to a lake surrounded by trees. An elderly couple walk past and smile at us. I fake smile back.

As soon as they're out of earshot Dom speaks.

'Look, you were one of us. I was trying to protect our daughter but wasn't going to let that posh James bloke haul you to jail. Grimey wouldn't like it – he still talks about you, you know? I told him I was keeping tabs on you, not why of course, I said that I wanted to make sure you're OK. Every now and then he gets paralytic and cries at losing you and his firstborn, even though he's got another one now, a son with his missus.'

I stop and turn to him square on. I don't want to know anything more about Grimey. Those days are long gone.

'Just tell me what you want Dom. As you said, I have a plane to catch.'

'I want your thanks, your respect. Money too would be great. You say you haven't got any but you can work can't you? You managed to get enough for a plane ticket. Or two, you *were* planning on taking Lily with you, am I right?'

I keep my mouth shut.

'Yeah, I was right. You know I felt sorry for you for years, bad about my part in it all but the truth is you were quite prepared to shag me in return for drugs, weren't you? I didn't force you. Then you buried your mobile phone in the park when you could have called an ambulance far sooner for Audrey. And now, now I find out you've been at it with her old man? Really, there's no stopping you is there? I'm thinking you're not fit to be a mum, not fit to have that child who is going to grow up not knowing its dad or half-sister.'

Anger surges inside me at Dom, a drug dealer and pusher, judging me! My muscles tense on standby.

'James and Tina aren't going to call the police but what would you do to stop me doing it, hey? One call and the police will be after you like a shot. Remember I've got your mobile, SIM card and photo evidence of what you did. As soon as that baby arrives the social will take it away. That enough for you to pay up?'

'No!' I shout but no one other than Dom hears.

'Don't worry, I don't want sex with you again, not now I know where you've been. After all we've got a lifetime to come to an agreement for you to pay me back. I'll take a monthly instalment. Don't think about trying to hide, I tracked you down here, I'll track you down there. It's Spain you're going to I bet. That's where your mum is. The prodigal daughter is going to return.'

I don't think, my body reacts with a couple of instinctive moves from my university self-defence class. I swiftly kick his groin then do a heel palm strike forcing him to stagger backwards and fall onto the ground by the edge of the lake, angled dangerously down the steep incline. Quickly I pounce on him, straddle him with my body weight and force his head to the right so his mouth is under water and with my other hand I pinch his nose.

Underneath me he struggles wildly, but his centre of gravity is against him and he doesn't have the strength to oppose it. I use all the force I can muster to keep him there.

'Nobody is stopping me having this baby,' I hiss, then as the bubbles coming up from his mouth grow fewer and fewer I let go of his nose and begin to relax my grip.

A few weak kicks more and then his body goes limp. I hold him down for a couple more minutes just to be sure and then let go, staggering back and letting out a silent scream.

I look down at his corpse in horror, my mind and thoughts returning to take my body back over. What have I done? At what point could I have stopped this terrible chain of events?

There's no going back now. I look round frantically but can see no one. I roll Dom's body further into the lake whilst trying not to get too wet myself, then walk swiftly to the car, smoothing down my hair, all the time scanning my vision for CCTV cameras or other people.

Back at the car I throw open one suitcase and pull out a hoodie to wear on top of my T-shirt and cover up the wet marks. My trousers will dry in the car.

I start the engine on autopilot and slowly pull out of the car park. What should I do now?

Really there is no choice to be made. All I can do is hope my luck hasn't run out.

Thinking of the child nestling in my womb I slam my foot on the accelerator and head for the airport.

This time I don't look back.

Questions for Book Clubs

1. What does the book tell you about the nature of friendship? Do you think that Claire was ever a friend to Audrey?

2. Could you relate to Audrey's situation as a stay-at-home mum? Was she right to resent giving up work?

3. How do Claire and Audrey's lifestyles show the differences in the situations of millennials and women a decade or so older?

4. Was Audrey too harsh on Claire when she was annoyed with her keeping contacting her?

5. Who did you think Audrey's stalker might be? Do you think she was overreacting?

6. Did finding out that Audrey has restricted growth change your opinion of her in any way?

7. How did the change of narrator from Audrey to Claire affect the story for you?

8. Do you think Claire was in any way justified to initially want to see her daughter again? Did she cross the line at any point in the story?

9. Audrey's friends aren't convinced that Claire is genuine. Which of Rob, Tina and Sophie is your favourite and why?

10. Do you have any sympathy for Claire, and if so, why?

11. Would you like to believe that Claire makes it Spain and has her baby? Discuss.

Acknowledgements

I'd like to thank everyone who read and enjoyed my debut novel, *My Perfect Sister*, and inspired me to keep going and write book number two, as this novel was called for a long time.

As always my love goes to my family for their support, encouragement and belief in me: my husband Chris, parents David and Beryl Batchelor, brother Paul, sister-in-law Anna, nephews Tom and Nic, stepdaughter Amanda and stepgrandson J.J.

Thanks also to Clare Christian at RedDoor Press for mentoring me and also to her brilliant team Heather, Lizzie and Anna.

My friend Richard Greenslade helped with brainstorming plots as did my husband. The friendship and advice from my fellow Thriller Women www.thrillerwomen.co.uk co-founder author E.C. Scullion, bolstered me through the tricky 40000 word mark and line edits, as did Paula Winzar who told me she knew I could do it. Without the WhatsApp messages and fun from both of you, lockdown would have been much harder.

The support and camaraderie of the D20 group of authors (@TheD20Authors on Twitter), who like me all debuted during the very difficult year of 2020, kept me going through the dark times and their advice on a storyline was invaluable. There's not the space to mention you all here but you know who you are and I'll raise a glass of wine to you at our weekly Zoom meetings.

The cover is the brilliant work of Emily Courdelle and the editing aficionado was Laura Gerrard.

Thanks go to all the bookshops, booksellers and librarians who have enthusiastically spread the word about my novel *My Perfect Sister*, particularly Judy and Tamsin at Kenilworth Books; Keiran at Waterstones Harrogate; and Emily at Warwickshire Libraries.

Also by Penny Batchelor

A COMPELLING FAMILY DRAMA WITH A DARK TWIST

my
perfect
sister

PENNY BATCHELOR

Thursday, 4th May 1989. 4.15 p.m.

Out in the garden Annie enjoyed the feel of the sun on her skin in the dappled afternoon sunlight, relishing casting off her red gingham dress and lying down on the grass in the back garden playing horizontal starfish. The grass tickled her as she moved her legs and arms sideways in tandem, pretending she was floating in the sea; a feared creature of the big, wide ocean. Free to float away to a desert island.

The school day was over. Above her head a cabbage white butterfly flapped its wings, teasing her by flying back and forth almost rhythmically towards her nose but never quite trusting to land. Annie giggled with delight and opened her mouth, pretending to swallow the butterfly in one. It flew away towards the fence separating their garden from next door and disappeared into the pink blossom on a tree.

Annie bathed in the warmth of the sun against her skin and started to doze, dreaming about chocolate ice cream. Perhaps her mummy would take her to the corner shop to buy one when she got out of bed. All would be well with the world.

Suddenly a shadow covered the sun, cooling her face, causing her to wake up and sit bolt upright.

'Oh!' she said, startled. 'It's you.'

I stand in my childhood bedroom, though little remains of what it used to be. On the walls where in my teenage years I had Blu-Tacked Nirvana and Oasis posters there's now

~ 1 ~
2014

I stand in my childhood bedroom, though little remains of what it used to be. On the walls where in my teenage years I had Blu-Tacked Nirvana and Oasis posters there's now pale blue wallpaper with a small, white peony pattern. The old cider-stained taupe carpet has gone, replaced by a dark blue plush version. Instead of my vanity table placed against the side wall there's a modern sewing machine on a stand, surrounded by neat, stacked plastic boxes containing threads and fabric. Lots of flowers and pink. Everything has a place and is rigidly in it.

The pencil marks on the door frame recording my height over the years have been emulsioned over. A white flat-pack wardrobe stands where my old wooden one used to be. Inside are empty hangers, the kind bought in a multipack, not plastic ones taken from high street shops on a Saturday afternoon shopping trip. No cast-off underwear destined for the laundry lounges on the floor. The childhood books I left behind are long gone, as is the small bookcase. Only the single bed remains as a remnant from what the room once was to testify that I slept here. Even that, pushed up against the back wall instead of jutting out into the room, is covered in a patchwork quilt no doubt sewn by my mother to show her crafting skills off to guests.

If she ever has any.

This is not my room any more; it's the spare bedroom. In fact, it's as if I never was here, as if I didn't exist.

On the contrary, it is Gemma who probably doesn't exist, but you wouldn't know it by looking in 'her' room. I shut the spare room door behind me and push open the brown door with a pottery multi-coloured 'Gemma' sign still stuck on it. Behind that door is a lost world, a museum piece from a distant decade that should be covered Miss Haversham-style in dust and cobwebs but is as spick and span as if it were cleaned yesterday.

No doubt it was.

Presents lie on the floor next to the bed where her shoe collection used to be – one for each birthday and Christmas she has been gone. For goodness' sake. Does Mother think Gemma is going to come back from the dead and open them?

Her pop posters still line the walls, her lipsticks, mascara and eyeliner neatly sit on the dressing table below its mirror (I hate to think of the bacteria on them), and from the back of her dressing table chair hangs her mini-rucksack, the black one she took out with her when meeting her friends. Scruffy, the mangy fluffy dog Mother said Gemma was given as a baby, guards her pillow. It's the same bed linen, purple with white swirls that she once slept in, but freshly washed and ironed. This is a sanitised teenage girl's bedroom, without the smell of perfume, freshly washed hair, sweaty cast-off clothes or a cup of once warm coffee. Without breath. Without life.

I look at the pinboard resting on top of the desk. There

are photos pinned there, photos I haven't seen for all those years I've been away. Photos from a real camera, the kind where you point, shoot and don't know what the picture will turn out like until it comes back from the developer's. In the middle of one faded rectangle Gemma smiles at the camera, her dark brown hair pulled back in a ponytail, her eyes laughing at something the photographer must have said. She is in the park, I think. The evening light dances on her cheekbones, striped pink in that eighties fashion; her cut-off T-shirt shows off a tanned midriff above a pair of pale blue ripped jeans; she's raising her arms in the air as if to say this is mine. This is all mine.

The other photos show a mixture of permed girls and mulleted boys in a variety of fading situations: someone's house, the park again, and one where they wear white school shirts with fat short ties. She smiles out from the pictures, frozen at sixteen.

As I turn to leave I notice another picture at the bottom left-hand corner, one of my parents looking much younger, sitting on the step outside the front of this house. Mother is curled up on Father's knee and they are smiling for the camera, their happy faces belying what I can remember from my childhood. I peer closer inquisitively then remove the pin and pull the photo away from the board. The corner of another photo had covered part of the image. I take a sharp breath when I see which part hasn't been viewed by the world for twenty-four years. Here the colours are bright and stand out next to their muted neighbours.

About the Author

Penny Batchelor is an alumna of the Faber Academy online 'Writing a Novel' course. She lives in Warwickshire with her husband. Her first novel, *My Perfect Sister*, was longlisted for *The Guardian*'s Not The Booker Prize 2020 and was a *Waitrose Weekend* book recommendation.

Keep in touch with Penny:

Facebook: @pennyauthor
Twitter: @penny_author
Instagram: pennybatchelorauthor
Website: www.pennybatchelor.co.uk.
Sign up here for Penny's email newsletter with giveaways and exclusive news.

Penny and fellow author E.C. Scullion run the Thriller Women blog, celebrating female thriller authors and introducing readers to new books.
www.thrillerwomen.co.uk

Find out more about RedDoor Press and sign up to our newsletter to hear about our **latest releases, author events,** exciting **competitions** and more at

reddoorpress.co.uk

YOU CAN ALSO FOLLOW US:

  @RedDoorBooks

  Facebook.com/RedDoorPress

  @RedDoorBooks